Unexpected Bond

New York Times Bestselling Author

KAYLEE RYAN

Cover Design: Sommer Stein, Perfect Pear Creative Covers
Cover Photography: Wander Aguiar
Model: Zack Salaun
Editing: Hot Tree Editing
Proofreading: Deaton Author Services
Formatting: Integrity Formatting

Prologue

SETH

Sitting in the grass in the backyard of Ridge and Kendall's house, I'm watching Knox show me his new ninja skills. This kid, he's a trip.

"Sef, see?" Knox asks.

"I see. You're the best ninja ever," I praise him.

"That's whats my mom tells me." He grins and kicks the air again, making me laugh.

"Finley!" I hear a female voice call out.

Looking up, I see a little girl with dark curls racing toward the pond. A woman, I assume is her mother, is chasing after her, but she's got a pretty good head start. There's a fence around the pond to help protect the kids, but I still jump to my feet and cut her off at the path. Bending, I lift her into my arms, and big green eyes stare at me. She's frozen in my arms. "The water is dangerous," I tell her. She's not very old. She's about Everly's size, so I'm guessing around two.

"Thank you," the woman says, reaching us. She holds her hands out for the little girl, but she makes no effort to move. Instead, the girl points her finger and touches the scruff on my face, making me laugh. "I'm so sorry. She's not really been around many men. I'm Mara." The woman

1

introduces herself. "This is Finley, my daughter."

"Hi, Finley," I say, keeping my eyes on the little girl, not wanting to scare her, especially since I'm a stranger who just scooped her into his arms. "My name's Seth. Can you say Seth?" Green eyes just watch me.

Tearing my eyes away from the little girl, I look toward her mother and my breath knocks out of my chest. From a distance, I could tell she had the same dark curly hair as her daughter. What I wasn't prepared for were her matching big green eyes. Finley's are beautiful. Her mother's... they're striking. Like a force of lightning straight to my gut. "I—" I clear my throat and try again. "I'm Seth."

"Thank you for your help." She gives me a kind smile.

"No worries." I force myself to look away from her before I reach creeper status. Or worse, her husband comes around the house and beats my ass for the thoughts racing through my mind. Although, Mara said she's not been around many men. A quick glance at her finger shows no ring. "The water is dangerous, sweetheart," I say to Finley again.

"You don't go near the water without Mommy," Mara adds. "Let's go grab some juice." Mara holds her hands out for her daughter, but she doesn't reach back. Instead, she lays her head on my shoulder. Wide-eyed, Mara's gaze flicks between her daughter and me. "I-I've never seen her like this. Not with a stranger or a man." She stares at me as if me holding her daughter is a miracle or something. However, the way she bites down on her bottom lip and shifts from foot to foot, tells me she's nervous.

"You want some juice?" I ask Mara's daughter. She nods her little head. I look up at Mara. "Let's go get some juice." I turn back to Knox. "Knox, buddy. I think the ninja needs some juice. Gotta stay hydrated," I tell him.

"Yeah, juice," he agrees, and takes off running for the deck.

"I can take her," Mara says when I follow him at a much slower pace.

"It's okay. You're my new buddy, huh?" I ask Finley. She doesn't answer. She's perfectly content to just rest against my shoulder. Leisurely, I take my time heading to the deck.

"Amelia and I went to college together. We were roommates," Mara offers after a beat of quiet.

"We all grew up together," I explain.

"Yeah, that's what she said. She's trying to get me to move here. That's actually why I'm here. For a job interview."

"What field?" I ask.

"Human resources."

"Lots of drama." I laugh.

"You could say that. What about you?"

"I work with Ridge, so does Tyler, Mark, and Kent."

"Beckett Construction?"

"Are you a mind reader?" I ask her playfully.

Reaching out, she points to the logo on my T-shirt. Her eyes rake over my arms in my cut-off sleeves before bouncing back to my face. "The shirt gives it away." She smiles and her green eyes sparkle.

Once we reach the steps of the deck, Mara says, "Thanks for your help." This time she doesn't give Finley a choice. She reaches out and takes her from my arms. I wave at her, and she gives me a smile over her mom's shoulder.

I stand still, frozen in time as I watch them walk away. I've never felt an attraction like this. Not ever. She's a single mom from what I gather, and I know that's a big deal. Hell, I like kids, love them actually. My friends are collecting them lately. I'm not sure if I'm ready to plunge into late-night feeds and stepping on LEGOs. No, as much as I'm attracted to her, and her beauty, I have to sit this one out.

Chapter 1

SETH

My head is pounding. I know that opening my eyes is just going to make it worse. Not to mention, the room is spinning. Sliding one leg off the bed to stabilize the spin, it doesn't fall far. And that's when I remember I'm on an air mattress at Mark's. Keeping my eyes closed, I run through last night again.

Mara.

I can't stop thinking about her. I stole her number from Amelia's phone the same day we met and texted her back in June. I blew it off as asking if she needed help moving. I was really trying to be nice, but at the same time, I couldn't stop thinking about her. Lucky for me, or maybe unlucky for me, she had not heard anything from her interview yet, so my offer to help her move was unnecessary. I have to admit I was a little disappointed. Her moving closer would mean getting to see her again. I was using the offer to help her move as an excuse. It was my way of finding out if she was moving here without asking Amelia or the wives. Hell, even asking the guys if they'd heard would open a can of worms I'm not really ready to open. At least I don't think I am.

Although, I about spilled them all over the floor when I spoke to Mark a couple of months ago about being with a single mom. I wasn't projecting. Okay, maybe a little, but it's a big fucking deal. It's something that has been on my mind since Memorial Day. Since the day I laid eyes on Mara for the first time.

We've started this... texting thing that we do. It's casual conversation, but it's the most riveting I've had with a woman. Ever. For example, I'll text her song lyrics and she tries to guess which song and the artist. In turn, she sends me quotes from movies, and I have to try and guess the movie. They're mostly romantic comedies. She'd be kicking my ass if we were keeping score.

I tried to get her to come up this weekend, but she said she and Finley had plans for a girls' night slumber party. I came close to asking if I could crash, but I stopped myself. That little girl needs stability, and I don't know if I'm the man to give it to her. Not only that, but no one knows we've been talking. At least, not that I'm aware of. Not that we need to tell them. We're just two people who talk frequently, text even more so. I'm just some random guy who texts her instead of going out and finding a warm body to fill my bed. Funny, since meeting her, just any old warm body doesn't appeal to me.

"Make it stop," a female voice whines.

Forcing my eyes open, I slowly turn to see Amelia in bed beside me. She's lying on her side facing me, looking about how I feel. "We're too old to drink like that," I tell her.

"We're not even thirty," she says, louder than she intended from the wince that follows.

"It's been a long damn time since I consumed that much alcohol," I admit.

"Yeah."

I know why I was drinking. To forget about Mara and those big green eyes. To forget about that long dark curly hair that I would love nothing more than to have splayed out on my pillow. That's why I was drinking. Amelia, on the other hand, I'm not so sure.

"You good?" I ask her.

"No," she says, deadpan, and even though it hurts like hell, I laugh.

"You're going to be fine."

"I need to pee." I watch her as she rolls over and slowly sits up. Her elbows rest on her knees as her hands rub at her eyes. "Ew," she says, standing and immediately lifting her foot. "What the?" She stares down at the floor.

"What is it?" I ask.

She turns to look at me, her face pale. That's when I notice she's wearing my shirt. The same one I had on last night. Why is she wearing my shirt? I think back and nothing comes to me. "What is it?" I ask again.

"Seth...," she says, shaking her head.

"What?" I sit up and the cover pools around my hips. The cold air hits my dick, and that's when the pieces start coming together. She's in my shirt. I'm naked. That could only mean... "Did we?"

She looks down at the floor then back up at me. "Yep. I'm guessing this used condom I just stepped on can confirm that."

"A—" I start, but she stops me.

"This never happened." She shivers. "Oh my God, I had sex with a guy I think of as a brother. That's like incest or something. I think I'm going to be sick." She rushes from the room.

I flop back on the air mattress and let the truth sink in. I slept with Amelia. One of my best friends growing up. How could I have let that happen?

"Kent's still sleeping," she says a few minutes later when she returns, looking just as pale. I watch as she picks up her discarded clothes and tosses me mine. "Close your eyes so I can change."

"Really? I was just in—" She holds up her hand to stop me.

"Nope. We are not going there. Never talking about this ever. Not. Ever."

"A, we have t—"

"No." Her voice is firm. "I'm sorry, but we're friends. That's all we're ever going to be."

"Okay."

"Okay?"

"Yeah. What did you think I would say?"

"I don't know. You want to talk and we don't need to talk. It was a mistake. The alcohol. We just need to pretend it never happened."

"And if Kent heard us?" I question. Even my foggy brain can work out the fact that it's a good possibility.

"We swear him to secrecy. *Or* we can deny it."

"Right. Deny, deny, deny."

"Fuck," she murmurs.

"This never happened. Got it." I feel the same way, but I thought she'd want to talk about it. That's what women want to do, right? Talk shit out?

"You're a great guy, Seth, really. But this—" She closes her eyes and takes a deep breath. "You're too much like family. We would never work, and frankly, I'm just not interested."

"Wow." I hold my hands up in defense. "Who said I was?"

She points at me. "You were all 'let's talk about this,' so I just assumed."

"You assumed wrong. It was a mistake."

"Agreed. Now. I'm going to go change and head upstairs to start breakfast. This never happened." She gives me a pointed look. I nod and she shuts the door. Not two seconds later, the door opens back up. "You might want to handle that." She points to the floor and the used condom I assume.

"I'll handle it," I tell her. At least we were not too far gone that we thought to use protection. What's a miracle is I had protection on me in the first place. I haven't had the need over the last six months. My phone vibrates and I grab it from the floor. Seeing Mara's name, I unlock the screen..

I feel sick.

I didn't cheat on her, but I feel as though I did. She's not mine, no matter how much I wish that were not the case.

Mara: *Happy New Year*

It's accompanied by a picture. A selfie she must have taken with Finley. Finley is sleeping in her arms, her head resting on her chest while Mara holds up a silly hat with fireworks on it.

Me: *Happy New Year. Looks like you brought it in alone.*

Mara: *She was out at eight thirty.*

Me: *Crazy party.*

Mara: *Us Reyes girls know how to do it. LOL*

Me: *LOL*

Mara: *Oh, I forgot to ask you. Is that offer to help me move still on the table? I know you offered months ago, but I was hoping you might still be available?*

I stand up and pace the room. I couldn't give a fuck that I'm buck naked and anyone could walk in on me. I'm nervous. Is she moving here? Further away? Only one way to find out.

Me: *Of course.*

Mara: *Thank you. I got the job. Can you believe that? Over six months later and they finally call and offer it.*

I can't believe it, but I have the sudden urge to call them and thank them. She's coming here. Moving here... that complicates things. Texting her is one thing. Knowing I can see her anytime I want is an entirely different ball game.

Me: *They finally called? Today?*

Mara: *No, they called two days ago. I've been trying to get things in order here. I keep forgetting to ask you.*

Me: *Tell me when and where and I'm your guy.*

Mara: *Thank you, Seth.*

Me: *Where are you staying?*

Mara: *I was lucky to find a cute little house. Just big enough for me and Finley.*

Me: *Renting?*

Mara: *Yes, for now anyway.*

This is a small town, so chances are I know the owners. I don't want the two of them staying at some shit hole.

> **Me:** *Do you remember the owner's name?*

> **Mara:** *Yeah. M. Adams. I can't remember what the M stands for.*

Mark?

> **Me:** *Mark Adams?*

> **Mara:** *Yes! Do you know him?*

I laugh.

> **Me:** *Yeah, so do you. That's Mark. You met him Memorial Day.*

> **Mara:** *Mark? Dawn's Mark?*

> **Me:** *That's the one.*

> **Mara:** *Wow. Small world.*

> **Mara:** *Gotta go. Finley and I are headed out to grab some boxes, and start packing.*

> **Me:** *Be safe. Let me know when you're ready to start moving.*

> **Mara:** *I start next week. So, this weekend?*

That's faster than I thought. Then again, she's told me before how she and Amelia are close and that she misses her. I have no doubt that's why she's willing to pack up and move her life a couple of hours away on such short notice.

> **Me:** *Send me the address. I'll be there.*

> **Mara:** *Thank you, Seth. I appreciate it more than you know.*

> **Me:** *Don't mention it.*

Grabbing my clothes, I rush to get dressed and remember I don't have a shirt. Cursing, I quietly open the door to go to the restroom. Kent is no longer on the couch, and there's no sign of Amelia. In the bathroom, I grab some toilet paper and spy my shirt folded on the counter. Reaching for it, I grab my shirt and pull it over my head and go dispose of the condom. I still can't believe we slept together. She's right when she said it feels like incest. It also feels wrong. Wrong because I'm falling for a woman I've only ever laid my eyes on one time. Other than the few pictures she sends me.

That woman and her daughter are moving here. To my town. Maybe some wishes do come true. Condom taken care of, I straighten up the room, pick up a few beer bottles, finish getting dressed, and then make my way upstairs. My friends look about like I feel, but it's obvious that Amelia and I are the worst of the bunch.

"Breakfast is ready," Kendall says, all chipper.

"Is she always this happy in the mornings?" I ask Ridge.

"She is. But today it's more than just her demeanor. We had a kid-free night." He grins, smacks me on the shoulder, and makes his way into the kitchen where all the wives are making breakfast.

"Thank you," I tell them, following Ridge.

"Oh, you're welcome, and don't thank us yet." Reagan grins wolfishly. "Y'all get to clean up."

"This smells so damn good, you're not going to get any complaints out of me." The guys chorus their agreements.

"Yes!" Amelia says, and we all stop to look at her. "Oh, sorry." She smiles. "Mara just texted me and she got the job."

"Wow, took them long enough," Reagan says.

"I know, but I'm so excited to have her close."

"It will be nice for Ev to have another little girl to play with." This from Kendall.

"Guys, do you mind helping her move? Mark, I guess she's renting your place," Amelia says, looking at her phone.

"Possibly. We have a new tenant. The leasing company sent over the details, but I haven't had a chance to look at them. That's what I pay them for. We've been kind of busy with Daisy and the wedding."

"Where's she working?" Dawn inquires.

I could kiss the wives right now. They're giving me intel without me having to ask for it.

"For me," Ridge says, shocking us all.

"What?" I ask.

"I hired her. Mom is helping more with the kids, and I want to be home more. It was time."

"What took you so long to decide?" I ask him. I know it's wrong to be pissed off that he could have hired her sooner, that she could have been here sooner, but I am all the same.

"I didn't know it was her. She was at our place over Memorial Day. That following Tuesday, I had an interview with her. I was on the fence opening the day-to-day operations of the business to someone outside of the family, but Kendall and I talked it over and it's time."

"Do we need a human resources person?" Kent asks.

"Yes and no. There are a lot of legal things as a business that Mom takes care of. I'd like to take that off her plate. She'll be taking care of payroll and paying the bills too. All I'm going to have to do is sign the checks. It will give me more time at home and more time on the job site that makes us money."

"She's going to be at the office all day fielding calls for new jobs. She'll be able to answer questions about how far out and schedule days for Ridge to go give estimates. It's well past the scope of human resources, which is her degree, but she seemed up for the challenge," Kendall adds.

"Your damn phone rings all day long," Tyler says.

"Yep. I'm hoping that this changes that, and I can actually get some work done. I love owning the family business, but a big piece of that is working with my hands. I hate the office stuff," Ridge confesses.

"So, what took you so long to decide?" I ask him again, trying not to let my irritation show that he left her hanging for over six months. Six months we've been texting when she could have been here. Although, I feel that that gave us a chance to really get to know each other. Besides, she's not mine.

"Mom. She was having a hard time giving up. It took us some time to convince her. All these years she's taken care of things. When Dad retired, she insisted she keeps doing them. It's time for them to enjoy life."

"And their grandkids," Reagan chimes in. "It took me and Kendall promising her she could have the kids more to get her to agree."

"She starts Monday, so yeah, if you guys are willing to help us get her moved, that would be great," Kendall says. "She's a single mom, and from what she's told us, no close family. She could use our help."

"I'll call Helen and see if she can keep Daisy," Dawn offers.

"Pft," Mark scoffs. "The problem is getting our daughter back from the baby hog."

"Mark!" she scolds. "That's your mother."

"Baby hog," he mutters.

"Mom and Dad are keeping Knox and Ev," Kendall says.

"And my parents are keeping the boys," Tyler informs us.

"Perfect," Amelia chimes in, looking up from her phone. "I really appreciate you all helping her out. You're going to love her. She's going to fit into our group perfectly."

That's what I'm afraid of.

Though my fear is feeling more and more like excitement.

Chapter 2

Mara

M oving day has my head spinning. I'm comfortable here, in my current life and home. Moving almost three hours away from my comfort is a big deal. A huge deal. Luckily, Ridge and Kendall have been amazing. They helped me find a place to stay, and Kendall's mom, Sonia, is going to watch Finley for me until I can arrange childcare. Amelia speaks highly of the family as she grew up with them. Since she's like family to me, her word puts me at ease that Fin is going to be okay with them. Although I'm comfortable, I'm ready to be closer to my best friend. I miss having her so close, and Finley needs more than just me and the ladies at her daycare. I want my daughter to have more people in her life; something I never had.

Sonia just recently retired and claims she has too much time on her hands, according to Kendall. She's been alternating days with Ridge's mom, who watches their kids.

Glancing at the clock, I see I still have an hour before Seth gets here. Well, Seth and the rest of the cavalry. Apparently, Amelia asked them all to help. I feel bad that they're all using their weekend to help me move, but she assured me it's fine. Seth too. I mentioned it to him in one of our text messages this week, and his reply was ***That's what we do for family.*** I didn't argue. Not because I didn't want to, but because I was too stunned to think of a good response. I've never really had someone outside of those who were paid to look after me take care of me. It's not something I'm used to.

I take a minute to survey my small home. Finley is playing on the living room floor. The house is all boxed up but a few of her toys. I packed the remaining toiletries and kitchen items after we had breakfast early this morning. Now, all that's left is a box of toys, which are currently strung out all over the floor.

The knock at the door pulls me out of my thoughts. It's just after nine, and everyone isn't supposed to be here until ten. Going to the door, I peek through the side window and my heart immediately starts to race.

Seth.

He's standing there, hands in his pockets; I assume to ward off the cold. I can't see his arms from his jacket, but I know what's underneath. I ogled him enough the one and only time I saw him to have the ridges of his muscles memorized. Don't judge. It's been a while for me, and never with a man who was as... defined as Seth.

"Hey," I say, opening the door.

"Morning." He gives me a boyish grin that does nothing to settle my already racing heart.

"Morning." I step back, letting him in. I hear the pitter-patter of little feet against the hardwood floor. Finley stops when she gets to me and stares up at Seth. I watch as he crouches down to one knee to talk to her.

"Hey, sweetheart, remember me?" he asks. She stares at him, not moving. "Are you excited to move?" he asks.

Still nothing from my daughter. "She's kind of shy around people she doesn't know. Especially men," I tell him, even though he already knows.

"You mentioned that," he says, looking up at me before turning his attention back to my daughter. "If Mommy says it's okay, I have something for you." He raises a bag from the local bakery that I somehow missed. "Mommy?" he prompts.

"Sure, but we had breakfast so she might not eat it."

"She's a kid and it's donuts," he tells me. "Finley." He sets the bag on the floor, reaches in, and pulls out a small box before opening it to show her. "You want one?" he asks her. She nods. Standing to his full height, he offers her his hand and she takes it. "Can you show me where the kitchen is?" he asks, even though the house is an open concept so he can see it from where he stands.

With more enthusiasm than I would have thought, Finley pulls him toward the small kitchen table that's bare, waiting to be loaded into the back of a truck and moved to our new place. I watch as Seth places the box on the table, takes a seat himself, and then holds his arms out for Finley. She goes to him as if she's known him for years and takes a seat on his lap.

"These are just your size," he tells her. Reaching into the box, he pulls out a small round donut hole. I watch as he pulls a stack of napkins from his jacket pocket and sets them on the table. Pulling one off the stack, he unfolds it and places the donut hole on it in front of Finley.

Stretching her arm, she pokes it with her finger, getting some of the white powder on the tip, then sticks her finger in her mouth. She looks up at him and smiles. "Good, huh?"

This time she grabs the entire thing and brings it to her mouth for a bite. She has powder all over her, and him, but neither of them seems to care. "Let me try," he says, and she offers it to him. I'm shocked when he takes a bite—just a small one—but some people, especially those without kids, are freaked out about eating after them. "Yummy."

"Yummy," Finley says, taking another bite.

I stand, staring at this man winning over my daughter like it's his job. Picking up the bag of remaining pastries, I carry it to the kitchen and rest it on the table. "Can Mommy have a bite?" I ask Finley. She offers me her soggy donut, but before I can lean in, she pulls it away and takes another bite, giggling. "You stinker." I tickle her side and she squirms on Seth's lap. "She likes you."

"I mean, I'm an easy guy to like, huh, Fin?" he asks.

Refocusing our conversation, I ask, "So, what brings you by so early?" I unpack the bag and grab a glazed donut from one of the boxes.

"I told them I'd stop and get breakfast. I guess I'm a little early." He offers Finley another and she greedily accepts. "Actually." He looks up at me, his brown gaze intense. "That's not true. I wanted to see you. Before everyone got here."

I can feel the blush coat my cheeks. "Look at you," I say to Finley, trying to change the subject. Grabbing a napkin, I wipe her mouth. She fights me on it by twisting her head, but I manage to get her face wiped off.

"Hey." His hand lands on my arm. "I'm sorry if I made you uncomfortable."

"No, I just… you didn't," I assure him.

"Good. I wanted to see you. I thought maybe one night this week we could do dinner. Maybe I could show you girls around town?"

"It's a small town."

He chuckles. "Can a guy not want to take two beautiful ladies for some dinner?" he asks.

"I'm a single mom." I state the obvious. I know he knows this already, but I felt as though it needed to be said.

"I'm a single guy." He grins.

"Bite," Finley says, holding her soggy donut up to Seth.

"Oh, no, that's all yours. I bought these for you. They're all Finley's."

"Mine." She reaches for the small box and starts to pull it from the table, but Seth manages to stop her in time.

"One at a time, munchkin." He taps her nose, and she grins, mouth full of donut.

"These really are hers," he tells me, sliding the box out of Finley's reach. "I thought they would be easier for her to hold onto."

My heart flutters in my chest at his thoughtfulness for my daughter. "That was sweet. Thank you."

"You're welcome. Was it sweet enough to get you two ladies to have dinner with me?"

"Seth—" I start, but a knock on the door interrupts me. "You okay with her?" I ask him. I'm just going about twenty feet, but still, I don't know him. Then again, I think that maybe I do. Our messages these past few months, although light, I feel like I know him. Pulling open the door, I'm immediately crushed in a hug from Amelia.

"Where's my Fin?" she asks, pulling away.

"Occupied!" Seth calls out from the kitchen.

Amelia looks around the corner. "What are you doing here so early?" she asks.

"I stopped to pick up breakfast. I was starving. It didn't take as long as I thought it would."

"Finley, come to Aunt Amelia," she says, walking into the kitchen and holding her hands out for my daughter. She shakes her head and snuggles into Seth.

"What's this?" Amelia says, crouching down to get eye level. "Can I have a hug?"

Finley ignores her, chomping another bite from her donut hole. "Fin," Seth says soothingly. "Aunt Amelia might cry if she doesn't get a hug," he tells my daughter. She looks up at him, then to Amelia. I watch in fascination as she sits up, holds out her arms, and gives Amelia a hug. It's short-lived before she's snuggling back up to Seth.

"How did you win her over so fast?" Amelia asks Seth, standing and taking a seat at the table. She reaches into the box and helps herself to a donut.

"Donuts." Seth shrugs.

"I don't know," I say, taking my seat. "She was pretty taken with you at the Memorial Day cookout too. Remember I was trying to catch her. You stopped her for me and picked her up?" I look over at Amelia. "She wouldn't come to me. He carried her back up to the deck."

"I think someone has a crush," Amelia says, her eyes quickly glancing at me before she begins tickling Finley's sock-covered foot. She giggles and pulls her foot away.

"You guys want something to drink? I have some bottled water in the cooler." I point to the small cooler on the kitchen floor. "It's on ice and ready." Now is not the time for my best friend to play matchmaker. Not with everyone here, all of them watching. Nope. Not today, Amelia.

"No thanks," they say at the same time.

I stand and grab Finley's sippy cup, and pour some water into it before handing it to her. She refuses to take it so Seth takes it for her. "You better drink up," he tells her. "Those donuts taste better with water." Once again under his spell, my daughter takes the cup she

15

refused from me and has a couple of big pulls.

"I'm starting to get a complex here," I say, laughing. Of course, I'm kidding, but I am surprised at how easily she's taken with him.

"The ladies love me," Seth boasts.

"Oh, brother." Amelia rolls her eyes. "If your ego gets anymore inflated, it won't fit out the door."

"You hear that, Fin? They're making fun of me." Amelia and I laugh, which causes Finley to laugh dramatically, even though she has no idea why.

Once the group arrived, they had my entire house loaded in the back of their trucks and trailers in about an hour. Of course, it was faster because I had everything packed and ready to go. It's sad in a way. This is the house that I brought Finley home to. Where her first words were spoken, and her first steps were taken. No one can take those memories from me, but it still makes me a little melancholy.

"You ready to go to our new house?" I ask Finley.

"New house," she says and nods.

I know she has no idea what I'm talking about, but her easy acceptance is nice all the same. We're not really leaving anyone behind. Sure, she has her daycare and her friends and teachers there, but she's still too young to feel the loss. At least I hope so. I have no family to speak of, at least none that I'm aware of.

"You got everything?" Seth asks.

"Yeah, I just want to do one more walk through just to be sure."

"Come here, sweetheart." He holds his arms out for Finley, and she practically leaps from my arms to his. "Let's walk with Mommy while she makes sure she's not leaving anything behind."

"We're going to head out," Ridge says.

"I'll stay back, and if she's forgot something, I'll toss it in my truck if it won't fit in her SUV," Seth tells him.

"Thank you all so much for your help today. You've made this process a lot less stressful."

"That's what we do," Kent says.

Seth and Amelia have both said something similar to me. "I have a key. You okay with us moving stuff in? We can move it where you want it later," Mark asks.

"That's perfect. Thank you."

With a wave from the guys and a hug from the girls, they all leave. "I'm going too," Amelia says. "I'll see you in a few hours."

"Drive safe." I hug her tight. Amelia and I were college roommates and she quickly became my best friend. I was sad when she moved home and missed her like crazy. I have to admit being close to her again is a big part of the appeal of this new position. Not to mention the flexibility for me as a single mom. I like the fact that if she's sick, I can bring her to work with me since I'll be the only one there for the majority of the day. Ridge and Kendall both assured me that needing time or adjusting my hours as needed was fine. I had them put it in writing. Not that I didn't believe them, but human resources is my background. If it's not signed and documented, it didn't happen.

"Okay." I look over at Seth and Finley. "I guess it's time." I start down the hall, and they follow me. I go into Finley's room and let the memories of my baby girl wash over me. Sliding open her small closet, I check to make sure nothing is left behind. It's empty. "On to the next room," I say, holding in my emotions. Seth and Finley follow me to the bathroom, where I find a drawer with extra hand towels. "Oops," I say, and Finley repeats me.

"Oops."

I don't find anything else in the bedrooms or bathrooms. Checking the kitchen, I don't find anything either. "The washer and dryer are loaded," I say, so I don't need to check them. "I think we're good." Grabbing my keys from my purse that's on the counter, I take the house key off the ring and leave it in plain sight. "My landlord said they would come by and pick it up."

"All set?" Seth asks.

"Yeah, just need to get this little one in her coat." With Seth's help, since she refuses to come to me, I get her in her winter coat and all zipped up.

"I'll carry her out for you." Seth grins.

"I really am starting to get a complex."

"Aw, babe. I'm sorry. Finley, Mommy needs some love," he tells her. Leaning her over, he prompts her to give me a hug and a kiss, which she does obediently before settling back in his arms. "I need to run outside and start our cars. Hang with Mommy for a minute, okay?" She nods and reaches her arms out for me. It's like my kid is in some kind of Seth trance. "Hand me your keys." He holds his hand out and I give them to him. "I'll be right back."

"What do you think, Finley? Do we like him?"

"I wike Sef." She grins, showing me her teeth.

I chuckle. "Yeah, Mommy likes him too."

"Shew, it's gotten colder out there." Seth walks back into the house, rubbing his hands together. "I'll follow behind you two. You remember the way?" he asks.

"Yes. You don't have to wait on us." He gives me a look that tells me he's going to follow us back to Jackson regardless of what I say. "Okay," I concede. "Thank you."

"Much better."

"Let's get you loaded up." He reaches his arms out for Finley, and she leans into him, letting him take her from my arms. "Ready?" he asks me.

I nod. I'm ready despite being sad; this is all so final. A new chapter is about to begin. "Yeah," I say, my voice giving me away.

"Come here." With his free hand, he pulls me into him. Finley loves this idea and wraps her hand around my head. The three of us stand here in an embrace.

"My go bye-bye," Finley says, and we pull away smiling at her.

"Yes. Let's go bye bye," I say.

Seth helps me load her into her seat, kisses the top of her nose, and closes the door. "Call me if you need to stop or anything. I'll be right behind you."

"Thank you, Seth. For everything."

He cups my cheeks with his large calloused hands. "I wanted to be here." That's all he says, but his eyes tell me so much more. He feels this too. I know he does. It sounds crazy to have this kind of connection to him this soon, only meeting him twice, but it's there all the same. After all those messages, I feel like I've known him for years.

Chapter 3

SETH

The guys' trucks are lined up on the street, and the driveway is open. I wait for Mara to park her Pathfinder before I back into the driveway. I take my time getting out of my truck. I was hoping there would be more to unload so I could stay busy, but the guys' trucks are unloaded. I know it surprised everyone I was there early today. They've known me long enough they can see right through me. It won't take much for them, especially Amelia and the wives, to put together who the girl is I can't stop thinking about. The one that I've only met one time.

Mara.

"Sef!" I hear my name being called. Turning, I see Mara and Finley standing outside my truck door.

Grabbing my keys and my phone, I open the door, careful not to hit them. "Let's get you ladies inside."

"You okay?" Mara's green eyes study me as if she can see right through me.

"You know it." *Unless you count this attraction that I feel for you. The way I*

19

want to crush my lips to yours, trace every inch of your skin, and make you mine. I'm just fine unless you count all that.

"Sef," Finley says again, and leans away from Mara, reaching out for me.

I take her into my arms and bounce her. "Look at your new house. Are you excited?" She just watches me for a minute, then turns to look at the house. With my hand on the small of Mara's back, I guide her to the front porch. I've been to this house more times than I can count. The guys and I have late-night poker nights; we take turns and end up crashing on the floor or the couch. Mark's old place was no exception. The guys are married off, well, all but Kent and me. They have wives and babies growing our family. I'm happy as hell for them and a little envious if I'm honest. We still have poker night, just not as religiously as we used to. I get that their lives are changing with wives and kids. I understand that, but the green-eyed monster of envy sometimes does not.

"Honey, we're home," I call out as we enter. Mara walks ahead of me, breaking our connection.

"Home," Finley says, mocking me.

"You little stinker." I tickle her belly, stealing Mara's word for her. Her laugh, it's the sweetest damn laugh I've ever heard. "You sound like a mockingbird," I tease.

"Come see Aunt Amelia." Amelia holds her hands out for Finley and she shakes her head and then snuggles into my chest.

"Aw, sweetheart, look, Aunt Amelia is sad." She turns just enough to glance at Amelia, who's playing along and has her bottom lip jutted out. "I think she needs a hug. Can you do that for me?" I ask her.

She nods and sits up, holding her hands out for Amelia. "You've captured her full attention, that's for sure," Mara says, coming back to stand next to me. "She usually can't wait to run around like a little tornado. With you around, all she wants to do is be carried."

"Just hers?" I ask before I can stop myself. Thankfully, Amelia is already out of earshot, taking Finley to see her new room. A faint shade of pink tints her cheeks.

For the second time, she says, "I'm a single mom." It comes out like the fact should scare me.

"I know. To an adorable little girl, who is already my biggest fan." I smirk and she laughs. I love this, seeing her eyes sparkle when she laughs. The way she tilts her head back just slightly. All things I missed when we were texting. I missed getting to see her like this. I can't seem to take my eyes off her now that she's here in the flesh.

"I'm sure you have women falling at your feet." She tries to deflect.

"Not the one I want." It's true. I want her. I've fought it, and I've thought about it long and hard. I know what it means to date a single mom. I know the responsibility that comes with it. I also know the consequences if I'm not all-in. One being that I'll eventually have to see her and Finley with another man. That's just not going to work for me.

"What are you saying, Seth?"

"I'm saying that for the last, what, six or seven months, you're all I've been able to think about. I know you're a single mom. I know what that means. That doesn't scare me, Mara. She's a part of you." At this point, I couldn't even envision Mara without Finley. They're a pair.

"I don't want her to get attached and then you walk away."

"She's already attached. You can't keep her from being hurt. You can't guard her from life. But," I say, placing my index finger under her chin to bring her eyes to mine when she looks at the floor. "I have no intention of hurting either of you."

"So, what? You want to date me?"

"Yes." My answer is immediate and there is zero hesitation.

"Slow," she says, surprising the hell out of me. "We take things slow. I know we've been getting to know each other, but over text messages is a lot different than in person. Finley is now involved. I can't hide you in my phone forever."

"You set the pace," I tell her. Her shoulders relax and a slow smile tilts the corner of her lips. I want to puff out my chest and tell the world that I put that smile there. What is she doing to me?

She nods. "I set the pace."

"What's got the two of you looking so serious over here?" Amelia asks with a giggling Finley in her arms.

"Furniture placement," I say, trying to diffuse the situation. I meant it when I said that she sets the pace. That includes telling our friends. Speaking of friends, things between Amelia and I are as if last weekend never happened. I still can't believe we were drunk enough to sleep together. I'm never drinking like that again. Ever.

"I'm going to go round up the guys and unload my truck." I give Mara's shoulder a squeeze as I pass by her. I want to kiss her, but our first kiss won't be a short peck in passing. No, I want to devour her.

The wives are in the kitchen unpacking boxes and setting everything on the counter when I walk in. "Hey, where are the guys?"

"Garage," Reagan says, pointing at the garage door.

"What's up?" I ask, joining them.

"Just staying out of their way." Mark motions toward the door that I just walked through.

"We're the muscle," Kent says, flexing his arms.

"Come on then, muscles. I have my truck backed up and ready to unload."

"We heard you pull in. What took you so long?" Tyler asks.

"Had to say hello to the women," I say as an excuse. Not that I was convincing the beautiful Mara to date me. One, they would never let me live it down, and two, she sets the pace.

"Let's get the rest unloaded. I'm sure she wants to get settled," Ridge says, opening the side-entry door and letting in the cool January air.

It takes the five of us maybe fifteen minutes to finish unloading my truck. "Now what?" I ask Mara.

She looks around at all the boxes and furniture and sighs. "I don't really know." She laughs.

"Tell us how you want the furniture arranged in here, and we'll get it moved for you. Then we'll go to your room and Finley's. That way all you have to do is unpack," I suggest.

"Okay." She looks at the room as if she's trying to work it out in her head.

"When Mark lived here, he had the couch here, the loveseat over there." Dawn points out how the room was laid out.

"I like it. Let's go with that."

"You sure?" I ask her.

She nods. "I'm not super picky and the layout makes sense. Let's do it."

"No, you move on to the next room, decide how you want it. This won't take us long." I avert my gaze to keep from watching her walk down the hall.

It takes us all of ten minutes to change the furniture around. The longest part was moving boxes out of the way. "Next?" I say, walking into the master bedroom.

"I think this room is good. I like the bed where they set it up. The dressers too. I'm going to go check Finley's room now." I follow her out of the room and across the hall to Finley's.

"I set her crib up," Tyler tells her. "It's solid."

"Thank you. I appreciate that so much. It took me days to put that thing together the first time."

I want to ask her where Finley's dad was. All I know is that he's no longer in the picture. She's never gone into detail and I've never pushed for more either. However, if we're doing this, we'll need to discuss it eventually. Just like I'll have to confess about sleeping with Amelia. I shudder at the thought.

Fuck, I'm seriously never drinking again.

"This room looks good too. I can't thank you all enough for the help. You've made this move so much easier."

"Anytime," Tyler says, turning to leave the room. "Reags!" I hear him call out for his wife. "I'm starving."

"I'm going to order some food," Mara says, heading toward the door.

"Hey." Reaching out, I hold her arm. "You're not feeding this brood." It would cost her an arm and a leg.

"Of course I am. That's the least that I can do with all the help everyone has given me."

"Nope. I'll order a few pizzas."

"Seth." She sighs. "You don't have to take care of me. I've been doing this on my own for a long damn time."

That's something else she's been vague about. I don't know her history, just that she's alone. I want to know why. How? How could a woman as kind and as beautiful as her have no one? Where's her family?

"Consider it a welcome-to-the-neighborhood offering. Better yet, we can chalk this up to our first date." I give her a wide smile and the corner of her mouth tilts into a grin.

"You don't give up, do you?"

"On you? Never." Placing my hands on her shoulders, I turn her body toward the door and walk with her out of the room.

Two hours later, we're sitting in the living room, bellies full of the pizza I ordered. The women are in the kitchen helping Mara put everything away that they unpacked, while the guys and I are sitting here on our asses. We did the heavy lifting. Besides, I have a dark curly-haired angel sleeping against my chest.

"Cute kid," Ridge says, pointing to Finley, who plopped down in my lap to eat and never left.

"Yeah." I agree she's pretty damn cute.

"She seems to like you," Tyler adds.

"You seem to like her," Mark chimes in.

"You seem to like each other." Kent laughs. "Hey, I wanted to be in on this too." He shrugs.

"I mean, I am irresistible," I say. I know what they mean, and I do like her, and it's the icing on the cake that she seems taken with me.

"It's Mara, right? The one you can't stop thinking about?"

Damn. "You a mind reader?" I ask.

"No." He chuckles.

"She's hot," Kent comments.

"Don't even." I point at him.

"Thank you for your help." I hear Mara say. Looking up, I find the ladies joining us in the living room. "I'm sorry. I'll take her," Mara says when she sees me.

"I'm good," I tell her, placing my hand on Finley's back. Her eyes lock on mine like she's trying to figure me out. Yeah, join the club, sweetheart. You have me doing and thinking things I didn't think I was ready for.

"Call us if you need anything," Amelia says, breaking us out of our trance.

"We'll come by tomorrow and ride over to my mom's together. Let

Finley get used to her and her house before Monday," Kendall tells her.

"I can't thank you enough. All of you. You've made this move so much easier."

I remain seated as she hugs everyone goodbye. "You want her in her bed?" I ask.

"Yeah, but I need to get her changed into some pajamas. Lay her on my bed. It's easier than her baby bed."

Carefully, I stand and take my time making my way to her bedroom. It already smells like her. I slowly inhale, memorizing her scent.

"Ready," she says, holding up a pair of purple pajamas.

Trying not to wake Finley, I place her on the bed. "I'll step out while you change her." I don't want to be a creeper.

"Thanks, Seth."

In the hallway, I stand with my head tilted back against the wall, waiting for her to emerge.

"Sef," a sleepy Finley says.

I feel her words in the pit of my stomach. It's like it's twisting and knotted up, but not in a bad way. It's a good feeling—knowing she's asking for me.

"Seth's still here," Mara assures her. "Lift up for Mommy," Mara tells her. "There. You ready to sleep in your new room?" Mara asks as they step out of the room.

"Hey, sweetheart." I wave awkwardly to Finley. However, not without reward. Her little face lights up with a smile.

"What have you done to my daughter?" Mara asks, her tone teasing and her eyebrows scrunched in confusion.

"We're buds, right, Finny?" She doesn't reply but rubs her sleepy eyes.

"Let's get you in bed," Mara says, stepping down the hall and entering Finley's bedroom.

"Sef," Finley whimpers, and her plea reaches in my chest and grips my heart.

"Hey." I step into the room. She holds her arms out for me where she's standing in her bed. I don't ask for permission as I lift her into my arms and snuggle her to my chest. "What's going on?" She burrows into my chest, her head on my shoulder. "You have to get some sleep. You get to meet Sonia tomorrow. Are you excited?"

"No sweep," she replies while yawning.

"How about I rock you?" I look over at Mara. "Or read you a story?" I ask, not really knowing what their routine is and not wanting to intrude, but damn, she's tugging at the strings attached to my heart.

"Seth, you don't have to," Mara says. She looks nervous and unsure. However, now that the offer is out there, I really want to do it. This little angel, I can't tell her no.

"I know. If it's all right with you, I'd like to." I look down at Finley. "I can't tell her no," I admit.

Mara's face lights up with a smile. "Yeah, I know the feeling." She walks over to a box sitting on the floor and shuffles around until she pulls out a book. "This is her favorite right now."

I take the book from her. "*Goodnight moon,*" I read the title. "All right, Miss Finley, it's story time." I take a seat in the padded rocking chair in the corner of her room. I open the book and begin to read and rock. I can feel Mara's eyes on me as she stands in the doorway watching us. I worry I'm overstepping a little, but telling this little angel no isn't something I'm capable of. Not to mention, it keeps me here longer. I'm not ready to leave. Either of them.

"She's out," Mara whispers after only a few pages.

Setting the book on the floor beside me, I carefully stand and walk over to her bed, laying her gently without waking her up. "Night, sweetheart." I cover her with a soft purple blanket and leave the room. I wait for Mara in the hallway. I've invaded enough of their time tonight. I'll give her time to say goodnight without me hovering.

"You're good with her." Mara pulls me out of my thoughts a few minutes later. She steps around me and heads down the hall.

"She makes it easy. She's a good kid." I follow her down the hall and into the living room.

"Thank you. It's not always been easy, but I wouldn't change it for anything. She is the best thing I've ever done."

She takes a seat on the couch, and I do the same, keeping some space between us. "Parenting's a hard gig, let alone by yourself. Where's her dad?" It's something that's been on my mind for months, but I never wanted to pry. As of today, I'm pursuing her. Pursuing both of them. I need to know what I'm up against with this guy.

"Ah." She tucks her legs under her. "I've been waiting for that question."

"I just figured I need to be able to size up the competition."

"No competition. He passed away. Army. Killed in the line of duty."

Damn. "I'm sorry."

"I was working at a bar right out of college. Amelia had just moved home and I was missing her something crazy. Blake was in on leave. We hit it off. I met him and a few of the guys at a club the next night. One thing led to another, one too many drinks, and you can figure out the rest." She waits for me to speak, but I don't say a word. "I'd never done anything like that before. In fact, he was only the second person I'd ever slept with." She shrugs. "I had his address as we agreed to keep in touch. We did for the first couple of months, by mail. And then I found out about my pregnancy and wrote to him. I told him I could do it on my own, but felt he needed to know. I waited for weeks and never heard from him. Almost two months to the day of sending the letter, I got a call from an attorney. He claimed his client Roger, who was a friend of Blake's, wanted him to reach out to me. He said Roger was in town and wanted to meet up. I agreed. I wanted to know what was up with Blake. We met at a small diner in town, and when I got there, he handed me the letters I had sent to Blake. They were unopened." She stops to collect herself and I remain quiet. Just taking it all in, trying to process the fact that she's been a single mom from the moment she found out about Finley.

"'He's gone, Mara.'" She wipes a stray tear from under her eye. "That's what he said. He told me he was killed in action. I didn't ask for specifics and he didn't volunteer them. From the haunted look in his eyes, it was better that way."

"I'm sorry." Reaching out, I place my hand on her leg, offering her comfort.

"I knew something was wrong. He wrote to me every day. Sometimes multiple times a day. Somedays I would get no letters and the others I would get four or five. Just depended on when he could get them to me. He never knew," she whispers. "He never knew he was going to be a father." She closes her eyes taking a deep breath. When she opens them, I swear I can see straight to her heart. "There was this connection between us, one I can't explain. Maybe I was just enamored with him because I was the center of his attention? Hell, I don't really know. I do know that neither one of us wanted to say goodbye, as unrealistic as that sounds." She pauses, collecting her thoughts. "I was falling for him, you know? I realize it sounds crazy, but you really get to know someone when you communicate with words."

My heart bleeds for her and Finley and the loss of Blake. One part of me wishes I could take her pain away and the other part, the selfish part, is glad that life brought them to me, to this moment. That I've been given the chance to do right by them. She sniffs, and I feel as though I need to send this conversation on an alternate path. I grin at her. "Does texting count?" I ask to lighten the mood, but honestly, I want to know her answer.

She laughs. "Yeah, texting counts."

"So, what did your family say? When they found out you were pregnant and going to be a single mom?" If I thought her eyes were sad before, that's nothing to the haunted look that fills her green eyes.

"Nothing like getting it all out at once," she says, taking a deep breath and slowly exhaling. "I grew up in foster care, Seth. I was a ward of the state from the age of two. I lost count of the number of foster homes I grew up in. I bounced from one to the next. Some of the families were nice, and others were there to get a paycheck. My last family, the Parkers, they had to move due to Mr. Parker's job. I was fifteen at the time. His job was moving him overseas and since I was a ward of the state, I couldn't go with them. They could have adopted me, but that takes longer than the time they had. I'd been with them for four years. They were the closest thing to a real family I ever had. I never heard from them after the move. I know life gets busy and all that. I went back to the children's home, and that's where I stayed until I turned eighteen."

Did you hear that crack? It's my heart splitting wide open for this incredible woman sitting in front of me. "Mara." I whisper her name because, honestly, I don't know what else to say.

"It's okay." She smiles through her pain. Smiles for me.

"Don't do that." I move closer to her and pull her into my arms. "It's okay to not be okay. I suck at this kind of thing but don't hide it from me. I want the real."

She lets me hold her for a few minutes before pulling away. "My *real* is that little girl down the hall. She's my only family. She's my heart and soul."

"You're an incredible mother."

"Thank you, but she makes it easy. She really is such a sweet girl."

"Trust me, I know enough about kids to understand that their parents help shape them into the tiny humans that they are. You've made her amazing."

"So, that's it." She changes the subject. "That's my real. I have no family to speak of, and Blake didn't either. None that he claimed anyway. Roger said he always told him he was alone, that the army was his family. I gave Finley his middle name and my last name. I left his name off the birth certificate. I could have listed him, but I wasn't willing to risk any family he might have coming to the surface and trying to take her from me."

"I can't imagine how that must have been. Being all alone."

"We made do," she says with a shrug.

I hold her a little tighter, not really knowing what to say. I could tell her that she's incredible and that her strength is beyond measure. I could tell her that I thought I was falling for her before, but now that I know her past, it makes me want to be with her even more. It makes me want to be there for her to help carry some of her burdens, to be the one to help wipe away the tears. Not just for her but for Finley too.

"I'm sorry." She pulls away and I miss her warmth immediately. "I shouldn't have sprung all of that on you in one night."

"I'm glad you did. However, if you thought it would get rid of me, you're mistaken."

"What about you?"

I feel bad talking about my childhood to this amazing woman, who has lived through things she never should have. "Well, my parents are still married. I'm an only child. Ridge, Tyler, Mark, Kent, and I all grew up together. We've been thick as thieves for as long as I can remember."

"I love that." She smiles. "What about the ladies?"

"Well, Reagan and Ridge are brother and sister, so she's always been around. Same with Amelia. She was always there too. Kendall lived here then moved away to college and came back. She brought Dawn with her." I go on to explain our dynamics and how everyone ended up together.

"So, Daisy isn't Mark's?" she asks.

"She is in all the ways that matter. They adopted her. Dawn's sister passed away, as did her parents. It was all in the same year. It was tough."

"I bet. I don't remember my parents. I imagine having them and loving them, then losing them would be far worse."

"I think every situation is unique. Both scenarios are terrible."

"Yeah." She places her hand over her mouth, covering a yawn. I'm not ready to go, but I know she has to be exhausted. Mentally and physically.

"So, I was thinking maybe tomorrow we could have lunch?"

"I have a ton of unpacking to do. I'm meeting Kendall's mom tomorrow too. She's going to keep Finley until I find more permanent childcare."

"Breakfast? Dinner?" I ask, hopeful she'll take me up on at least one of them. "I can even bring it over, so you don't have to leave. I'm more than happy to help unpack." I flex my arms, showing her my muscles. "I need to give the guns a workout anyway."

"Whatever." She laughs, shaking her head.

"I'll take that as a yes. What do you ladies want to eat?"

"Honestly, Finley would be happy with a Happy Meal from McDonald's."

"What about Momma?" I tuck her hair behind her ear as I speak.

"Where do you think she got her love of chicken nuggets?" she asks, making me laugh. "Actually, we're on a budget, so things like McDonald's are a treat for her. For both of us. She'll love it. But you don't have to do that."

"Mara." I wait until I know I have her full attention. "I want to. Next time though, I'm taking you ladies out."

"Who says there's going to be a next time?" she sasses.

"Trust me, beautiful." I lean in and kiss her cheek. "There's going to be a next time." Standing before I make a fool of myself and attack her lips with mine, I hold out my hand to help her up. "Get some sleep," I say as we walk toward the front door. "Make sure you lock up behind me."

"I can handle it."

"Yeah, I know you can." Stepping in close, I wrap her in a hug. "What you don't realize is that you no longer have to do it alone." Pulling back, I give her a wink and rush through the cold out to my truck. I should have started it earlier, but I had to leave before I begged her to let me stay.

Chapter 4

Mara

Today could not have gone any better. Sonia, Kendall's mom, was amazing with Finley. My girl took to her right away and they were immediate friends. It takes a lot of the worry from my shoulders, with moving away and starting this new job. However, it feels like I have more friends here than I did back home, and we've only spent one night in our new place. Amelia was right—her friends are great. I'm so glad I took a leap of faith and moved.

When I pull up to the house, I see his big blue truck in the driveway. I drive past him and into the attached garage. This isn't a luxury we had at our old place. I love not having to take Finley out in the cold snow and rain. This house is definitely going to have me spoiled with this garage.

"Sef!" Finley claps when he opens her door for her. He has her out of her seat and in his arms before I'm even out of the car.

"How is it she's taken with you so fast?" I ask, shaking my head. "She even remembers your name." I know I sound like a broken record, but it's astonishing to me. This isn't like my daughter at all.

"The ladies love me, Mara." I have to fight to not roll my eyes.

"Come on, ladies' man, let's go inside where it's warm." I hit the button to close the garage door, and then lead the way into the house.

"I got you something, but I have to run out to my truck," Seth tells Finley. "I'll be right back." He sets her on the couch and makes eye contact with me, I'm assuming to make sure I'm there to keep an eye on her before rushing out the front door to his truck. He's back in a flash carrying a small black soft-sided cooler.

"What's that?"

"Dinner." He places the cooler on the table and then holds his arms out for Finley, and of course, she reaches for him. He's her new best friend, after all. Aside from Sonia, that is. My girl is making all kinds of new friends. It makes my heart smile to see her so happy.

"Dinner?"

"Yep. I got my girls their favorite." He grins. "Chicken nuggets." He says it like he's telling us we won the lottery with flair and a pitch to his voice. Finley giggles. "These aren't just any chicken nuggets. No, these are the best nuggets." Reaching into the bag, he pulls out a small white Chick-fil-A box. "Now, your mommy said you like McDonald's, but I wanted you to try my favorite nuggets."

He carries her into the kitchen, and puts her in her booster seat, and pushes her chair up to the table. "You're going to spoil her," I say, gripping the back of one of the chairs. This is only a four-person table; it's just Finley and me, so we don't need anything bigger than that.

"And?" he counters. "Be right back, kiddo." He ruffles her curls and rushes back to the living room with the cooler.

I watch him as he unpacks four more boxes of nuggets and three containers of their waffle fries. "Uh, Seth, it's just the three of us."

"I know. I should have gotten another nugget," he says, opening one of the boxes and popping a nugget in his mouth.

Finley does the same thing. "Finley, small bites," I remind her. She reaches into her mouth, pulls out the now soggy nugget, takes a bite, grins, and offers the rest to Seth.

"I've got my own. Those are yours." He grabs another nugget from his box, only this time he takes a small bite, which prompts Finley to mimic him and do the same with her soggy nugget.

"I wasn't sure if you were still stopping by," I say, taking a seat when he points at the box of nuggets and fries he slid in front of me on the table.

"I told you I'd be here."

"Thank you for dinner," I say, opening my box of nuggets.

"Anks," Finley says, grinning at Seth with a mouthful of french fries.

"Don't talk with your mouth full of food," I tell her. Not that it does any good.

"You're welcome, Finny." Seth smiles at her. "So, what's left to unpack?" he asks, his eyes darting around the kitchen.

"This room is done, thanks to the girls yesterday. I have most of my room done as well. I did that after Finley went to bed last night. I have a few boxes with pictures to hang on the walls. I should probably ask Mark before I do that, though, huh?"

"Nope. We're in construction; that's what we do. He's not going to be upset over a few nails. I brought some tools, so I can hang them. Just tell me where you want them."

"You're pretty handy to have around," I tease.

"Mara, Mara, Mara, we haven't even scratched the surface." He gives me a wicked grin.

I cross my legs to ward off the ache he causes. I can only imagine what he's capable of. "Well, regardless," I say coolly, effectively hiding my body's reaction to him. "Thank you for your help. I appreciate it very much."

"You ready for tomorrow?" he asks.

"Yes and no. I'm nervous leaving Finley, but Kendall's mom is wonderful and Finley took to her right away."

"She's great. They're good people."

I nod. "I can't believe I'm here," I say, my eyes surveying the room. "All these months we've been talking and texting, and now here we are. Having dinner in my new place."

"I'm glad you're here." I raise my eyebrows and he grins wolfishly. "What? I am. Not that I didn't like our texting marathons, but this is so much better. I get to see you, and..." He reaches out and runs his index finger down my cheek. "…touch you."

I shiver. "Yeah?" I ask, breathless.

Finley drops her sippy cup on the floor, and Seth bends over to pick it up. "Here you go, sweetheart." He holds it out for her and she grins.

"Anks."

"So polite." He glances over at me. "You really have done a great job with her."

I smile at my daughter. "Thank you. We've muddled through the best way we know how."

"Well, you're kicking a—butt and taking names," he says, catching himself.

Finley starts playing with her food instead of eating it and I know she's done. "All right, little miss, it's bath time for you." I stand and remove her from her booster seat. "You want to stick around?"

"I'm not going anywhere. I'll clean up in here while you take care of bath time." He stands and starts gathering our trash. I stand here with my daughter in my arms, just watching him. I was a little worried about the move for so many reasons, but Seth, he makes me forget all of them.

"Seth." I wait for him to look up at me. "I'm glad you're here." The confession comes freely. I really like this guy, and for some reason, he likes both me and my daughter. I'm going to take a leap of faith and see where this goes.

Abandoning the trash, he walks around the table until he's next to me. He bends and kisses Finley's cheek and then mine. "Me too, baby." Finley pats his cheek, breaking our moment, but he just laughs and tickles her side, effectively moving her little hand without a fuss. "You stink," he tells my daughter. He's overly dramatic when he holds his nose and waves his hand in front of his face. "It's bath time."

Finley giggles.

My heart smiles.

"You go with Mommy, and I'll come say good night when you're done." He rubs his hand softly over her curls, and goes back to gathering trash.

On shaky legs, I carry Finley to the bathroom and fumble my way through her bath. I've never met a man who's literally made me weak in the knees. He's so good with my daughter, and the sincerity when he's with us, it shines from his eyes, his words, his actions. This man is unlike anyone I've ever met. We have a routine, but tonight, I let her play a little longer than usual. My mind's racing with thoughts of Seth. It's been a long time since I've felt this way. This nervous, excited flutter in my belly. It's been just as long since I've let a man into my life, into my daughter's life. In fact, it's never happened. Finley's dad, Blake, was the last man I was with. Most men run when they find out you're a single mother, not that I even bothered; my priority was my little girl. I've never brought a man into her life.

My gut tells me that Seth is different, and I want to see where this goes. Seth slowly crept in, and now here we are. The chemistry between us is electric, and for the first time in a hell of a long time, I want to feel it racing through my veins.

I want Seth.

"Sef." Finley points over my shoulder and I turn to see him. His ankles are crossed, as are his arms over his chest as he leans against the doorjamb.

"Hey, sorry it took so long," I say over my shoulder before turning back to Finley. "You, little miss, it's past your bedtime," I tell her, leaning in for a kiss goodnight.

"Sef," she says again, holding her arms open for him. It's on the tip of my tongue to tell her that's enough and it's time for bed, but his voice stops me.

"What's up, Finny? You giving your momma a hard time?" He looks over at her bed.

"Night night," she says, standing and holding her arms out for him.

He chuckles, a sound from deep in his chest. "Come here, sweetheart." As if he's done it a million times, he lifts her and gives her a hug. "Now, it's time for you to go night-night." He places her back on her mattress, and my deviant child lies down and allows him to cover her up. "Sweet dreams, Finny," he whispers with a small wave.

"Momma loves you," I tell my daughter.

"Wuvs you," she replies, hugging her bear to her chest and closing her eyes.

Checking to make sure the monitor is on, I close the door softly behind me. "She's a handful," I say when I find Seth in the hall waiting for me.

"She's a cute kid."

"Thanks." I don't really know what to say. This has all been out of my comfort zone. Seth makes the decision for me when he holds out his hand for me. I take it, allowing him to lace our fingers together and pull me into his chest.

"What else needs to be done?"

"You've done enough. I can get it."

"Mara," he says softly. I look up at him, and his brown eyes are smiling down at me. "Let me help you. I want this transition to be easy for both of you."

"What's in it for you?" I blurt before I can stop myself.

"You. The pleasure of your company. And Finley and her goodnight hugs." He wraps his arm around my waist and leads me down the hall to the living room. He waits for me to sit on the couch, then takes the cushion right next to mine. "So tell me what's next?"

"I'm good, really. I mean, eventually, I want to paint Finley's room and get her a toddler bed. Mark said we could paint the walls any color we wanted."

"Okay, do we know what color? Do you have a bed?"

"I'm thinking a teal green. That's the color she pointed at when we were browsing color options. And her bed, I know which one I want. I just have to order it and put it together. I'm actually considering a princess twin-size bed so she can sleep in it longer."

"That's a good idea. I know Ridge and Kendall did that with Knox as well. His is a race-car bed. Kid loves it."

"I've been looking online."

"How about we take her shopping, see which one she likes?"

I can't help it. I laugh. "How many times have you taken a two-and-a-half-year-old shopping? Well, she'll be two and a half next month."

"Never. But how bad can it be?"

"Trust me on this one." I reach over and pat his arm. "We're better to shop online."

"Grab your computer, we can do it now. We'll get the bed ordered and then we'll know what color of paint for sure."

I mentally calculate my bank account. Moving didn't cost what I thought it would with the guys helping. I hate dipping into savings because you never know what could happen, but I will make a good salary at Beckett Construction. My little girl deserves her dream room at our new house. "I'm exhausted," I say, because I am. "If I start down that rabbit hole, I'll never get to sleep, and tomorrow is my first day. I don't need to roll into the office looking like a zombie."

"You'd make a beautiful zombie." He winks.

I playfully roll my eyes. "I'll start looking and let you know. How's that?"

"Fine." He sighs dramatically. "I guess I should head out so you can get some sleep."

As if his words have a direct connection to my brain, I yawn, covering it with my arm. "I'm sorry."

"Nothing to be sorry for. It's been a long weekend." Leaning in, he kisses the corner of my mouth. "Lock up behind me." He stands and I do the same, following him. "I'm actually going to go start my truck. I'll be right back." He rushes out the door. I hear his truck fire up, and then he's back, shivering from the cold.

I want to wrap my arms around him to warm him up, but that's too much, right? He has my head all jumbled. "Thank you for dinner and for all of your help," I say instead, keeping my hands to myself.

"You're welcome. How about I take you and Finny to dinner tomorrow night to celebrate your first day?"

"You don't have to do that."

"I want to do that," he says, mocking me. "What's our girl's favorite?"

My heart stutters in my chest at his "our girl" remark. "Chicken nuggets, french fries, oh, and she loves cheese pizza."

"Pizza it is. I don't know what time I'll get off tomorrow, but I'll text you and we can plan from there."

"Seth."

"Mara." He grins. "I'll see you soon. Sweet dreams, and lock up." He taps my nose and turns to leave. I shut the door behind him, holding off the frigid air. "Lock up," he calls through the door. I flip the lock. "Night, Mara," he says, and then all I hear are his heavy footsteps as he walks away.

I don't need to look in the mirror to know my face is lit up with a smile. Seth Jennings is a force to be reckoned with.

Chapter 5

SETH

I know as soon as I pull into the parking lot and the only vehicles are Ridge's and Mara's, that I'm in for a day of nagging from the guys. I also know that I don't have it in me to give a fuck. Grabbing the box of donuts and the two coffees, I climb out of the truck and make my way inside.

Ridge looks up when I walk through the door, then glances at the clock on the wall. "What are you doing here so early?" he asks, confused.

So, I'm about thirty minutes early. Sue me. I couldn't seem to help myself knowing she was going to be here. "I brought breakfast," I say, placing the donuts on the corner of the desk.

"And those." He points to the small carrier holding two coffees.

I take one out and walk around the desk. I place one of the coffees in front of Mara before I bend down and kiss her temple. "Morning, babe," I murmur.

"Oh," Ridge says, exaggerating the word. "I see how it is."

"I'm so sorry," Mara says, giving me a look telling me to back off.

"I'm the one that should be apologizing. You're going to have your hands full with this one." He gestures at me and my grin grows wider.

"You're not mad? I mean, we're not really… we're talking I guess you could say. Have been talking," she confesses.

Ridge looks over at me and I nod. Everything falls into place with that simple act. "Not at all. As long as it doesn't interfere with your work."

"It won't." She's quick to assure him. "Right, Seth?"

"Have a donut," I say, indicating the box. She glares at me, which makes Ridge laugh. It's not that I don't want to answer her, but I don't know how without coming on too strong. She's what's most important, not the job, and I know she won't see it that way. I know the guys will be good to her—that's not an issue—but still, I can't promise I won't ever interfere if that's what's best for her. I can't lie to her, and I know she's not ready to hear that, so changing the subject works best.

"Don't mind if I do." Ridge lifts the lid and pulls out a donut before sliding the box to Mara. "Have one. This is a treat."

"Oh, so you don't bring donuts to work every Monday?" she asks, and I can hear the snark in her voice.

"Only on my girl's first day." Her eyes widen as does my smile.

"As I was saying," Ridge focuses on Mara, "you already know QuickBooks, and pretty much everything else will come with a learning curve. Mom has been handling a lot of it. Kendall only works a half day today, so Mom will be here this afternoon after Kendall picks up the kids."

"I'm sure I can figure it out," Mara assures him with confidence.

"That's what I'm hoping. I'm shit at all of this." He waves his arm around the small office that will be hers. "I'm much better out of the office bidding jobs, or keeping the monkeys from getting out of hand."

"Hey," I say, pretending to be offended. "Who are you calling a monkey? Is that how you treat a man who brings you breakfast?"

"Like you even have to ask." He laughs. "Besides, you're too little too late. Kendall made cupcakes for her first day. They're in the kitchen." He points to the door that leads to the small kitchen area in the building.

I shrug, because it's the thought that counts, and I know Mara well enough that my good deed is already catalogued in her mind.

The door opens and heavy footfalls sound throughout the room. "Wait? What are you doing here?" Tyler asks, joining us. He's also carrying a box of donuts.

"I brought my girl some breakfast for her first day."

I swear his damn eyes light up. "Your girl, huh? This is a new development. What happened to the chick you've been pining over for months?" Tyler smirks. I know Kendall told Reagan, I can see it in his eyes. Fucker knows it was Mara. "And my wife suggested I bring donuts as well." He places the second box on the desk.

"Good. I'm starving," Kent says as he enters the building kicking snow off his boots. He reaches for the box Tyler just placed on the desk. He chooses one and shoves a huge bite into his mouth. "I heard vat," he says, talking with a mouthful of donut.

"You mean the one he only met one time?" Ridge asks, indicating toward Mara.

"No kidding," Kent says after swallowing his half a donut. "Damn, here I was thinking of asking her out."

"Nope," I say, popping the *p*. I want to tell him to keep his damn hands to himself, but surprisingly, I keep my cool. He knows what this means; they all will. I also know they would never try to go after my girl. I'm taking a page out of Mark's book and finding my inner calm.

"You sure? It's not too late to kick his ass to the curb," he asks Mara.

"We've got your back," Tyler chimes in.

"You do have an in with the boss." Ridge chuckles, grabbing a donut.

Her face is flushed, but she's still amused by our banter if the small smile that tilts her lips in any indication. "It's new."

It's not that new. Sure, it's been texting, and the odd phone call here or there, but this intensity that I feel, that I know we both feel, that's not new.

"What's new?" Mark asks from behind us. He walks over to the desk where Mara sits and places a small bouquet of flowers. "These are from Dawn." He then reaches into the box and pulls out a donut. "What's new?" he asks again before taking a huge bite.

"Mara and Seth," Kent answers.

"No kidding. What about the one you've been saving yourself for?" he asks, laughing, and winks at Mara. Looks like Dawn was in on that phone tree as well. If Kent had a wife, I'm sure he would have been in the know as well.

"Mara," I say by way of explanation.

"Really?" he asks, faking being surprised.

"Why the shock?"

"We should have seen that one coming," Tyler says. "How did we miss it?"

"You were all occupied with your families."

"I should have seen it then," Kent counters.

"You were occupied with the kids. I believe they used you as a jungle gym most of the day."

He smiles. "I'm the favorite uncle."

"Keep telling yourself that," all four of us reply at the same time, causing Mara to laugh.

"We need to load the trailer to start on the drywall today." Ridge diverts the conversation back to work.

"On it, boss." Kent grabs an entire box of donuts and heads back outside.

"Thank you, all of you and your wives, so much for everything," Mara says.

"Welcome aboard." Tyler taps the desk and turns to leave.

"This one gives you any trouble"—Mark points to me—"you let us know." He winks and then follows the others.

"Call me if you need anything," Ridge tells her. "Here's Mom's number, and Kendall's as well."

"You can call me too," I tell her.

Ridge nods. "Any or all of us if you need anything." He grabs a donut from the other box. "Chances are the guys are gone by now," he explains before sliding into his coat and leaving us alone.

"That went well." I don't have to wait long for her reply.

"Seth," she hisses. "It's my first day."

"I know that. I also know that they need to know about us. I won't hide it."

"No. I don't want to either, but do you really think this was the time or place?"

"I do. We're family. Have been since we were small. They know I've not been going out as much and that there was someone I was interested in. I never told them who, because I wasn't sure if what I was feeling was a figment of my imagination. Then we started to text and I liked you even more. I still kept quiet, wanting to know for certain. I understand the implications of dating a single mom, and I wanted to know for me, that I was all in with you, with both of you before I said anything."

Visibly, her shoulders relax. "Okay."

"Okay? That's it?"

"That's it. I understand, and while I would have done it differently, it's out there, which is for the best and we can move on."

"Wow? No arguing? Nothing?" It's not that I think she's a drama queen, quite the opposite, in fact. However, I didn't expect for her to let go of this that easily. Just another thing to add to the ever-growing list of things I like about her.

"Life's too short. You explained yourself and I understand. There's nothing to argue about. Now, you better get moving so I can get to work. I have a lot to read through and learn."

Bracing my hands on the desk, I lean in toward her. "Have a good day." My lips connect with her cheek, and I pull back. Not because I want to, but because we both need to get to work. "Pizza tonight?" I remind her.

"Yeah. I didn't tell Finley, but she's going to be excited."

"Good. I'll text you and let you know what time we're done."

"Have a good day," she calls after me.

I want to puff my chest out and slap my hands against it at her attention. I'm fucked when it comes to her. Lucky for me, I watched Ridge, then Tyler and then Mark fall, so I know what I'm up against. I see what's happening for what it is.

I'm falling for her.

The guys didn't give me shit as I expected. With three of them married, I guess they get it. They understand the spell she has me under. Kent, on the other hand, he's still living his best life as a single guy. He'll be the last of us to fall, and I, for one, will be happy to sit back and watch it happen. Hell, that's exactly what Ridge, Tyler, and Mark are saying about me. That was pretty much their exact words. However, what they don't realize is I'm ready for it. I want that special bond with someone else. I want what they have with their wives.

"You want to head to Bottoms Up for a beer?" Kent asks.

"Sorry, man, I have to rush home and shower. I've got plans."

"With Mara?"

"Yeah, I'm taking her and Finley out for dinner."

"You need to hear the speech?" Mark asks.

"What speech?" I ask, confused.

"The one you gave me about dating a single mom."

"No. That was a little bit of projecting on my part. I had to make sure I was on board as well."

"Well?" Tyler asks as he closes the toolbox he was just loading.

"Well what?" I play dumb. I know exactly what he's asking.

"What was your conclusion?" Tyler questions.

"I know what it means, and I've thought about it. Trust me, it's not something that I'm entering into lightly."

"She's Amelia's friend," Mark points out.

"And she's my employee. My wife likes her too, so don't screw this up." Ridge slaps me on the shoulder as he walks behind me to gather the rest of the tools as we pack up for the day.

"I don't plan on screwing it up."

"But maybe scr—" Kent starts, and I punch him in the shoulder to shut him up. "What was that for?" he asks, grinning.

He knows damn well what that was for. "Don't say it. Don't even think it," I warn.

"Come on, you know you're thinking about it," he counters.

"Kenton." My voice is stern and his smile grows even wider, and I didn't think that was possible.

"Fine." He holds his hands in the air in mock surrender. "I got it.

46

Mara and her… Mara's off-limits."

"Asshole," I mutter, and Ridge throws his head back and laughs.

"Each and every one of you deserves this and so much more. I should have recorded y'all when I was falling for Kendall. You were relentless with the shit you gave me."

"Anyway," I say, changing the subject because he's right. I might be ready for it, but that's not going to stop me from calling them assholes when I see fit. "We're having dinner tonight, so I gotta jet." Looking at the time on my phone, I see it's just after six. I know she left at four thirty, so I hope I'm not too late and they still want to have dinner.

Rushing out to my truck, I climb in and am grateful I started it earlier. Actually, it was Kent who started all of ours. Fucker, I can't help but shake my head and smile. Pulling my phone from my pocket, I start to type out a text but decide to call instead.

"Hello." Her sweet voice answers after one ring.

"Hey, I'm just leaving the job site."

"Long day?" she asks.

"Yeah, but that's the norm for us. Are we still on for dinner?"

"Seth, it's fine. You've had a long day."

"You're right, I have. I'd like to end that day with you, Finley, and some cheesy extra sauce pizza."

"How did you know that?" she asks.

"Mara." I chuckle. "I remember every one of our conversations." She doesn't reply, so I push on. "I'm going to stop by my place and grab a quick shower. You ladies be ready in thirty."

"Okay," she says, surprising me. I was prepared for her to try and argue out of going.

"See you soon." I end the call, not giving her the chance to change her mind, and point my truck toward home. Lucky for me, the job we're on is only ten minutes from my place.

Pulling into my driveway, I leave the truck running and head inside. I strip naked in the laundry room, tossing my clothes in the washer to start later. I then take the world's fastest shower, towel dry my hair, slide into some jeans and a hoodie, and call it good. I find some tennis shoes in the laundry room, slip into them, grab my keys, wallet, phone, and lock up, racing back out to my truck.

I make it to Mara's with time to spare. Again, I leave the truck running as I bound up the front steps and knock on the door. I shift from one foot to the other, warding off the cold. It doesn't help that my hair is wet. I should have used the blow dryer but didn't want to risk being late.

"Hey, get in here. You're going to freeze." Mara steps back, allowing me to pass her and enter the living room.

"You ladies ready for dinner?"

"We are, but you need to do something about that wet hair. You're going to get sick."

"I'll be fine." I grin. She's worried about me.

"And we can eat here." She places her hands on her hips and gives me what I can only guess is her "mom" look.

"Fine. Do you have a hairdryer?" I ask. "Oh, and we're going out," I say, giving her a look that tells her I'm ready to argue if she is.

She sighs. "Yes, come with me." She reaches out, takes my hand, and pulls me behind her, leading us to her bathroom. She drops my hand and bends to open the cabinet under the sink, and I can't help but stare at her ass in those leggings she has on. "Here." She stands and hands me the hairdryer. "Handle that." She points to my head. "I'm going to get Finley ready to go."

"I left my truck running."

"We need to take mine for the car seat."

"I'll move it over."

"That's a lot of work just for dinner. I'll go start mine now." She turns on her heel and leaves me standing in her bathroom holding her hairdryer and thinking I need to get a car seat.

Shaking out of my thoughts, I plug the dryer in and run it over my hair. It's still damp, but not as bad. Running my fingers through it, I tuck it behind my ears. Good enough. Once I've wound up the cord and placed it back under the cabinet before shutting off the light, I follow the sounds of Finley's giggles.

"Sef!" Her eyes light up when she sees me.

"Hey, Finny. You ready for some pizza?"

She bobs her little head up and down, wiggling in her seat on the chair.

"Hold still." Mara laughs. "We have to get these boots on you or no pizza." Immediately, Finley stops wiggling and cooperates with her mom. "There." Mara stands and lifts Finley from the couch. She reaches out for me and I grin, taking her from her mother.

"How was your day with Sonia? Did you have fun?" I ask her.

She doesn't answer; instead, she rests her head on my shoulder. Her little eyes take me in as if she's trying to figure me out.

Mara collects Finley's coat and stops to stand in front of us. "We have to put your coat on so we can go."

Finley folds her little body into mine and refuses to let her mom help her into her coat. "Finley," Mara says, her tone of voice a clear warning.

"Hey, Finny. You want to go get pizza?" She lifts her head and nods. "Okay, you have to listen to your mommy and put your coat on. It's really cold outside, so if you don't wear a coat, we can't go," I explain, having no idea if she understands what I'm telling her. She's almost three, but I'm not sure reasoning with a two-and-a-half-year-old is the right thing to do. I only know what I've seen the guys and their wives do with their kids. I hope it works.

Moving to the couch, I set her down and take her coat from Mara. She holds out one arm and then the other, allowing me to help her into her coat and zip it up. As soon as her hood is up, she holds her arms out for me, and I pick her back up. "Ready?" I ask her.

Again, she bobs her little head. "Peza!" She cheers.

"How about you, Momma? You ready to go?"

She smiles a watery smile and nods. "Yes."

"Hey." I reach out and place my hand on her shoulder. "You okay?"

"I'm fine." She shakes her head and her smile grows.

"Tell me." I step closer.

"You're so good with her, and she's enamored with you."

"I'm sorry if I overstepped." I'm not really. I want to help her. She's been raising this little lady all on her own, and I want to be there to support her. Give her a break now and then. But, I also don't want to piss her off. Finley is her daughter, after all. I have no claim to either of them—something that doesn't sit well with me.

"It's not that at all. I worry about letting her get too close to you. You're the first man to ever really be in her life." She waves her hands on the air. "You know that already. I'm rambling. Never mind, let's go."

"Mara." I wait for her to look at me. "You don't have to worry about her getting close to me. I'm not going anywhere. I know that it's more than just your heart I'm vying for, it's hers too. I understand this is a package deal. I wouldn't be here if I was any less than all in."

"Momma, peza," Finley says, demanding our attention.

Leaning in, I kiss Mara's forehead. "All right, let's get moving." I bounce Finley in my arms and head outside, making sure I cradle her close to my chest to ward off the cold. I buckle her without any issues as I've had practice with the guys' kids.

"Let me shut my truck off," I say to Mara once I've closed the back door to her SUV. Rushing to my truck, I switch it off, pulling the keys from the ignition and locking the doors before climbing into the passenger seat.

"Sef," Finley says, pulling my attention. I turn to look at her and she smiles at me.

"Silly girl," I say, making a funny face. She laughs, as do I. Turning back around, I look at Mara. "She's a ham."

"She's showing off for you."

I chuckle. "Let's go, woman. We're starving here," I say to change the subject. I know it's hard for her to see Finley connecting with me this easily. It's going to take some time for her to get used to this and for her to be convinced that I want them both.

Chapter 6

Mara

We're sitting in a booth in the back corner of Small-Town Pizza. Seth is on one side of the booth while I'm on the other. Finley sits in a booster seat next to Seth. She insisted, and he didn't even balk at the idea. Instead, he slid into the booth, helped her remove her coat and made sure she was settled in her seat. Our waitress brought over a plain white paper placemat and a small cup with a few crayons in it. Finley is scribbling on the paper with not a care in the world that the man next to her is virtually a stranger.

"How was your day?" Seth asks, resting his back against the booth.

"Overwhelming. There's a lot to learn, but the systems I can handle. It's just learning the processes for Beckett Construction and the ins and outs of the business."

"Well, if you have questions or need any help, you know who to call." He points to his chest. He grins at me and I can't help but return it with one of my own. He's so easy to be around.

"What about you? You put in a long day."

"Yeah, nothing new really. We like to keep on task. If it's a job that we need to get under a roof or is outside, we try to work ahead of the weather. In this case, it's snow. We're supposed to be getting a big storm on Friday afternoon. Ridge wants to head out early, and we all agreed."

"I think it's great that you all have been best friends for so many years and still work together."

"Since we were not much older than Finley if you can believe it. And we're more than just best friends. We're family. I know that sounds strange, but the more you're around us, you'll see what I mean. It's hard to explain it. They're my brothers, their wives are my sisters-in-law, and their kids are my nieces and nephews. I can't imagine it any other way."

"I've never had that, so it's hard for me to grasp. I had very few friends growing up. I was the outcast as the girl in foster care. Most of my foster families basically took me in for the money, and I got the minimum of what I needed. Hand-me-down clothes, nothing new. I wasn't allowed to get my driver's license until I was eighteen and moved out of the home. It's not like I could invite a friend to spend the night at the home. And in order for me to go to someone's house, they had to have extensive background checks and home visits to be approved. That's a lot just for some kid to hang out at your house. The upside is that my college was paid for, so there's that. Well, there would have been that had I not gotten a full-ride scholarship. It was still nice to know that option was there, to not have that financial burden over my head.

"The foster families I lived with, they never allowed me to have people over, and they never let me go anywhere either. I think they were worried I would run off. What they failed to realize is that living with them, in a clean home with solid meals, was better than living in the children's home. They weren't mean to me. We just never really connected, you know? All that changed when I went to live with the Parkers, they had planned to at least let me get my license when I turned sixteen. They always offered for me to have friends over, but I didn't have many friends, I was the outsider, the girl with no real family."

"You've never told me what happened to your parents."

"My parents, well, let's see. I don't know who my father is. My social worker said my mother never listed him on my birth certificate. My mom, she's an addict. *Was* an addict. She died when I was two. I went to the children's home and bounced from a few foster homes. I was lucky in that respect. None of the homes I was in were bad. No drugs, or abuse. I just never seemed to... bond with them. Something was always missing. Until the Parkers, but I only had them for four short years before they had to move away."

"And Amelia? I know the two of you met in college," he says as he reaches out and pulls Finley back into her seat where she was starting to slip.

"Yeah. So when I turned eighteen in May, I also graduated. I busted my ass in school to get a full-ride scholarship. I was even granted a summer scholarship, so I started as soon as I graduated. Amelia did as well and we were roommates. We hit it off and have been close ever since."

"We all grew up together, us guys and Amelia. She went away to college and we never really heard from her. Not until she came back last year."

"She was there for me when I found out about Finley, and Blake. I don't know that I could have made it through without her. When she called and told me about the possibility of a job closer to her, I wanted to know more. She's my dearest friend." Something flashes in his eyes, but it's gone before I can decipher it.

"Sef, wook." Finley slides the placemat toward him and shows him her scribbles.

"Finny, you're an artist. How about this?" He grabs a crayon and writes F-I-N, in big letters. "Can you write that?" he asks.

She sticks out her little tongue and concentrates really hard to mimic him. He watches her with a smile on his face as she makes her attempt. "Wook," she says proudly.

"Strong work, Finny." He holds his large hand up and she places her little one against it for a high-five.

"Peza!" Finley cheers as our waitress approaches. She drops her crayon and claps her hands, making all three of us laugh.

"All right, little lady, this is hot, so you need to be careful," Seth says, placing a piece of pizza on her plate. He looks over at me. "Should I cut it up for her?"

"Yeah, I can do it." I start to reach for the plate, but he picks up a fork and starts to cut it.

"I can do it. You go ahead and eat. I eat fast so I'll catch up, trust me."

53

I put a piece on my plate and cut a bite with my fork, all while watching him work to cut up my daughter's food and keeping her entertained at the same time. He even blows on a piece and shows her that she can start eating while he works on the rest.

"For what it's worth," Seth says, adding two slices to his own plate, "I'm really glad that you took the job, and that you're here." He glances over at Finley then back to me. "Both of you."

"Me too." I don't just say the words; I mean them. All these months Seth and I have been talking, and I feel like I've known him forever. Sitting here with him, watching him with Finley, it confirms what I already knew. Seth Jennings is one of the good ones. I'm not sure what I've done in life to stumble upon Amelia and her friendship, and now this. Her sharing her friends and family with me. Bringing me into their fold. I feel as though Finley and I can actually be a part of something. That it isn't just the two of us against the world anymore. The thought is scary and exciting all at the same time.

"Finley, let's go potty before we leave," I tell my daughter once we've finished eating. "We're potty training. She's been doing great, but I have to remind her frequently to avoid any accidents," I explain to Seth. Some date I am. I can feel the flush on my cheeks as I stand here awkwardly discussing my toddler's bathroom habits.

"No worries. You ladies do what you need to do. I'm going to take care of the check and get a box for the leftovers."

"Here, let me." I reach for my purse and he shakes his head.

"Not happening, babe. Go take care of Finny. I'll take care of this. It was my treat." He lifts Finley from her seat over the booth and into my arms. I don't bother to argue. One, I don't want to make a scene and two, he doesn't strike me as the type of man who's just going to give in on something like paying for dinner. I make a mental note for it to be my treat next time.

Next time.

I'm already anticipating the next time I get to see him. "Momma's in over her head, Finley." She smiles up at me like she gets it. "Yeah, you are too, sweet girl. I hope he doesn't break our hearts." I've been living but not *really* living. Living for Finley, but I want to live for both of us. I want her to see what it's like for a man to be a part of our lives, to see the connection between a man and a woman. I'm risking both of our hearts taking a leap with Seth, but I can't shelter her from heartbreak. Hell, I can't shelter either of us. We're diving, hoping for the best, but if it's the worst, well, we have each other and we'll muddle through. "It's time to take chances, Finley."

"Sef."

I can't help it. I laugh. I know she doesn't know what I'm talking about, but her reply couldn't be more perfect. "Yeah, sweetie. Seth." I help her use the potty and praise her when she does. After washing our hands, we find Seth waiting for us just outside the restrooms.

"Let's get you bundled up." He helps Finley into her coat, then takes her from me, handing me mine. Once I'm in my coat, he passes me the small box of leftovers that were sitting on the ledge nearby and then laces his fingers through mine. Together, the three of us linked, hand in hand and Finley in his arms, make our way outside. "You mind if we make a stop?" he asks. "Or does she need to get home and in bed?"

"How long of a stop are we talking?" I ask, mentally wondering what time it is. I know it's getting close to her bedtime.

"Just about ten minutes tops. I actually need your help."

"Sure, we can do that."

"How about I drive?" He doesn't wait for an answer as he opens the back door to my Pathfinder and buckles Finley into her seat. I reach in and start the car and move around to the passenger side, climbing in. As if he's done it a million times, he slides behind the wheel, adjusts the seat, reaches for my hand, and rests it on his thigh before pulling out of the parking lot.

"So, where are we going anyway?"

"I want to get a seat for my truck."

"Why do you need my help with a truck seat?"

"Not for my truck, for Finley for my truck. That way, we don't always have to take your car. I can take you ladies out on a date with me driving."

"Seth, you don't have to do that." I'm quick to shut him down.

"I know I don't have to. I want to. Just humor me, will you?"

I don't say anything else as he drives us to the nearest Walmart. I'm trying to wrap my head around how my life has changed so quickly. I went to depending on no one, to wanting more than anything to depend on Seth. I want more than anything to embrace him and this new life filled with anything but loneliness he's offering. Even more so, I didn't really understand how lonely I was until moving here. I love my daughter, but having someone to lean on isn't what I'm used to. No one other than Amelia has ever been in that role for me.

Seth parks the Pathfinder and pulls the keys from the ignition, handing them to me. He hops out and has Finley unbuckled from her seat before I can offer to do it myself. He meets me in front of the car and, once again, laces his fingers with mine as we make our way into the store.

"You want to ride in the cart?" he asks Finley.

"Cart."

"Cart it is." He chuckles and sets her in the front. "Okay. So, first we get a seat for you for my truck, and then we hit up the toy aisle."

"My want toy."

"Let's get the seat first." He begins to push the cart to the back of the store, where the baby section is. I know because I made a visit to this very store early Sunday morning for supplies for the new place. "You need anything else while we're here?" he asks.

"Sef, toy," Finley says.

"I know, sweetheart. We have to get your new car seat first. You can help me and Mommy pick it out."

"'Kay." Just like that, she agrees to whatever he says. Don't get me wrong, she's not a bad kid. In fact, she's very well behaved, but at this age, she tends to be opinionated and wants things how she wants them. However, she doesn't appear to be that way when it comes to Seth.

"All right, tell me which one."

We're standing in front of a long line of car seats. "This is the one that I have." I point to the third seat on the left.

"Perfect. What do you think, Finny? Should we get a seat like the one in Mommy's car?"

"Dat one." She points to the same seat I did.

"Looks like it's unanimous." Seth pulls the box from the bottom shelf and places it in the cart. Even though he's bundled up in his coat,

I can imagine his muscles flexing underneath. Everything seems so effortless for him. His question pulls me away from ogling him.

"Now, Momma, you sure you don't need anything?"

"Actually, yes. I need some fabric softener. I forgot it when I was here yesterday."

"Okay, well, you go get what you need. Finley and I are headed to the toys."

"Toy, Mommy." Finley grins.

"Don't spoil her." I point at him.

"Sure thing," he says, grinning, and I know damn good and well he's not going to listen. "We'll be in the toys." He pushes the cart in the opposite direction of where I need to go. My chest tightens, watching him leave with her, but I trust him. Regardless, I haul ass to grab what I need and head straight back to the toys. We've been separated maybe five minutes at the most by the time I reach them. Finley has two stuffed animals and a baby doll in her arms.

"Seth." His name comes out as a sigh.

He throws his head back and laughs. "She can't decide." He defends his actions with a small shrug.

"One." I hold up one finger. "Finley, you can have one."

"I wuv dem," she says, trying to squeeze them all to her chest.

"You choose one." I look up at Seth. "You can't spoil her like this. I can't do this every time I come to the store, and I don't want her to expect it."

"I'm sorry." I can see it in his eyes that he gets what I'm trying to tell him without saying the words. I can't afford to spoil her like this. Not to mention, I don't know that I would if I could. I want her to grow up understanding not everything is just handed to you in life. I want her to earn it, appreciate it.

"Okay, sweetheart. You have to pick just one."

"Mine," Finley says, pouting.

I can see Seth wavering, but he surprises me when he stands his ground. "Pick your favorite." He takes them from her and she whines but doesn't throw a fit. "Let's pick." He holds all three of them to his chest. "You can only have one, so which one will it be?"

Finley furrows her brow as her eyes move to the stuffed animals and the small baby doll, then back to Seth. "Dat one," she says, pointing to the teddy bear that's light brown with a pink nose.

"Excellent choice." Seth hands her the bear and places the other two back on the shelf. "Did you get what you needed?" he asks me.

"Yeah." I hold up the small bottle of fabric softener, and he takes it from me, placing it in the cart. He pushes the cart, talking to Finley about her new bear all the way to the front of the store and through the checkout line. He pays for everything, including my fabric softener, even though I told him not to. He didn't listen, but I've decided I need to pick my battles. I know he's doing it to be nice, and I appreciate the gesture. What's a small bottle of fabric softener in the grand scheme of things? Is it worth starting an argument? Not to me.

Seth wheels the cart out of the store and pushes Finley fast through the lot. Her laughter echoes, making me smile.

"I'll get her," I tell Seth. He nods and gets to work loading the car seat and the fabric softener in the back. He slips in behind the wheel and turns to hand Finley her bear.

"Here you go, sweetheart."

"Ank you, Sef."

"That right there could thaw any cold heart," he says before turning back around.

I don't say anything as he drives us home. Finley yammers in the back to her new friend, while I work on getting my heart to stop stuttering in my chest. Is this what all the authors mean when they say swooning? It has to be. This is not a feeling I've ever experienced, but one I could quickly grow accustomed to.

"Two stories, but she's finally out," I say, taking a seat on the couch next to Seth. He's got his shoes off and his feet propped up on the coffee table. He looks relaxed, like he belongs here.

"You don't have to apologize. Finley is your priority, I get that. Speaking of Finley. I'm sorry about the store. She's hard to say no to. I shouldn't have overstepped."

"You didn't. I just don't want her to think everything she wants is going to be handed to her. Special occasions or situations are fine, but I want her to learn the value of money and gifts. You know, things like that," I say, to stop my rambling.

"What else needs to be done tonight?" he asks.

"What do you mean?"

"Laundry, packing bags for tomorrow—what?"

"Oh. No, I packed her bag before you got here, and laundry is never-ending with a toddler."

"So I get some Mara time?" he asks hopefully.

"Depends. What exactly is Mara time?" I can't help but laugh.

"Just time with you. Come here." He lifts his arm and I slide in a little closer, resting my head on his chest. "This is Mara time."

"Hmm, Seth time sounds better."

"How about us time?" he counters with a low chuckle.

"Us time sounds perfect," I say, covering a yawn. He flips the channel to some movie I've never seen and begins to softly trace circles on my back. It's not long before I feel sleep pulling me under. I'm too tired to even try to resist as I drift off.

Sometime later, I wake to the evening news. It takes me a minute to get my bearings and realize I'm in the living room, lying on top of Seth, where we're both stretched out on the couch. I move to get up but his arms tighten around me. "Stay."

I don't fight him; instead, I snuggle into him, resting my head back on his chest, right over his heart.

"I know I need to go, but I don't want to," he whispers.

"I don't want you to go either, but—" I stop, letting my reasoning hang between us.

"I know, babe," he assures me. "I know you don't want her to wake up and see me. And this is new, you and me, well, not really, but the being together in person part is new. Not the way I'm feeling about you."

I lift my head to look at him, resting my chin on his chest. "I feel it too," I confess.

"Good." He tucks my hair behind my ear. "I'm going to go, but can I kiss you first? I really want to kiss you," he whispers, his eyes following the movement of my tongue as I wet my lips.

"I'd be mad if you didn't." I lift up and meet him as his lips press to mine. The kiss starts off slow, just the pressure of his lips on mine. Once, twice, three times, he kisses me before his tongue peeks out and traces my bottom lip.

"So sweet," he murmurs, kissing me again. This time, his hand finds its way to the back of my neck as he holds me close. I open for him, and he wastes no time sliding his tongue past my lips to caress mine.

Needing more, I move to straddle him, never breaking our kiss. My hips rock against his, and his body reacts to me. Somehow, he manages to sit up and rest his back against the couch. My hands go to his shoulders as I grind against him.

"Fuck," he murmurs, letting his head fall back against the couch. I freeze, and his hands land on my hips. "Don't stop, baby. Take what you need."

Embarrassed, I bury my face in his neck. I don't know what's come over me. I feel his arms wrap around me as he holds me close.

"Mara."

Knowing I have to face the music, I lift my head, grateful that the room is dark with nothing but the glow of the TV. "I'm sorry," I say sheepishly.

"I'm not. I never want you to be shy about asking or taking what you need from me. No matter what it is."

"That's not me. I don't know what's come over me."

"That might not be you, but that's us." His hands move to my hips and he guides me to move up and back, up and back. "Take what you need. There are no pretenses, no worry about what you'll have to give in return. Not with me." His hands move from my hips to cradle my cheeks in the palms of his hands. "I want to give you everything." His lips connect with mine in a kiss so sensual, it sends electric currents throughout my body. I rock my hips and he pulls away. "Take what you need. I wanna see you come, Mara." His softly whispered confession does nothing to limit my desire, this hot inferno building inside me. My hands brace on his shoulders once more. His hands land back on my hips, and together, we chase the high that is just within my reach. His eyes, dark brown pools of desire, never leave mine. I close my eyes, his stare too intense. "Open for me, Mara. I want to see you when you lose control."

"I can't." I keep my eyes closed and lower my head. Just… feeling.

"It's just me, baby, and I'm here for you. Take what you need, but let me see. Let me watch you. Give me those big green eyes." He lifts his hips and his hard length hits my clit. Slowly, I lift my head and stare into his eyes. "There she is. Now show me."

The sensation is too intense, the friction feels too good, so I do as he asks. I grind against him, seeking release, something I've been missing in my life since the night I last slept with Finley's father. Since the night my daughter was conceived. Sure, I take matters into my own hands, but there is nothing that compares to strong hands roaming your body, or Seth's deep voice telling me to let go.

"S-Seth," I pant.

"I'm right here, gorgeous. I'm right here." His grip on my hips tightens as he guides me to my release.

"Oh my…." I bite down on my bottom lip to keep from screaming out his name, mindful that my daughter is sleeping just down the hall. Once the final tremor leaves my body, I slump against him. Spent, sated, and too damn blissed out to feel embarrassed.

Seth holds me against him. I can feel how hard he is, but he never once takes it any further. That alone makes me want to. I pull away, stand, and try to drop to my knees, but he stops me.

"Not tonight. Let's get you tucked into bed."

"That's got to hurt," I say, looking at the bulge in his jeans.

"Don't worry about me. I got exactly what I wanted. I wanted to spend time with you and your daughter, and I wanted to see you come. I got both."

"Seth—" He stops me with a kiss.

"No. We have time for more another time. This isn't one and done, Mara. There's no rush. Come on." He walks me to the door. "I wanted to tuck you in, but damn it, I know if I see you in your bed, I'll never be able to leave. So I'm going to say goodnight here. Lock up behind me and I'll see you at work in the morning."

"Thank you for dinner."

"My pleasure. Get some rest."

"Be safe. Will you text me when you get home? So I know you made it okay."

"I don't want to wake you."

"I'll be up until I hear from you."

"Okay. Lock up behind me. Give Finley a hug from me in the morning."

"Night, Seth."

He leans in and kisses me. "Night, baby."

He opens the door and quietly slips outside. I turn the lock and hear his footsteps pound down the front steps. I'm sure his truck is freezing cold, but I'm afraid if he was here any longer, I might force him to stay. Turning off the TV, I make my way to my room and decide I need a shower to clean up. I rinse off quickly, knowing I'll take another in the morning since I'm going to bed with wet hair, and change into some pajamas. Picking up my phone, I see that I have a missed call.

Amelia.

I quickly send her a message.

Me: *Sorry. I fell asleep.*

With Seth. Of course, I leave that part out, even though it's the most interesting. I know my friend and she's going to want all the details, and I'm still processing them myself.

Amelia: *I figured. How was your first day?*

Me: *Great. It's a lot to learn about the business, but I'm feeling good about it.*

Amelia: *I knew you would. Get some sleep. We'll catch up tomorrow.*

Me: *Night.*

Amelia is working at temporary jobs for an agency. I'm not sure why. She's got the education and the skill to do so much more. I feel like I'm missing something important with her. Maybe it's just the time we spent apart, but my gut tells me that it's more. I'll have to plan dinner or something so she and I can catch up, and I can try to figure out what's going on with my dearest friend.

I'm lying in bed staring at the shadows on the ceiling, thinking about tonight, thinking about Seth, when my phone vibrates in my hand.

Seth: *Made it home.*

Me: *Good. Night, Seth.*

Seth: *Night.*

Plugging my phone in to charge, I drift off to sleep with thoughts of Seth and this new life I'm living on my mind. I'm excited for once to see what's yet to come.

Chapter 7

SETH

It's Saturday night and I'm sitting on the floor of Finley's room watching her dance around in circles. We spent the day painting it a light and dark teal. I thought Mara was crazy when she told me, but I have to admit, it turned out great.

"You like it?" I ask, laughing as she spins so fast she gets dizzy and crashes into a pile of pillows in the middle of the floor.

"I wuv it." She crawls over to me and into my lap. "Ank you." She wraps her little arms around my neck in a hug. I hug her back, my heart splitting wide open for this little girl.

"All right, miss thang, it's time for you to go to bed."

"No." She clings to me.

"Hey, remember I have a surprise for you tomorrow."

Her little head lifts from where she had it buried in my chest. "You have to go to sleep so you can wake up and I can take you to your surprise."

She shakes her head. "No."

"Come on, Mommy will read you a story." Mara tries to coax her.

"Sef," she says defiantly, holding onto me.

My eyes find Mara, and she sighs. I raise my eyebrows in silent question, and she nods, giving me her permission. "Okay, but one story, and then you have to promise to have sweet dreams." In a flash, she's off my lap and rushing to the small bookshelf that's sitting away from the wall allowing the paint to dry. She grabs a book and brings it to me. I lie down on the floor, resting my head on the pillows and she lies down next to me. "*Five-Minute Princess Stories*," I read the title of the book. I glance at Mara to see that she's no longer there. "Okay, one story, you ready?" I ask Finley. She nods her little head and yawns. If I was a betting man, I would guess she won't last through one full story. She's played hard today and only slept for a little while. According to Mara, she usually takes at least a two-hour nap, so I'm sure she's ready to crash.

I'm barely a minute into the story when her breathing evens out, and I know she's out. I read a little longer, just to be sure, before putting the book off to the side and sliding away from her. Once on my feet, I bend to pick her up and place her in her crib. Kissing the tips of my fingers, I place them to her forehead. "Night, Finny," I whisper before turning off the light and switching on the small lamp, just like I've seen Mara do every night this week.

Every night I've been here for bedtime, and I don't hate it. In fact, I enjoy it more than I ever thought I would. I also enjoy the time with Mara after. Nothing like Monday night, but lots of kissing and her in my arms, so that's a win in my book.

Quietly making my way down the hall, I find Mara on the couch, with tears in her eyes and a tissue in her hands. "Hey." I rush to her, sitting as close as I can. "What's going on?"

"Nothing." She laughs through her tears. "I'm just emotional, that's all."

"Why don't you let me be the judge of that? What's causing these tears?" I ask gently, wiping them from her cheeks with my thumbs.

"She's never wanted anyone but me," she says sadly. "It's a new concept for me."

"I'm sorry," I say. I hate that Finley wanting me to read to her has caused this.

"Don't be. It's silly. I love that you're so good to her. I love that she has someone other than me in her life who she can turn to. I just…. It's hard when it's been just the two of us. Amelia moved home when she was still pretty young, and she was still in the mommy stage. She really likes you."

"I like her too. She's a good kid."

"I really like you too." Her confession is whispered. "It's fast and overwhelming, and I don't know how to handle it all."

"One day at a time. There is no timeframe we have to live by. We do what's best for us."

"Thank you for being so good with her."

"She's a part of you," I say, cupping her cheek. "How could I not be?"

She laughs and her smile overcomes the sadness that shadowed her face just moments before. "She's going to love you even more once she sees her big-girl bed and that you're the one putting it together for her."

"All in my master plan."

"Oh, yeah? Care to enlighten me?"

"Easy." I shrug. "I get Finley to fall in love with me, and then by default, you won't have a choice but to follow suit."

"Is that what you want? For me to fall in love with you? For both of us to fall in love with you?" she asks. Her tone tells me she's cautious of my answer, but not so much that she's afraid to ask.

"I don't hate the idea." I wink, and her face lights up.

"Thank you for today. I'm sure you had better things to do than hang out here and paint all day."

"It was fun. A challenge to keep Finny's hands out of the paint, but it was a good time. I like being here with the two of you."

"She's going to be so excited tomorrow when we go shopping for her big-girl bed. You sure you don't mind going?"

"Not at all. I'm invested at this point. Not to mention, I promised her a surprise."

"That's right. She never forgets either. A few weeks before we moved here, she saw a commercial for ice cream and was determined to get some that night. It was way too close to bedtime, so I appeased her, saying she could have some the next day. She woke up asking for ice cream."

"What did you do?"

She shrugs and grins. "We had ice cream for breakfast."

"What? No, I can't see you doing that." I laugh.

"Normally, I wouldn't. She looked so sweet with her hair a tangled mess, rubbing her eyes, asking for ice cream. It was a Saturday, and I knew we would be cooped up all day packing, so I figured why not. It's okay to live a little. I want her to be spontaneous and adventurous. I just don't want her to be a wild child and eat ice cream for breakfast every morning."

"She's too sweet to be a wild child."

"Don't let her innocent looks and that pouty lip fool you."

"I think it's her eyes. They're just like yours, and that makes it even harder for me to say no to her."

"When have you ever tried to tell her no?"

"At the store when we bought her seat. I really wanted to buy her all three that night."

"Well, thank you for not."

"I said that night."

"What did you do, Seth Jennings?" She playfully smacks my arm.

"What? I had to. I ran to the store after work the next night to pick up the other two. I'll save them for a rainy day. She *wuved* them all," I say, mocking Finley.

"Sucker." Her grin is wide as she speaks.

"It's those eyes, I'm telling you."

"Wait until I tell the guys." She chuckles.

"Go right ahead. They'll all get it. Well, Kent will, but not to the extent that the others do. They all have kids. Ridge and Mark specifically with little girls. I mean, how do you discipline her? One wobble of that little lip and a bat of those eyelashes and I'd be toast."

"If it's to teach her right from wrong, I don't have an issue with it. It's my job to make her a functioning member of society, but if it's something like repeating a cuss word, it's hard to keep a straight face."

"No. No way does my little Finny cuss."

"She does when she hears her mommy say it when she stubs her toe.

I was so afraid that she was going to go to daycare and sing 'shit' all day long. I've learned to watch my mouth."

"Yeah, we've all gotten better as well. The wives keep on top of us when the kids are around. It was hard with Knox, but now, between the five kids, there is always one lingering and we're getting used to it. At least I am."

"Yeah." She places her hand over her mouth to cover her yawn. "Sorry."

"Don't be. We've been at it all day. I guess I should head home. What time do you want to leave tomorrow?"

"The store opens at eleven since it's Sunday. So sleep in."

"How about I take you girls to breakfast?"

"How about I make us breakfast instead? You don't have to keep taking us out. You took us out Monday, brought dinner Wednesday and Friday, and then paid for takeout yesterday."

"I want to."

"Well, I want to make you breakfast."

"Okay. What time do you want me here?"

She thinks about it while biting on her bottom lip. "Ten? I think we should be at the store when it opens. I have to go to the store tomorrow for next week as well."

"Ten it is. You need me to bring anything?"

"Just you, Seth. You've already done too much."

"Never." I lean in and kiss her softly. "I don't want to leave you."

"I thought maybe it was just me."

"Definitely not."

"One more," I say, pressing my lips to hers. I kiss her lips, then trail my kisses across her jaw and down her neck.

"Seth."

I'm not sure if it's a warning or a plea, but I pull back and kiss the tip of her nose. "I'm going to run out and start my truck. Be right back." I stand and rush to the door, sliding my feet into my boots and head out the door. The cool wind does nothing to cool my body's reaction to her. At this point, I don't know if anything ever will.

"You should have worn your coat," she says, standing by the door when I get back inside. "You're going to get sick."

"Me? I'll be fine." I wrap my arms around her and she shivers from the cold.

"I forgot that Amelia is coming over tomorrow for breakfast so we can catch up."

"Okay. So I'll come a little later." Not an issue. Sure, I want all their time, but I know she hasn't been able to catch up with Amelia this week, because she's been with me.

"No, I still want you to be here. I'll text her and tell her to come a little earlier because we're going bed shopping."

"You sure? I know you've been missing her calls all week."

"I'm sure. I'm not going to shut you out to see her or shut her out to see you. Although you're so distracting I'm sure that's how it seems."

"Distracting, huh?" I ask, my lips nipping at her ear.

"So distracting."

"I'll be here," I whisper in her ear. "Sweet dreams, Mara." Standing to my full height, I pull her into my chest and hug her tight.

"Drive safe. Let me know when you make it home."

"Will do, babe. Lock up behind me." It takes everything I have to pull away from her and walk out the door. This week has been more than I can describe. Spending time with them and getting to see them together as a family. I long to be a part of it. The more time I spend with them, the more that becomes clear to me.

I want them to be *my* family.

In the living room, I flip through the TV channels, but nothing is gaining my interest. It could be because my interest is about ten minutes across town. The Walmart bag with the doll and the other stuffed animal are staring at me from where I dropped the bag on the chair earlier this week. I don't know when I'm going to give them to her, but I knew she had to have them. Sounds crazy now, but at the time, all I could think about was making that little girl smile. Both of them.

Glancing at the clock, it's just before nine. I have another hour before I have to be there. I should have slept in, but that's impossible. I'm used to getting up early for work, so the weekends are ruined for me. Turning off the TV, I toss the remote on the couch cushion next to me and call my parents and check-in.

"Seth, how are you, son?" Dad answers.

"Hey, Dad. Good. How are things?"

"Can't complain. How about you? Anything new?"

I hesitate for maybe a second before blurting it out. "Yeah, Mara and I are dating."

"Mara? That's Amelia's friend, right?"

"Yeah, she and her daughter, Finley, just moved to town. She's working at Beckett for Ridge."

"And the two of you are dating?" he clarifies.

"Yeah, she and I've been talking since she was here over the summer. Nothing official, just texting back and forth, a phone call here or there. Now that she's here, we're seeing where things go."

"She's a mom."

"I know."

"You know what that means?"

I chuckle. "Yeah, you can ask Mark all about that conversation. I was battling with it in my mind, and when everything went down with Daisy, I gave him the same speech. I know what it means. I know it's two hearts on the line. But it's actually three. I really like her."

"Well, you're going to have to bring them over for dinner. I'll have your mother call you to set it up."

"Where is Mom? I assumed she'd already be listening in to our conversation by now."

"Oh, she's out shopping with Sonia. They went to the outlet malls today. What are you getting into?"

"Mara and I are going to buy Finley a big-girl bed. Well, I mean a twin-size bed. Sorry, that's what we called it all day yesterday when we painted her room."

"Sounds like you're settling in."

"I hope so."

"Just be yourself, son. She won't be able to resist you. Your mother will be thrilled. She's been yacking about grandkids since Knox was born."

"Like she's the only one," I say, chuckling.

"Fine, we both want them while we're still young enough to enjoy them."

"Well, maybe I can talk Mara into a date night, and you and Mom can watch Finley for us?" I ask.

"You tell us when and we're there. I'm not going to mention it to your mother. I wouldn't put it past her to call Sonia and have her help convince Mara to let us keep the tyke for a couple of hours."

"Well, if I need backup, I'm definitely calling Mom." I know the power of persuasion when our mothers band together. Sonia and Mom will be no match for Mara. "All right, I'm heading over there now, I just wanted to call and catch up."

"Good to hear from you, son. I'll have your mom call and set up dinner. We need to meet Mara and Finley again now that things are official. Welcome them to the family."

"Will do. Talk to you later." I end the call with a smile on my face. My parents are nothing short of amazing. I don't know how they've put up with me all these years and still laugh about the shit the guys and I used to do back in the day. Nothing illegal, but we were always getting into something and eating them out of house and home. Not once did they complain. They just welcomed my friends with open arms. All five of us were lucky in that department. Amelia too. Although her parents were a lot older than ours, so they were kind of the outcasts of the group, staying to themselves, and we hardly ever went there. She was always with us.

That was a good way to spend fifteen minutes, but I can't wait any longer. Grabbing my phone, I slide it into my pocket, collect my coat, and head outside to start my truck. I mess around outside, shoveling the small amount of snow that fell last night from the sidewalk while the truck warms up, and fifteen minutes later, I'm pulling into her driveway, parking my truck beside Amelia's car.

I knock once and hear Finley yell, "Sef," which brings a smile to my face. I hear her little feet pad across the floor and Mara's voice telling her to not open the door. When the door finally opens, I'm greeted by my girls.

"Sef." Finley holds her hands out for me, and I don't hesitate to take her from Mara.

"Hey, Finny." I tickle her side, making her squirm.

"You're letting in all the cold air." Mara laughs as I step in and toe-off my boots. Leaning down, I kiss her forehead. "Morning, babe."

"Oh, how the mighty have fallen," Amelia chirps from her spot at the kitchen table.

"I'm enjoying the ride," I say, my eyes never leaving Mara. "You need any help?"

"No, I've made a breakfast casserole. It should be ready in another twenty minutes."

"Well, Finny, what do you say we go do some coloring so Mommy and Aunt Amelia can catch up?"

"Cowor." She cheers and wriggles until I let her down, and she races to the coffee table where her coloring books and crayons are laid out.

"Missed you," I say, kissing the corner of Mara's mouth while Finley is occupied before joining her in the living room. I can hear Mara and Amelia chatting, but Finley demands my attention as she shows me each color, and she changes them frequently. I hear laughter and look over to find Mara with her head tilted back and a huge smile on her face. Amelia is laughing and waving her hands in the air, telling a story. A knot twists in my gut. I'm going to need to tell Mara about New Year's Eve. Even though I can't remember it—neither one of us can—and it meant nothing, I still have to tell her.

I didn't cheat on her, although it feels like I did. We weren't dating. Hell, we weren't anything at that point, but the thought of us being more was there in the back of my mind. I never should have drunk that much. If I had been sober or less trashed, I would have known better. I slept with one of my best friends. Not only that, she's my girlfriend's one and only friend as well. I'm scared as hell that she'll push me away. I won't go quietly, certainly not without a fight. I fought myself for long enough, worried I wouldn't be enough for them, both her and Finley. Now that they're here and in my life, I want more time with them. I will strive each day to be what they need.

"Seth." Mara's soft voice accompanies her hand on my shoulder, bringing me out of my thoughts. "You okay?" she asks when I look up at her.

"Yeah, just dazed off there for a minute. Are you ready for us?" I look over to discover Finley is no longer sitting beside me.

"She heard me yell that it was ready. Are you sure you're okay?"

"Yes." I stand and kiss her temple. "Just lost in thought."

"Anything you want to talk about?"

"Not really." I lie. "Just thinking about how much I like us, you, me, and Finley." That is not a lie.

Her face lights up in a smile. "I like us too."

Snaking a hand around her waist, I guide us to the kitchen. Amelia is already eating, as is Finley. I take a seat next to the high chair, and Mara sits on the other side.

"Bite." Finley offers me her spoon with a bite of her casserole on it. Leaning in, I pretend to eat it and she cackles with laughter. "Bite, Sef," she says, holding it out again. I pretend again, but she's not having it. "Bite." She grins.

Taking the hint, I wrap my lips around her spoon and exaggerate a moaning sound like it's the best food I've ever tasted. It's not too far of an exaggeration; it's pretty damn good. "Yummy." My real bite must appease her because she goes back to shoveling in her breakfast. "Morning, A," I say to Amelia as I make my plate.

"Morning." She grins. "I've been hearing all kinds of things about you, Seth Jennings."

"Oh, yeah? All good I hope." I focus on taking my first bite instead of looking over at Mara.

Amelia laughs. "Surprisingly. I'm actually kind of disappointed. I wanted to watch you sweat over the fall, but you jumped in feet first."

"Do you blame me?" I ask her.

"Nope. Treat them right," she warns, pointing her fork at me.

"You have my word."

"Good. Now, what's this big surprise Finley keeps yammering on about?" she asks.

"I told her I had a surprise for her today."

"Oh, I love surprises."

"You're welcome to go with us," Mara tells her. "We're going to buy

74

a b-e-d." She spells it out. "For the big girl." Mara nods toward Finley, who is completely focused on her breakfast.

"You're buying it?" Amelia asks me.

"Right." I laugh. "Like this one would let me get away with that. She made me be the bad guy and tell Finny she could only have one stuffed animal the other day." I fake a pout, and Mara chuckles under her breath.

"You poor thing," Amelia coos. Well, she tries to. Her laughter wins out.

"Finny, you see the way they treat me?" I ask, leaning in close. Her reply is to laugh dramatically and shove her spoon in my mouth.

"That's one way to shut him up," Amelia quips.

I swallow my bite and grin at Finley. "Thanks, Finny."

"Anks," she replies.

We laugh and talk while eating our breakfast, and it's after eleven, later than we wanted to leave the house. Amelia declined our invite to join us, claiming she had to help her mom with a few things. So, me and my girls headed off to buy a big-girl bed. If you had asked me a year ago if this is where I would be, I would have denied and laughed at you. Now, there is no other way I'd rather spend my day than with the two of them.

Chapter 8

Mara

It's hard to believe today is my third week at Beckett Construction. These past few weeks have flown by, but I must admit I've loved every minute of it. I love my job. Ridge is great to work for. Kendall's mom, Sonia, has my daughter on a pedestal, and she's thriving because of it. She's always babbling about whatever it was they did during the day. I went from it just being the two of us to feeling as if I have this huge support system.

Every day since the day he helped us move in, I've seen Seth. He's been a constant in our lives the last few weeks, and already I know I don't want that to change. Tonight, however, he had to help his dad move some things around in the garage, so Finley and I had dinner just the two of us. She asked for Seth multiple times. That alone speaks volumes that I'm not the only one growing attached to him.

"Time for bed, Fin," I say, turning off the TV. I let her watch about twenty minutes of her favorite movie after her bath.

"No." She crosses her arms over her chest and pouts. "I want Sef."

"Honey, Seth had to help his daddy. He couldn't come and see us tonight. I promise you'll see him tomorrow."

"No."

At two and a half, there is no reasoning with her. "It's bedtime." I stand and lift her from the couch. She begins to cry. The closer we get to her room, the louder her cries are. "Look, you get to sleep in your princess bed Seth made you." He didn't really make it, but he did assemble it and that's all she cares about.

"Sef," she cries, her bottom lip quivering with her tears.

My heart splinters when I see her big fat tears roll over her cheeks. I try to put her in her bed, and while she clings to me, her cries are for him. For the first time, I'm not who she wants, and that's a hard pill to swallow. I rock her back and forth in my arms, but it does nothing to console her. My mind races with how to calm her down. How can I console her? Then it hits me. Reaching into my back pocket, I grab my phone and swipe at the screen. "Finley, how about we call Seth? You want to talk to him?"

Her cries quiet and she nods. Deciding that a video call is the better option, I tap on the screen and it starts to ring.

"Hello." His face appears on the screen and Finley calls out for him.

"Sef," she says in her pitiful, heartbroken voice.

"Finny? What's the matter, sweetheart?" he asks soothingly.

"Night night." She shudders as she tries to catch her breath.

"Mara?" he asks, his eyes darting to me.

"She's upset that she didn't get to see you tonight. She's been asking for you since we got home."

"Finny. I miss you so so much," he says, focusing back on her. "I'm sorry I had to miss tonight. I'm helping my daddy. You want to see him?" She nods and he turns the phone toward his parents. It appears that they're in their kitchen. "Finley, this is my mommy and daddy, Steve and Shannon Jennings." My heart stutters in my chest as we're introduced to his parents for the first time. From their expressions, they know all about us. I don't know why that surprises me; he's been open and honest about not hiding this relationship from the very beginning.

"Hey there, Finley. Why the tears?" Steve asks.

"My Sef," she says, pointing at the phone screen.

That small declaration does something to him. He stands and our view becomes the floor. I hear him tell his parents he has to go, then he's back on the screen. "Finley, I'll be there in about fifteen minutes. Pick out a book and I'll read you a story, okay?" he asks softly.

"'Kay," she replies, sniffling.

"Babe, I'm going to head your way. I'll see you soon." With that, the screen goes black.

"Sef story," she says with another shuddering breath.

"Yeah, sweetie. Seth can read you a story." She wiggles out of my arms and runs to her bookshelf and takes her time digging through her books. In the end, she chooses her *Five-Minute Princess Stories* and races back to her bed. I watch as she pulls her soft princess blanket over her and up to her chin. She hugs the book to her chest and looks up at me.

"Sef story, Mommy."

"He's on his way. How about I read you a story until he gets here?" I offer. Again, reasoning with a two-and-a-half-year-old is not the easiest thing in the world.

"No. My want Sef."

"Okay," I say, holding back tears of my own. "Well, we need to go wait for him to get here. Mommy has to unlock the door." Just as I say the words, lights shine on her bedroom window as a truck pulls into the drive. "There he is," I tell her. "Let's go let him in." She launches herself in my arms and I carry her down the hall and to the front door. Just as his hand is up to knock, I'm pulling the door open to greet him.

"Sef!" Finley cheers and jumps from my arms to his. Luckily he was ready for her.

"Hey, Finny. What's going on? You giving your mommy a hard time?"

"Sef story." She pouts, and I know that look alone will have him giving her anything she wants. Not that he wouldn't otherwise. Seth is a big ole softy when it comes to my daughter.

"Do you have a book picked out?" he asks. Her reply is a nod. He pulls his attention from her to me. "Hey, baby." He surprises me when he snakes an arm around my waist and pulls me into him, landing a kiss on my lips. "I missed my girls."

I lean into him just as dazzled by him as Finley is. He never kisses me like that in front of her, so I'm a little shocked, but I'm not angry. My daughter, on the other hand, she's not impressed as she pushes at my arm to get me away from him.

"My Sef."

"I'm your Seth and Mommy's Seth," he tells her. "And it's past your bedtime, little lady. Let's go read you a story." He kisses the top of my head, giving my hip a gentle squeeze before releasing his hold on me, and disappearing down the hall to her room.

In the past when he's done this, I've stood at the door and even lain in bed with them, but tonight I do neither. Instead, I head to the living room and curl up on the couch, throwing a blanket over me as I lick my wounds. I'm not hurt that she wants him. I want him too. It's just hard to see her not want me. I have to process the fact that he's just as big a part of her life as he is mine. This is happening fast and I should be worried, scared for our hearts, but I'm not. Instead, I want to race toward him, jump in his arms just like my daughter does, and beg him to never let me go.

"She's out," Seth whispers, taking a seat next to me on the couch. "You good?"

"Thank you."

"Never thank me for needing me, Mara. You didn't ask me to come over. I made that decision on my own."

"I know, but it would have been a crying fit until she wore herself out, so thank you."

"Those tears and the little lip get me every time." He places his hand over his chest.

"I'm afraid you've created a monster. She's going to want you every night from now on."

"How do you feel about that?"

"About her wanting you?" I shrug. "You're the first man in her life and you treat her like a princess. Of course she's going to latch on to you."

"That's not what I asked you, Mara." He waits patiently for my reply.

"It hurts, but not for the reasons you might think. If anything, I'm glad she has you. That we have you. She and I have been a twosome far too long, and suddenly we're surrounded by more. It's a lot to process, but at the same time, it's welcome. I'm not mad. It's just hard to see her want someone else. There has never really been anyone else in our lives for her to want. Until now."

"I'm glad it's me. When I got that call… I can't explain it. It's as if there were a million butterflies dancing in my gut. She was crying for me. That little girl—" He pauses. "And her momma—" He reaches out and cups my cheek. "—you're both under my skin. I want nothing more than to be the man who you both turn to, no matter what the situation or the reason."

"She's really bonded with you."

"Yeah, I'm glad. I'm just as attached to her."

"It's unexpected, but it makes me happy."

"Yeah?"

"Yes. I'm just an emotional momma bear who just realized her baby has other people in her life she can count on. I love that for her. It's just going to take some time to get used to it."

"I love that for both of you." Leaning in, he kisses me. It's slow and soft, and he makes no move to take things further.

There's only one problem with that. I want him too. "Seth," I murmur against his lips. "Can I ask you something?"

"Anything."

"Will you stay?"

"Stay as in here? Tonight?" he asks for clarification. I'm sure he's wondering what the hell is wrong with me when all I keep telling him is that he can't be here when she wakes up. However, that's exactly where he needs to be. It's where all three of us want him to be, so why fight it?

"You sure you want that?"

"I'm sure. I'm too raw right now. My emotions are a mess, and well, I just want you here."

"Then I'll stay. Go get ready for bed. I'll lock up." He stands and offers me his hand to pull me up from the couch. I go to my room while he locks up the house and turns off the lights. By the time he's standing in the doorway of my bedroom, I'm already under the covers. I'm fully clothed in the same pajamas as when he got here, but I feel naked.

Exposed. The only light in the room is a small bedside lamp. My eyes follow his every move as he walks to the side of the bed with the lamp, the opposite side I'm lying on, and unbuttons his jeans. I watch as they slide to the floor, leaving him in nothing but boxer briefs and a T-shirt. Turning off the light, he climbs into bed.

"Come here," he whispers.

With no hesitation, I slide as close to him as I can get and rest my head on his chest. He wraps his strong arms around me, and I melt into him. I can't remember the last time a man held me. In fact, I don't recall it ever happening. My hookup in college were just that, and Blake, Finley's dad, that was… different. He wasn't a loving, let me hold you close kind of guy. We spent one whirlwind week together before he had to ship out. At that time, I didn't think I needed that. Besides, our time was so limited we didn't get a chance to get to this point. Now, over three years later, it's exactly what I need, and I've been lucky enough to find a man willing to give it to me.

"Night, baby."

"Night." I whisper my reply as his strength surrounds me, and the steady rhythm of his heart lulls me to sleep.

When the alarm goes off at 6:00 a.m., I will it to stop. Unfortunately, my superpowers must be on vacation because the blaring sound refuses to relent until I roll over and shut it off. Flopping back on the pillow, I hear heavy breathing.

Seth.

Turning to take him in, my heart flips over in my chest at what I see. Seth is curled on his side facing me, and my daughter is snuggled up tight against his chest. He has his arm around her, cradling her to him almost protectively. I don't know what transpired that she's in bed with us, but I do know that seeing him with her like this, knowing that sometime in the middle of the night he took care of her, that little tidbit of information, their unexpected bond is what pushes me over the edge. It's the fine line between falling for him and knowing that this man owns a piece of my heart.

I'm in love with him.

I've been falling for him for months.

Careful not to wake them, I grab some clothes and make my way down the hall to the bathroom. My shower is quick as I rush through my morning routine. When I open the bathroom door, I hear giggles. Not just any giggles, but Finley giggles. Pure joy and happiness radiating in the sound.

"There's Mommy." Seth indicates to where I stand in the doorway of my bedroom.

"Mommy, Sef." Finley points to Seth.

"I see. What are you doing in here?" I ask her.

"Monsters." She scowls, and I have to bite my lip to keep from laughing.

"She woke up around one crying. I went in to check on her and she latched on and wouldn't let go, so I brought her in here. I was just going to wait for her to fall back asleep and then take her back to her bed. I've heard Kendall preach routine enough to know sleeping in your bed, let alone with both of us, is a bad idea, but I fell asleep," he says sheepishly.

"I'm sorry. I didn't hear her."

"She was barely whimpering when I heard her. I had to use the restroom so I was awake, waiting as long as possible to climb out of bed, not wanting to leave you when I heard her."

It's as if he fell from the pages of a book. Is this guy for real? "Thank you."

"We had a sleepover, huh, Finny?" he asks. "Now, how about you go with Mommy to get ready and I'll make us some breakfast." He looks up at me. "Eggs and toast okay?"

"You don't have to cook for us."

"Are you kidding? The thought of taking care of the two of you makes my day. You ladies do what you need to do. I'll handle breakfast."

"Don't you have to get ready?"

"Yeah, but I can shower and throw on some clothes in no time. Don't worry about me." He kisses the top of Finley's head and climbs out of bed. My eyes rake over him as he bends over and slides into his jeans. "Mara," he growls.

My head jerks up to his face. "Seth," I counter.

"Baby, you can't look at me like that. Not when Finny's in the same room."

"Sorry." I shrug. I'm not. Not even a little bit am I sorry for looking at what the good Lord gave him.

"This weekend. I don't care if it's Friday or Saturday, hell, it can be Sunday. My parents offered to watch Finny so we can go out just the two of us. Will you consider it?"

"I don't know. She's only met them once and that was months ago."

"They'll spoil her rotten while we're gone, that I can promise you. It's not that I don't want her with us. I do. It's the look you just gave me and how that makes me feel. I can't... touch you like I want while I know she's here."

"Married couples do it all the time."

"Yes, but they have time to grow used to it. I need time with you, Mara. Adult time," he says, emphasizing the word adult.

"I'll think about it."

"Thank you. Call Amelia, ask her about my folks. She'll vouch for them."

"It's not that—" I start, but he holds up his hand to stop me.

"She's your daughter. It's your right and job to be cautious of who she spends time with. I understand that. If you're not comfortable with my parents, then maybe Amelia?"

Amelia would be a good choice, but she's been acting so strange lately. I guess strange is the wrong word. She's more... closed off. There's something going on with her, and no matter how many times I ask, I get the same "nothing's wrong" reply.

"How about Saturday afternoon? That way we can pick her up in time for bedtime here?"

"Perfect. Or if you wanted, the two of you could stay at my place. I know all her stuff is here, but I'd like my girls to be in my space too. I want to see your hair splayed out on my pillow, and I want Finny's toys all over my living room."

"Okay."

"Yeah?"

"Yes." I'm too far gone to pretend otherwise. Besides, I'd like to spend more time at his place. Finley and I have been there a couple of times for dinner, but this is different. We're both going to be staying with him.

"Thank you." He kisses my cheek and disappears down the hall to start breakfast.

"Sef," Finley says, smiling and pointing where he just disappeared down the hall.

"Yeah, sweetie. I know. You love him too." Lifting her into my arms, we go to her room to get her ready for the day. All the while, Seth's deep timbre flows down the hall as he sings "My Girl" while making us breakfast.

SETH

It's been two months since she moved here, and it's hands down been the best two months of my life. Mara and I grow closer every day, and Finley... well, that little angel has my heart on a string. Who am I kidding? So does her momma. They make my life better. They make *me* better.

"Yo, Seth, you home?" Kent calls out.

"Back here," I call back.

"This the one?"

"Yeah." I pull my phone from my pocket and open my Pictures app. "This is her room at their house now. I want to create that here."

"This is an awful lot of work to get them to move in with you."

"It's a couple of cans of paint, and you get beer and pizza out of the deal. What are you complaining about?"

"Oh, I'm not complaining. I'm just curious as to why you're going through all the trouble. Not to mention, you've rehabbed this entire house the exact way you wanted it. Now you're changing it."

"I'm not changing it. I'm painting the walls so Finley will feel more at home here."

"So, you popping the question or what?"

"Not yet. At least not the marriage question. I am going to ask them to move in here. We're either at her place or mine. No point in her paying rent when I have more than enough space for all three of us here. We just re-did Finny's room, and I know she's going to counter with that. Finny loves her room. So I'm going to create it here too. Not to mention, the bedrooms here are much larger than Mark's rental."

"Where is your woman today? What does she think you're doing?"

"I told her you were coming over and we were going to hang out. She's with Kendall, Reagan, Dawn, and Amelia. They're all having a girls' day/play date for the kids over at Mark's."

"Are those jokers coming to help us?" he asks.

"Yep. They'll be here soon."

"All right, boss, put me to work."

That's what we do. Between the two of us, we have the room taped off and ready for paint when Ridge, Tyler, and Mark show up. Within an hour, the five of us have the room painted.

"What else is on the list?" Tyler asks.

"Pizza and beer. Thanks for your help," I tell them as the doorbell rings. "That would be our pizza." Rushing to the front door, I pay the delivery guy and compensate him with a generous tip. Seriously, pizza delivery is the best invention ever.

"Going all-in, huh?" Ridge asks after our appetites are satisfied and the six-pack of beer is all but demolished.

"Is there any other way?"

"Nope," Mark says. "Happy for you, brother."

"It's different, you know? Caring so much about them that I wonder how their days are going. I find myself texting at random times just so she knows I'm thinking about her. I've watched the three of you and knew it was different. I could see it change you, but I never really understood it until Mara."

"You just hadn't found the one," Tyler comments.

"Find them! Hell, they seem to fall in y'all's lap," Kent chimes in.

"Your day's coming," I tell him.

"Nah. I think I missed that train. It left the station without me on it."

"I thought I was going to a barbecue with family. Then I walked around the side of the house and there she was. You never know when it's going to happen."

"So when are you asking her?" Kent asks, clearly changing the subject.

"Tomorrow probably. My parents are taking Finley to the aquarium, so we have the day to ourselves."

"Good luck, man." Mark slaps me on the back. "It's not always easy, but once you get there, to where you're both on the same page, nothing's better."

"That's the plan."

"Hey, sweet girl," Ridge says, drawing our attention. "Okay. We're heading out too. You need me to bring anything home?" He waits for her answer. "Sounds good. Drive safe. I love you." He hangs up and stands. "Kendall's on her way home. The kids are all worn out so your women are headed home too."

"I'm out," Kent says, standing. Mark and Tyler do the same.

"Thanks, guys. I never could have gotten this done while they were gone without your help." They wave off my thanks and make their way to the door. Kent is pulling out, the last one to leave just as Mara's Pathfinder pulls into the driveway.

"Hey," I say, racing down the steps to greet them.

"Hi. I hope it's okay that we stopped by. Finley was asking for you."

"Just Finley?" I ask, leaning in and pressing my lips to hers.

"We missed you." She shrugs.

"Go on inside. I'll grab our girl." I walk to the passenger side and open the back door. Finley gives me a sweet smile and holds her arms out. I don't care what else is going on in life, a smile from this little girl will always light up my world. "Hey, sweetheart. Did you have fun today?"

"I pwayed."

"You did? That sounds like so much fun."

"I see fishes?" she asks.

I chuckle. Mara was right; we never should have told her until the day of our visit. "Yes, tomorrow you're going to the aquarium. You're going to see lots of fish." I bounce her on my hip all the way to the house. She's giggling when I set her on her feet.

"Have you been painting?" Mara asks.

Damn. I was so excited to see them, I forgot all about the evidence of my surprise. "Yeah, want to see?" Might as well go for it. Maybe it will help if Finley sees her room and is on my side.

"Finley, let's go see what I've been painting." She hops off the couch where she was settled in and more than likely ready to crash after her eventful day. She reaches me and slides her tiny hand in mine. Bending down, I scoop her up in my arms and hold my hand out for Mara to take. Together, the three of us walk down the hall and stop at the spare bedroom. "Go on in," I tell Mara, following her.

"Seth." She gasps as she stands in the center of the room and turns a full circle.

"Mine," Finley says, taking in the room that looks just like hers.

"That's right, sweetheart. This is your room."

"Seth?"

"I want you both to feel at home here." She continues to stare at me with a confused look, so I push forward. "We're never at my place or yours without the other. I own this place free and clear. I bought it when it was worn down, and I rehabbed it with the guys' help. There is no point in you paying Mark rent when you and Finny can stay here."

"What are you saying?" she asks, her voice wobbly.

"I'm saying I want you to move in with me. I know Finny loves her room, and I thought maybe making it the same would ease the transition."

"Seth, we can't just move in with you."

"Why not?"

"Because that's crazy. It's crazy, right? I mean, it's been what, two months, that's—No, we can't do that."

"It's been two of the best months of my life." Finley is resting her head on my shoulder; poor thing has had a long day. She snuggles into me as we get closer to Mara. Reaching out, I slide my hand behind Mara's neck and make sure I have her full attention. "I'm in love with you, Mara. Both of you. I want you here. I want this to be our home. If you hate it, we can find something new. You can change anything you want. I don't care as long as at the end of the day, we're all under the same roof. Permanently."

Her eyes well with tears. "Seth—I...." She stops and swallows back her emotions.

"I'm going to love you no matter what your answer is. Take some time to think about it." Leaning down, I place a kiss on her forehead, then drop my hand to my side. "How about a movie, Finny?" I ask. She's going to be asleep in minutes. "Take all the time you need." I turn and walk out of the room.

In the living room, I grab the remote and pull up Netflix to find a movie for Finley. As I suspected, she's sound asleep within ten minutes. I settle her on the chaise longue section of the couch, prop some pillows around her, and cover her with a blanket before going to find Mara. I find her sitting in the middle of the bedroom that I painted for Finley.

"Are you doing this so I'll sleep with you?" she asks, sensing my presence.

"What?" I take a step further into the room.

"How do you know you love me? We've never even had sex."

"Mara." I want to laugh at how ridiculous that sounds, but I can see she's 100 percent serious. I take a seat next to her on the floor. "I love you. Not because of what I think those three words will give me, but what you give me. I miss you as soon as you walk out the door. I think about you and that little girl in there twenty-four hours a day. I think about a future with you. More babies. Finley on Christmas morning. I could go on for days. The heart of that matter is just that. My heart. There is a huge tattoo across it that reads *Mara and Finley*." I stop and collect my thoughts as her eyes well with tears. I keep going. "We haven't slept together, but that's okay. I know what you mean to me, and when we do add sex to that, it's going to increase tenfold. I love you both for the happiness you bring to my life. I want you here. I want us to start our life together."

"We hardly know each other," she counters.

There is only one thing she doesn't know about me, and now might not be the best time to bring it up, but I've been putting it off and I need to tell her. I can't let her decide to move in here without her knowing. "There is only one thing in my past that I've never told you." Her worried eyes find mine. "Something happened. I don't even remember it, but it happened all the same. I've avoided telling you because I didn't want to lose you. However, I can't let you move in here without knowing everything."

"Tell me."

"I'm going to tell you, but you have to promise me you'll stay. That we'll talk about it."

"I'll stay," she agrees, although hesitantly.

"I remember the day I first laid eyes on you. You were sitting on the deck, Finley was in your lap and you were laughing at something one of the girls had said. I remember that it felt as though the air had been knocked out of my lungs. You were beautiful, the most beautiful woman I'd ever seen." I take a breath and begin again. "I pulled Ridge aside to ask who you were. 'Amelia's friend,' he said. 'She's here for a job interview.' He didn't tell me that it was for Beckett Construction.

"I watched you that day. The way you were with Finley, the way your hair would blow in the breeze. I memorized as much of you as I could. I remember we made small talk about the weather, and I fought to memorize every word of our conversation. The sound of your voice, all of it. I wanted you then. However, you were a single mom and I know what that means. I know that it's not just your heart on the line, but that little girl's as well. So, regardless of how bad I wanted you, I kept things friendly. I went to bed that night with my cock in my hand and memories of you. I woke up the next day still thinking about you."

"I thought about you too. I remember wanting to run my fingers through your hair." She reaches out and does just that.

Grabbing her hand, I pull it to my lips and kiss her palm before gripping it in mine. "I thought maybe it was a fluke, but then it happened every day for the next two weeks. You were all I could think about. So I managed to steal your number from Amelia's phone and sent you a bullshit text asking how the job interview went. It's not that I wasn't interested. I was hoping you would get the job, so I could see you again. I took a chance, and over the next few months, your messages were what I looked forward to. I didn't go out. I didn't look for anyone else because

I knew it was you."

"I looked forward to those messages." She smiles softly. "And the few times we actually talked, I would hear your deep voice for days after."

"I wanted you. I knew that for certain. Mark and Dawn were in the middle of gaining custody of Daisy, and I gave him this big lecture on the importance of knowing what he was getting into dating a single mom. I was projecting, but in a way, it helped me see that you being a single mom wasn't a burden; it's a gift. Finny is an extension of you, and that little girl—" I tap my hand over my chest. "—she's right here next to you. I wanted to be certain this was what I wanted. I didn't want to come into your lives only to turn around and leave. Then I found out you were moving here. That first day, I knew there was no going back. I knew you and Finley were my future."

"Is that so bad?"

"No. It's not bad, but what comes next is." I take a deep breath and just go for it. "New Year's Eve, Mark and Dawn had a get-together. It was just us, the family. I was torn up because I wanted you, but you lived so far away. I had all kinds of things running through my head. I was still pissed you didn't get the job that would have brought you closer to me. At the time, I still didn't know it was Ridge who was hiring you. If I would have known, I would have given him shit for it. Anyway, I was pissed that you didn't get the job. I was considering leaving Beckett Construction and finding a job near you, to see if we could make it work. My head was all over the place, and I know that sounds crazy because you had no idea. I never told you that I had fallen for you."

"Seth." Her eyes soften.

"Anyway, the kids were all with the grandparents so the adults could kick back. I watched my friends with their wives, and the more I watched them, the more I drank. I was jealous of what they had. I wanted that... with you. I drank until I couldn't remember."

"That's not so bad."

"That's not all." I take a deep breath, keep my grip on her hand, and force myself to continue. "We all stayed there. There was more than enough space, and we had a couple of air mattresses. Anyway, I woke up in the basement in the bedroom on an air mattress." I pause, fighting off the urge to be sick as I put the nail in my coffin. "With Amelia."

"With Amelia?" she repeats. I nod, giving her time to let my words sink in. "Oh my god." She tries to pull her hand from mine, but I hold strong.

"Neither one of us remembers what happened. We were naked, and the uh, the condom was there."

"You slept with my best friend?" she murmurs.

"She's one of my best friends too, and it didn't mean anything. Hell, we don't even remember it happening. It's not like that between us. Kent said we were both out-of-our-minds wasted. We ended up in the downstairs bedroom and crashed. None of them know what happened because it was a mistake. One she and I both regret." I hold tight to her hand, letting her process my words.

She's quiet, too quiet as a single tear trails down her cheek. "I have to go. I need to process this."

"No, you said you wouldn't go. We have to talk about this."

"Damn it, Seth. I just… I need a minute."

"Finny's sleeping," I say in an attempt to keep her here.

"Can you keep an eye on her for me? I just need to go. I'll be back, I promise. I—Please, Seth. I just need some air."

"I don't think you should be driving when you're upset."

She wipes at her cheeks. "I'm okay to drive. Trust me. I would never do anything that would leave my daughter alone in this world. I never want her to feel what I did growing up."

"Okay." What else can I say? "I'll watch her. Take all the time you need, just… come home to me."

"I'll be back. I just want to take a drive and clear my head. I need to process all of this." She pulls her hand from my grip, and this time, I let her. She stands and I follow her down the hall and to the living room. She peeks in on Finley and then grabs her purse, coat, and phone before sliding her feet into her boots.

"I love you, Mara. Please be safe. Check in with me, okay?" Fuck me, I don't want her to leave, but she's leaving Finny with me. That's a good sign. At least I hope so. Regardless, she'll have to come back for her.

"I'll be back." She turns and walks out the door. It's not a declaration of love, but I'll take it. She could be running away with Finley.

Through the window, I watch until I can no longer see her car. Making my way to the living room, I settle on the couch and watch Finley sleep. I love this little girl as if she were my own. I can't imagine my life without Mara or Finley in it. I'll fight for them. Every day of forever I'll fight for them. After all, they're my heart.

Chapter 10

Mara

He slept with my best friend. The man I love, the one who treats my daughter as if she were his own, the man who just asked me to move in with him. He slept with my only friend. I've been driving around for almost an hour, and I still can't seem to wrap my head around this new information.

My phone vibrates from its spot in the cupholder. I assume it's Seth, but a quick glance at the screen tells me I'm wrong. It's Amelia. Taking a deep breath, I swipe at the screen and place the phone to my ear. "Hello."

"Mara, we need to talk."

"Yeah," I say, because I know it's true. I've just been in denial and wasting gas.

"Seth called me. Are you okay?"

"Fine."

"Where are you?"

"Out driving."

"I'll meet you. Where do you want to go?"

"My place."

"I'll be there in ten."

"I'm about twenty minutes away."

"Okay. I'll stop and grab us a couple of coffees. We're going to need them." She ends the call, and I sigh, dropping my phone back into the cupholder and turning around, pointing my car toward home.

Eighteen minutes later, I'm pulling into my driveway. Amelia is sitting on the front step with a carrier holding two coffees and a small bag next to her. "It's freezing out here. Why are you not waiting in your car?" I call out as I walk toward her.

"I've only been here for a minute or two. I knew you had to be close. Besides, I like the fresh air."

"Get inside before you get sick," I admonish. She mumbles something I don't catch and follows me inside. We take off our coats and sit on opposite ends of the couch. Amelia leans forward, grabs a coffee, and hands it to me, taking the other for herself.

"It meant nothing. If anything, I'm a little disgusted. It's like sleeping with my brother." She shudders.

"I want to believe that, but come on, Amelia. You don't sleep around."

"I drank way too much that night. I remember dancing in the basement, but after that, things go black… until we woke up the next day."

"That's not like you. You never drink that much. What's going on?"

"Nothing. Just had some things on my mind lately."

"Like sleeping with my boyfriend?" I ask snidely. I know it's rude, but I can't help it. She's hiding something from me, and I can't help but think that it might be her true feelings about Seth.

She smiles softly. "I deserve that. But no, I promise you it has nothing to do with Seth."

"Then why can't you tell me? We used to tell each other everything." I think back to the night she was attacked in college. As far as I know, I'm the only person she's ever told. "I've kept your secrets," I say as a reminder of what we've been through.

"I was so scared he was going to…." Her voice trails off. She doesn't need to finish her thought for me to know what she's thinking. It's a blessing she was able to get away when a group of students rounded the corner. That night could have ended so much worse than just having a fear of the dark and a distrust in men.

"Whatever it is, you can tell me."

"Don't be mad at Seth. Please. I've never seen either of you this way. He loves you."

"I love him too."

"It was one night, a drunken mistake never to be discussed again. I don't feel anything for him except for long-time friendship. Please don't let this get in the way of your happiness."

"Technically we weren't even dating. I mean, we were texting back and forth but as friends. Neither one of us had said we were interested. That didn't happen until I moved here. Sure, I guessed and some of the things I said, some of the things he said implied it, but we never spoke the words until… after."

"After I slept with him. I'm sorry, Mara. I had no idea you two were even talking to one another. Not that I could have prevented what happened. Well, I could have not drunk myself into oblivion, but I wanted to forget," she says, and her eyes widen at her confession.

"Tell me, Amelia."

"He loves you."

"I know that."

"Don't take this out on him. You've seen us together. Did you see anything between us?"

I think back to the day she was there and we had breakfast. That's happened a few times over the past couple of months, and she's right. I never would have guessed that anything ever happened between them. "No."

"Exactly, because there's nothing there. I want you to be happy, both of you. He called me and I swear he sounded on the verge of tears."

My eyes well up just at the thought of him being upset. "I told him I was coming back. I left my daughter with him. Of course I'm coming back."

"Yes, but are you going to stay?"

"I want to. I want to believe that this life he has dreamed up is one we can live happily ever after. I've never felt this kind of love before. I love Finley with all that I am, but this… it's different. I can't think about him without getting this warm tingly feeling. I know it sounds crazy, and I can't even explain it to you. I just know that it's there and no one has ever made me feel that way but Seth."

"Then love him, Mara. Let him love you. Don't punish him for this. It meant nothing to either of us."

"He wants us to move in. Did he tell you that?" She nods. "Did he tell you that he spent the day painting one of the bedrooms to match Finley's room? He said he wanted her to feel at home." I wipe a tear from my eye.

"He didn't tell me that, but I'm not surprised. I know you're scared, but there is nothing to be afraid of. That man will be by your side until the end of time. That's who they are, Mara. All five of them. You've found a good one in Seth."

I know she's right; I feel it deep in my soul. The love he has for me and for my daughter. I don't want this to get in the way of what we're building or the future he sees for us, or the one I've dreamed of having one day. Seth is the man who's making my dreams come true. As soon as I figure out what's going on with my friend, I'm going to pack Finley and me a bag and I'm going home. To my family.

"I know you're scared, but there is nothing to be afraid of. I'll be here for whatever you need. That's who we are, Amelia. You came into my life and gave me a person. You were there for me when I had no one, and now it's my turn to be that for you. I'm here for you. No matter what's going on, I'll be by your side."

I watch as she loses the battle with her emotions and a sob breaks free from her chest. Taking her coffee and mine, I set them on the table and pull her into a hug. Her sobs bring tears to my eyes. I've never seen her like this. Not even the night back in college when she was almost raped.

"I'm right here," I tell her, holding her and offering her comfort. "You can't hold this in. Whatever it is, you have to talk about it." I don't know how long I hold her, but eventually, her cries quiet down and she shudders, pulling away from me.

"I'm sorry."

"I'm not. That's what friends are for." My phone vibrates and I know it's Seth.

> **Seth:** *Please tell me you're safe.*
>
> **Me:** *I'm good. I'm at my place. Amelia is here. I'll be home in a little while.*
>
> **Seth:** *I love you, Mara.*
>
> **Seth:** *Finny just woke up so we're going to eat some dinner.*
>
> **Me:** *Thank you for taking care of her.*
>
> **Seth:** *I love her, Mara. You girls are all I want.*
>
> **Me:** *I'll be home soon.*

I almost told him that I loved him, but I don't want to do it with a text message. I'll do it tonight when I get there and show him that Finley and I are staying. I'm moving forward in life, and there is no one else I want by my side.

"Seth?"

"Yeah." I place my phone back on the table. "Tell me what's going on with you."

She opens her mouth to speak, but more tears flood her cheeks. Reaching out, I take her hand in mine. I wait, giving her the time she needs. She takes a deep breath, and the words she says have me gasping for air as they knock the air out of my lungs.

"I have cancer."

"Cancer?" I repeat the vile word as my mind tries to process what she's telling me.

"Cancer."

"When did you find out?"

"Officially about a month ago. Unofficially, New Year's Eve."

"Amelia," I say softly when it all clicks together. She was drinking to forget.

"I'd been feeling bad for months. Just run-down and drained. Then I got this cold, and the cough lingered. It just wouldn't go away so I finally broke down and went to the doctor. They did X-rays, and he found a spot on my lung. He told me I would need further testing, but he'd seen it many times before and that there was a chance I had cancer."

"Oh my God," I say breathily. "You should have told me. I could have been there for you."

"I was in denial at first, you know. I'm not even thirty. I've never smoked. I couldn't have lung cancer. That night, I just wanted to forget. I didn't want the fear or the worry. I just wanted to forget."

"How are you feeling? What are they telling you?"

"I'm doing okay. I have good days and bad. I had a biopsy a few weeks ago and they confirmed it's lung cancer. Small cell carcinoma." She pauses, then her tired eyes find mine. "I'm stage 2. Life expectancy of five years is about 33 percent. Mara, I'm dying." Her voice cracks.

"No. You have to get a second opinion. There are other doctors, other hospitals we can take you to," I say, wiping the tears from my eyes.

"Mara." She reaches out and places her hand over mine. "I've gotten a second and a third opinion. There is no cure for the cancer that I have."

"But things change every day. You have to fight this, and then maybe there will be a cure. Miracles happen every day."

"Mara, I love you. I grew up with mostly guys as friends, and when I met you freshman year, you were a breath of fresh air. I never knew I was missing female companionship until then. Reagan was really the only girl I hung around and she was two years younger than us, so we were not always in the same circles."

"This can't be happening."

"Now you sound like me." She laughs humorlessly. "I was in denial for a long time. However, after three different specialists give you the same diagnosis and prognosis, denial is no longer possible."

"So when do you start treatment?" I vow to be there for her for whatever she needs.

"Next week. I have to go in for some more tests and then I'm supposed to start the first round of chemo on Friday."

"What do you mean supposed to?"

"I'm not sure I want to."

"What?" I stand from the couch and start to pace. "How are you not sure? You have to fight this, Amelia."

"Mara, there is no cure. Chemo kills your body. It makes you so sick, just to what... prolong my life a few months? Maybe a year or so if I'm lucky? I don't know that I want to be that sick my final days."

"You are not giving up. You hear me, Amelia. I won't let you."

"This isn't your choice to make."

"The hell it isn't. You're not thinking clearly. You have to fight this."

"I'm going for the testing and have an appointment with my oncologist on Thursday. That's when I'll make my final decision."

"I can't—" My voice cracks. "I love you. I'm here for you for whatever you need. What time is your appointment? I'll go with you." I'm rambling but I can't help it. I'm in shock and my mind is racing with how I can help her. My best friend.

"You don't have to do that. You just started your job."

"Right. And do you really think Ridge is going to tell me no?"

"You can't tell him. Any of them."

"Are you out of your mind? You have to tell them. Let them support you. You don't have to do this on your own."

"I-I can't—" She breaks and tears race down her cheeks again. "I haven't even told my parents. Dad's health is going downhill, and his heart... he doesn't need the stress."

"Amelia, you could be dying. They deserve to know that. They're going to want to spend as much time with you as they can and be there for you."

"They're so much older. I don't want them having to take care of me, to clean up after me. I just... I can't do it, Mara."

"I know you're scared, but you have to. I'll do it with you. I'll be there every single step of the way."

"I don't know."

"How about we have everyone over to Seth's tomorrow afternoon and tell them? Then you and I can go tell your parents together?"

"They're getting older. Mom was in her mid-forties when they had me. I don't want to put this pressure on them."

"Trust me, as a parent, they'll want to know. I'll be right there with you. You're not in this alone."

"How did this night turn into this? I just wanted to keep you from making the biggest mistake of your life by letting Seth go and now this." She waves her hand between the two of us.

"I'm here making sure you don't make the biggest mistake of yours. You told me to let Seth love me, and I plan to do exactly that. But, Amelia, you need to let us love you too. All of us. You have this huge support system that I'm just now experiencing for the first time in my life. It's incredible and you've had it all along. Let them help you. We've got you. No matter what the situation, no matter how sick you get. We're all going to be right there by your side."

"Okay. Tomorrow."

"Noon. I'll take care of getting everyone there. How about you and I sleep here tonight?" I suck in a breath trying to keep myself under control. I can't think about what this really means. My chest hurts. There is literally an ache in my chest as I process what I've learned.

She's dying.

My best friend is dying.

"No, you have to get home to Finley and Seth. I'm sure he's pacing the floors."

"I'll call him and explain. I don't want you being alone right now."

"I'm going home. I'm exhausted even more so after this conversation. I'll meet you at Seth's tomorrow at noon." She stands, and I do the same, hugging her tight.

"We're going to fight this," I say with conviction. She has to fight this. I won't let her give up. I'll be there for her, and I know they all will. They'll rally because that's what they do.

"You are the strongest person I know, Mara Reyes." I fight the urge to scoff. She's been dealing with this all on her own. She's a fucking rock star. I can't imagine how hard this has been on her.

"Right back at ya. Drive safe and call me anytime night or day if you need me." I bite down on the inside of my cheek to keep from breaking down.

"I will. Thank you, Mara."

"Thank you." With one final hug, she disappears out of my house and I fight the urge to make her stay. As soon as the door is closed, I lose my battle with my tears. This can't be happening. I can't lose my best friend. Not now. Life is just starting to work out for me. I have so many people in my life, friends, my daughter is thriving and now this.

Cancer.

I hate that fucking word. That fucking disease. So many lives have been altered and touched by it. Wiping at my eyes, I go to Finley's room and pack her clothes, pull-ups, her bear that Seth gave her, and her soft princess blanket she sleeps with every night. I grab the nightlight out of the hallway outlet, just in case. In my room, I do the same, making sure I have clothes for work for at least the first few days this week, toiletries, my cell charger, and call it good. That will have to do for now. Besides, I'm sure Seth will waste no time getting us packed up and moved. I take the bags out to my car and grab my reusable grocery bags. I go to the kitchen and clean out the refrigerated items and bring them too. I don't want them to spoil, and besides, I went to the store early this morning for my lunches for this week. No need to go again when I can just bring it with me. Satisfied that I have what we need for now, I lock up and make my way to my car.

Me: *Headed home.*

Seth: *You're my home.*

Ten minutes later, I'm pulling into his driveway. He has the garage door lifted and is standing on the step that leads into the house waiting for me. As soon as I pull inside and shut off the engine, he pushes the button to close the door and comes toward me. I'm out of the car and meeting him halfway as I wrap my arms around him and let his warmth comfort me.

"Let's get you inside," he says softly, guiding us into the house.

"Where's Finley?" I ask, noticing the house is way too quiet.

"She's asleep in her bedroom. We blew up the air mattress for her."

"I brought a pull-up. They're in my car."

"I had one here. Pajamas too. She didn't get a bath, but she's fed and comfy in her room.

"Mara—" I hold my hand up to stop him.

"I cleaned out my refrigerator and brought my groceries over. We need to get them out of my car."

"Okay." I can hear the caution yet hope in his voice.

"There are two other bags as well. One for me and one for Finley." This isn't uncommon when we spend the night. "I'm letting you tell Mark I'm breaking my lease."

"Wait. What?"

I smile up at him. "I love you, Seth Jennings. Thank you for being open and honest with me. It was before we were... what we are, and after talking to both you and Amelia, I have a better understanding of what happened that night."

He lifts me from the floor so we are eye-to-eye. "Say it again."

"I love you." He kisses me quickly before setting my feet back on the floor. "I want the life you've imagined for us. I want to take a leap of faith with you."

"You're moving in?" he asks, a smile as wide as a country mile on his face.

"Yes. We're moving in."

"Fuck yes!" he shouts, lifting me off my feet and spinning us in a circle.

"Shh." I laugh. "You're going to wake Finley." He stops spinning, kisses me hard, and once again sets me back on my feet.

"I'll get the bags. Be right back." A swift kiss and he's rushing out to the garage, only to appear a few minutes later still smiling as if he's just won the lottery. He quickly puts all the groceries away and leaves the two other bags filled with our things in the hallway.

"Can we talk?" I ask him.

"Sure." He guides us to the couch.

"I have something to ask you. Can you call everyone and ask them to meet us here tomorrow at noon?"

"What's going on?"

"C-Can you do that for me? After, I'll tell you. I just... I want you to

106

be able to get through the calls. Just call them for me. Family meeting, our house at noon."

"Our house." He leans in and kisses me. I watch as he calls each of the guys, asking them to be here with their wives, well, all of them except Kent—he's still flying solo—tomorrow at noon.

"Now, tell me what's going on."

So I do. I tell him about my conversation with Amelia, how she described their night together as a drunken mistake, and he nods, not at all taking offense. Then I tell him about the cancer. His body is rigid and his face is a mirror of shock and concern. "That's why she was drinking so heavily that night. She was told that day that something was wrong and that there was a chance it could be cancer."

"Fuck," he says, running his hands through his hair. "What does she need?"

"Well, I convinced her to tell everyone tomorrow, that's why I wanted you to invite them over. She has some tests this week, and she gets the results on Thursday. Right now, she's supposed to start chemotherapy on Friday, but she's considering not going through with it."

"What? What do you mean she's considering not going through with it?"

"She said that there's no cure for the type of cancer she has. The life expectancy is only 33 percent that she'll live five years." I repeat the stats that Amelia gave me.

"So, what? She's just going to give up? Miracles happen every damn day."

"I know. I told her the same thing. Maybe everyone can talk her into it tomorrow."

"She needs a second opinion."

"She got a second and a third. All three told her the same thing."

His reply is to pull me close and bury his face in my neck. When he angles away, his eyes are misty with tears. "If I've learned anything over the past few years, it's that life is short. You have to live each day as if it could be your last. I love you, Mara. I love Finley, and I want us to be a family. I'll give you time to let that sink in. Give you time to process what I'm telling you."

"What exactly are you telling me? I'm not fishing for compliments, but I just want to make sure what I think you're saying and what you mean are the same thing."

"I want to marry you. If you'll let me, I'd love to be that little girl's daddy. I want more babies and memories and… I want it all, Mara."

"I'm—" I start, but he stops me.

"I know you're not ready, but please think about it. It's fast I know, but when you know, you know. And I know you and Finley are my heart." He leans in and kisses me. "Now, it's been a long day and tomorrow is going to be even longer. Let's go to bed. I need to hold you."

He gets no complaint from me. Together, we lock up the house, turning off all the lights. Stopping at her door, we check on Finley and then head to his room.

Our room.

As promised, he holds me close all night long.

Chapter 11

SETH

There's something wet on my lips, and I think I'm dreaming until I hear a shouted whisper, "Sef, wake up." Slowly, I peel one eye, then the other open to find Finley sitting next to me on the bed. She's on her knees leaning over me. She's smiling wide, and her green eyes—the ones she got from her momma—are sparkling. "I go to fishes," she says, pulling on my hand to get me out of bed.

With everything that happened yesterday, I forgot that my parents are stopping by to take her to the aquarium. That works out because she doesn't need to be here to see all of us upset. "Shh, don't wake Mommy." I place my finger to my lips.

Finley mocks me, but her "shhh" is not quiet at all.

"Morning," Mara says, rolling over to face us.

"Momma, fishes." Finley bounces on her knees.

"That's right." Mara chuckles.

"Let's get some breakfast and then a bath. What time are they going to be here?" she asks me.

"Mom said around eleven."

"Good, we don't have to rush. Come on, kiddo. Let's go get some breakfast." Mara throws the covers off and climbs out of bed.

"Sef, go." Finley pulls on my hand again, trying to move me.

"Uh-oh," I say dramatically, gaining her full attention. "You just woke up the tickle monster." I hold my hands in the air, fingers spread wide, and sit up. When I start for her, she squeals, climbing off the bed laughing. I take my time chasing her in slow motion, letting her get ahead of me. "Here comes the tickle monster," I say, my feet hitting the hardwood floor. I walk toward her, mimicking a zombie, and she cackles with laughter and rushes out of the room yelling for her mommy to save her.

When I reach the kitchen, she's hiding between Mara's legs and her laughter fills up the entire house. Bending down, I lift her into my arms and place a wet sloppy kiss on her cheek. "I love you, Finny." It feels good to be able to tell her. To tell them both. "I love you too, Momma." I lean in and kiss Mara on the cheek as well.

"Wuvs yous," Finley says, kissing my cheek and leaning out of my arms to do the same to Mara.

We eat eggs and toast for breakfast, then Mara takes Finley to give her a bath and get ready to spend the day with my parents. They've met Finley a few times over the last couple of months, and they're both thrilled to have a grandchild to focus on. Mom's words, not mine. Finley took to them right away. I'm glad she has them and that my parents are so supportive. She needs all the love life has to give. I work on cleaning up from breakfast before going to our room and taking a shower. By the time I'm done, Finley is ready, and I take over keeping her entertained while Mara gets ready.

"We make a good team," I say, snaking my arm around her waist and kissing her quickly.

"We do." She smiles and wriggles out of my hold to go shower.

An hour later, my parents are knocking on the door. "Come in," I call out. The three of us are on the couch watching cartoons.

"Finley girl, you ready to go see some big fish?" my dad asks.

"Fishes!" she cheers, jumping off the couch and running to him. He's ready for her, bending to lift her into his arms.

"That's right. All kinds of fish, and sharks and turtles," my dad says with extreme enthusiasm.

"Thank you for offering to take her. It's all she's talked about," Mara says.

"We're just glad you're letting us take her. They're such a joy at this age," Mom says affectionately. "Okay, down to business. Any rules or allergies we should know about? You know, like to ice cream?" Mom asks.

"Fishes and ice cweam." Finley nods, making us all laugh.

"No allergies, and I trust you."

My mom steps forward and wraps Mara in a hug. "Thank you, dear. I promise she's in good hands. We're going to take our time. You two enjoy your day together."

"We actually have everyone coming over at noon." I don't need to clarify everyone; my parents know how tight-knit our group is.

"Really?" she asks, surprised.

"Yeah, Amelia's sick." I pause before saying that vile word. "Cancer."

"Oh my." Mom places her hand over her heart. "What can I do? What does she need? How is she?" she fires off.

"I'm not sure, I don't know, and as good as can be expected," I answer. I run my fingers through my hair. "She hasn't told anyone else, so that's what today is about."

"Please give her a hug from us. Oh my, I just can't believe this," Mom says, more to herself than to us.

"Yes. Let us know what she needs," Dad chimes in. He wraps his arm around Mom and pulls her close.

"Now I see where you get it," Mara whispers just for me.

"Why don't you guys take my truck, so you don't have to move the seat back and forth?" I offer my parents. I need to change the subject. I don't want to be upset when she gets here, making this day harder for her.

"Oh, we bought one."

"What?" Mara asks, not able to hide her surprise.

"Yeah, that way, if we ever need to pick her up or want to take her with us, we'll have it." Mom shrugs like it's no big deal while Mara sags against me. The weight of my family's acceptance hits her hard.

"Give Mommy a kiss," Dad says, stepping forward and allowing Finley to kiss her mom and give her a hug.

"Bye-bye, Momma."

"Don't forget Seth," Dad tells her, stepping to the side, bringing her closer to me.

"My Sef," she says, kissing my cheek and hugging me as well.

"Bye, Finny. Be good," I say, then address my parents. "Thanks, guys. We can come and pick her up. Just call us when you're home."

"Oh, we'll bring her home. You two do what you need to do. Send Amelia our love," Mom says before they walk out the door.

"Oh my God. Seth, your parents." Mara shakes her head. "I can't believe… they're just… they're amazing. She's never had grandparents in her life," she says, wiping at her eyes.

"Now she does."

"I love you."

"I love you too."

"We're all here," Ridge says as Kent takes a seat in the last remaining chair. Mara, Amelia, Tyler, Reagan, and I are on the sectional couch, Ridge and Kendall are in a chair, Kendall on his lap, while Mark and Dawn are on the loveseat. "Care to tell us what's going on?"

"Yeah, you didn't give us any explanation. Kept me up all night," Kent grumbles.

I look over at Amelia as she chews on her bottom lip. "Amelia has something to tell you, but when she got here, she asked if we would tell you for her." Mara leans into me on one side, while Amelia is on the other doing the same. "There is no easy way to say this, so I'm just going to put it out there." Reaching over, I lace my fingers with Mara's and then do the same to Amelia, offering her support. "Amelia has cancer."

The room is silent. Not a single word is spoken as they process the news. Amelia squeezes my hand, and I give hers a gentle squeeze back, giving her my silent support.

"I'm dying," she whispers. Her whisper might have well been screaming for the silence in the room.

"Tell us everything, A," Mark says, pulling Dawn into his side.

"I haven't been feeling well. Just… off, you know? I came down with a cold a couple of months ago and I couldn't seem to shake the cough. New Year's Eve I'd had enough, so I broke down and went to the doctor. They did X-rays and found spots on my lungs."

She takes a minute to collect herself. I stand and go to the bathroom to grab a box of tissues. Reaching under the cabinet, I grab two more. This is going to be hard to get through. When I get back, Mara is sitting next to Amelia, and they are huddled close, holding hands. I pass out the boxes of tissues, making sure Amelia has one and then take a seat next to Mara.

"I had to have some more tests. It was confirmed that I have lung cancer."

"We'll get a second opinion," Ridge tells her.

She smiles through her tears. "I did that, Ridge. I got a second and a third. All three doctors gave me the same diagnosis and prognosis. Small cell lung cancer. Stage 2."

"What does that mean?" Kent asks.

Amelia takes a deep breath and slowly exhales. "That means the maximum life expectancy of up to five years is 33 percent." She sounds like a robot, a crying robot, as she relays the information.

"Explain that," Reagan says, barely able to get the words out.

"There is no cure, Reags. Not for small cell, and five years is a generous guess. Most barely make it two."

Kendall, Dawn, and Reagan stand, and head our way. I lean in and kiss Mara on the cheek and move to sit next to Mark, where Dawn was. The girls huddle around Amelia, offering her hugs and support while the five of us watch. Memories of growing up together, time at each of our houses, the park, playing ball in the street of Mark and Tyler's subdivision. Everything comes flashing back like a movie reel. To look at her, she looks healthy. A little tired, but healthy. You would never know that cancer is eating away at her from the inside.

Fuck cancer.

"So what do we do?" Ridge asks, his voice thick. "How do we fight this?"

Mara and Amelia share a glance. "I-I'm not sure I want to."

"What?" Kent stands and starts pacing. "What do you mean you don't want to? You can fight this fucking thing, A. I know you can."

"Kent." Her voice breaks on a sob. "Th-The treatments are brutal. The chemo and the radiation kill your body. My quality of life will be shit."

"You're fighting for your life!" he booms.

"Hey." Tyler stands and places a hand on his shoulder. "Calm down. Give her time to explain."

"Do you hear her?" Kent makes eye contact with each of us guys. "Are you hearing what I'm hearing? That she's just giving up?" He runs his fingers through his hair, his frustration and fear evident.

"Amelia, you have to fight this." Ridge's voice is pleading.

"What about an operation? Can they not remove it?" Tyler asks.

Amelia shakes her head. "No. They dumbed it down for me, basically saying that if they open me up, air hits this cancer, and it grows. Trying to remove it would be the worst course of action."

"Amelia." I pause, waiting for her to look at me. "We need you to fight."

Tears roll down her cheeks. "I've talked to three different oncologists. They have all told me the same thing. The treatments are harsh. They will break me down. Sure, they may give me a few extra months, but I'll be sick all that time. If I don't do anything, I still have time where I'm me. The me you know. Not a me who's too sick to come out of her house. I could live, for what time I have left, until it gets too bad, like I want. If I do these treatments, I'll be sick all the time, drained of any and all energy."

"How much time?" Dawn asks her. "If you don't treat it, how much time?" It's the question that I'm sure all of us have wanted to ask but didn't have the courage. Dawn and Amelia grew close while Daisy was in the hospital. Their relationship is different from ours with Amelia, and even Mara's.

"I don't know. I didn't ask. I'm not sure I want to know. I just want to 1-1 -live." She stumbles over her words. "I just want to live," she says again, this time her voice stronger.

"Why are you just now telling us?" Mark asks.

She looks over at Mara and sighs. "This one." She motions her head toward Mara. "She wouldn't let up until I told her what was going on."

"I'm sorry," Reagan says softly. "We knew something was up, but we didn't want to pry."

"You have nothing to be sorry for. I know I should have told you. Hell, I haven't even told my parents yet. Their health is not the best and I didn't want to worry them until I was 100 percent certain. Now I am. I'll be telling them tonight."

"You want us to come with you?" Mara asks.

"We'll be there," Dawn says.

"We've got you," Reagan chimes in.

"You're not alone in this," Kendall tells her.

"My heart is so full," she says as more tears begin to fall. "I love you guys so much." She makes it a point to look at each of us. "You all have been there with me since we were kids. I'm so happy that you've found these strong women to stand by your side." She stops at Kent. "You all love so deeply."

"We love you," Tyler says confidently.

"I know. I also know that you don't understand my reasoning, but I ask that you respect it. I'm going to die, no matter what I put my body through. That's the outcome I have to face."

"What about the tests?" I ask her. "You have more this week, right?"

She nods. "Yes, but those are to test my blood levels for treatment. If I'm not strong enough or my levels are not high enough, I can't start treatment. They have me scheduled to start chemo on Friday. I do five rounds and then off a week, and then thirteen rounds of radiation. Then more tests, then more chemo. I don't want that. I don't want to be sick all the time. I'm going to go for the tests, but I'm canceling my chemo on Friday."

"Please think about this," Ridge says.

"I have. It's all I've thought about. I know what I want. My mind is made up."

"We'll come with you," Mara says. "To all of your appointments. You won't have to do it alone. We'll be there."

"I know that. I love you all for it, but let me ask you something. Can you still be there? If I don't go through with treatments? I need you." She scans the room with her red-rimmed eyes. "All of you."

"Yes," all nine of us chorus in unison.

"Can you promise us something?" Kent asks. "Can you promise us you'll think about it? That you'll consider taking treatments? Everyone responds differently. You're a fighter, A."

She's quiet as she processes his request. "I'll give it further consideration, but, guys, I've had a couple of months to process this. To seek out second and third opinions. I've not come to this decision lightly."

"Think about it," Tyler says. "That's all that we ask."

"Okay." She nods and wipes at her eyes. "Now, enough of the heavy. Jennings, what do you have to eat around here?"

"To feed this brood?" I ask, knowing she's trying to lighten the mood. "Not enough," I say, and the guys chuckle. "Are we going out or do we want to order in?"

"Order in," the ladies say immediately.

"Just order pizza. They deliver and none of us have to leave," Dawn suggests.

"Pizza it is." I make my way to the kitchen to make the call. As soon as I hang up, the guys are there. All five of us stand around the island looking forlorn.

"How do we convince her to fight?" Tyler asks.

"I don't know that we can," I say, running my fingers through my hair. "It's ultimately her choice. I mean, I get what she's saying."

"She has so much to live for. She's young, she has so much life ahead of her," Kent says.

"I agree with you, but like Seth said, it's her choice," Ridge counters. "All we can do is be there for her."

"Fuck, can our family not catch a break?" Mark says.

"We've been through some tough times," Ridge agrees. "We have to be there for her no matter what she decides."

"So, we just watch her die?" Tyler chokes on the words.

"From the sounds of it, that's inevitable."

"Fuck me, I can't believe we're discussing her death like the damn weather," Mark grumbles. "I hate this. I fucking hate cancer."

"She just told us last night, so I haven't had time to research it myself. But she's been consistent with her information and her decision. She's never wavered. Not even once."

"I'm sure Kendall and Dawn will be all over it," Ridge says. They're both nurses, so they probably understand this better than any of us.

"Fuck," Tyler murmurs.

"We have to go out there and treat her like we always do," Kent says. "That's what she wants. She wants to live life to the fullest, and fuck me, but we're going to give her that. Regardless of what she decides to do, we're going to do that for her."

"Agreed," the four of us reply.

We compose ourselves, go back to the living room, and talk like one of our best friends didn't just tell us that her time here on earth is limited. We act as though everything is normal as it should be. We don't talk about cancer or tests or treatments. We pretend for our old friend that everything is how it should be.

Chapter 12

Mara

On Seth's couch, I grip my phone in my hand as I wait for Amelia to call and tell me that she needs me. We all offered to go with her to tell her parents, but she insisted that she do it alone. Reluctantly, we all agreed with the understanding that if she needed us, she would call. That was two hours ago. Not a word from her since.

"Hello," Seth says, and I turn to look at him, wondering if it's Amelia or news about her. "Hey, Dad," he says, and I sigh.

His parents taking Finley today was a blessing. They've sent us a few pictures and videos of their day, and my girl looks like she's being spoiled rotten. I love that for her, and I'm so grateful they are wanting and willing to spend time with her. They're giving her something I never had, something I haven't been able to give her. Not until Seth came into our lives.

Seth chuckles, once again drawing my attention. "Sounds like you've had a good day, Finny. Thanks, Dad. Sure, we'll be here." He ends the call and looks over at me. "They had me on speakerphone. Finny was going on and on about the fishes." He smiles. "They're taking her to get ice cream, then they'll bring her home."

"Okay."

"How are you?" he asks.

"I'm hanging in there. I just hate this for her, you know? She's never going to experience falling in love with a man who deserves her. She's never going to be a mom, to experience her child growing inside her." My voice cracks. "She was there for me when I found out I was pregnant. She was in the delivery room when Finley was born. I don't— I don't know how to be okay with this."

"Come here." He takes a seat next to me on the couch and pulls me into his arms. "I know, babe. It's hard for me, hell, for all of us to wrap our heads around it. All we can do is be there for her. If she wants to get drunk, we get her drunk. If she wants to jump out of a fucking airplane, we make that shit happen. That's all we can do. Respect her decision and make these final days the best for her. For all of us."

"I hate this," I say, tears forming. "I hate that I'm losing my best friend. I hate that I can't make her fight to stay with us. Miracles happen every day. What if they come up with a cure, and—" I break off on a sob.

"Baby, if they were close to any kind of breakthrough, the doctors would know about it. I hate it too, but it's not our decision. We can try and convince her, but in the end, we have to respect her choice."

"I do, but I don't," I say, wiping at my tears. "I know I'm being selfish, but she was my rock. Life after foster care was scary, and I met Amelia, my new roommate, and suddenly it wasn't. I know it's hard to explain, but she guided me through life, through pregnancy, delivery, and I was going to do the same for her."

"We'll get through this. We'll get her through this. All of us will." He holds me close to his chest, and I let myself relax into his warm embrace. "You're not alone, Mara. Not now, not ever. As long as I have breath in my lungs, you and Finley will never be alone."

I lift my head to look at him and my heart bursts with love for this man. Sliding my hand behind his neck, I pull his lips to mine and kiss him. He kisses me back, slowly, softly, but I want more. Suddenly, I need all of him. I can't get close enough. Moving, I straddle his hips and kiss him again. This time he takes control. He tenderly holds my face in his hands and slides his tongue past my lips. I rock my hips and he moans, a sound ripping from deep in his chest. Dropping his hands to my hips, he guides me over his erection.

"More," I say, kissing across his stubbled cheek and down his neck. My tongue traces the column to his collarbone. He grips my ass.

"Mara," he warns.

"Make love to me, Seth."

"Finley."

"She's with your parents."

"They'll be back soon."

"Then you better get with it."

"I need to take my time with you." He brushes my hair out of my eyes.

"Next time. I need you. I need to feel you. I just need... to be connected to you."

"You are connected to me." He places my hand on his chest over his heart.

Something happens. My insides feel like mush as his words and their meaning wash over me. "Make love to me," I say again. I can see the indecision in his eyes, so I take matters into my own hands.

Literally.

Sliding my hands under the waistband of his sweatpants, I grip his hard length. "You're ready. I'm ready."

"Jesus," he pants, letting his head fall back against the couch.

Pulling his pants back a little further, I stroke him. "Make love to me."

"Not here." I yelp when he stands from the couch with me in his arms. "Hold on, Mara." With long strides and a firm grip on my ass, he carries me down the hall to his room. He kicks the door shut with his foot. "Lock it." He steps close so I can reach out and turn the lock on the door. "This is going to be fast. I didn't want it to be this way. Not the first time I feel you."

"If all we have is now, I want this. I want you." I can see it in his eyes he's thinking about Amelia, and that none of us really know how much time we have left. "Even more reason," I say, I'm sure reading his mind. "I don't want to wait another minute not sharing this connection with you. The intimacy. I need it. I need you, Seth."

"Fuck," he murmurs before standing me on my feet. "Strip." Not needing to be told twice, I peel off my clothes. Seth kicks off his sweats and boxer briefs. I watch as he reaches behind his neck and pulls off his T-shirt. "Mara," he growls, and I smile then jump back into action by removing my bra and panties. He reaches into the nightstand and grabs an unopened box of condoms. He tears into it, and condoms fly everywhere, but he manages to snap one. Bringing the small foil packet to his mouth, he tears it open and makes quick work of sliding it along his hard length. He surprises me when he sits on the bed, moving back. "Take what you need from me."

Stepping between his legs, I run my hands through his hair. One leg then the other, I climb onto the bed, straddling him. Reaching between us, I fist his cock and lower myself onto him. "Ooh," I say. It's been too long and he feels so good.

"Fuck," he whispers harshly.

Opening my eyes, I see him biting down on his bottom lip. His eyes are glued to where our bodies are connected in the most intimate of ways. I lift off him slowly, then slam back down. "There," I say, repeating the process over and over again.

"Mara," he grits out.

"I need more. I'm so close, I just... mmm." I can't even finish a sentence from the electric current rolling through my veins.

His grip on me tightens, and the next thing I know, I'm flipped over with Seth pistoning in and out of me. Never missing a beat. Over and over he's relentless, and it's perfect. My hands grip his biceps as I hold on, enjoying every thrust, every inch he's willing to give.

"D-Don't stop. P-Please don't stop." I clench down on him just as my orgasm steamrolls through me. Wave after wave of pure ecstasy courses through my veins.

Seth stills suddenly and throws his head back as his own orgasm washes over him. He leans down and presses his sweaty forehead against mine. "That's not how I imagined it would happen, but fuck if I would change it."

"Seth?"

"Yeah, babe?"

"I love you." Life is too short to not tell the ones you love just how much every single day.

Pulling back, he stares into my eyes. "I'm madly in love with you, Mara Reyes. You and your daughter."

I hear a noise that sounds like a car door and freak. "Shit! We have to clean up." I push at his chest, making him laugh.

"Way to ruin the moment."

I stop and pull him back to me, kissing his lips. "I heard every word you said, but this is not how I want your parents or my daughter to find us."

"Hey, this was your idea." He kisses the end of my nose then pulls out, taking care of the condom.

Quickly, we clean up in between kisses and get dressed. Seth grabs us both a bottle of water and is just sitting on the couch when there's a knock at the door. "Come in!" he calls out. "They're only knocking because they probably assume we were up to something." He winks.

"That was close," I whisper. He leans over and kisses me.

"Mommy, Sef!" Finley races into the house. "I saw fishes and yummy ice cweam."

"You did?" I ask, catching her when she jumps on my lap.

She nods.

"Tell them about the stingray you got to pet."

"Papaw pet stinwray," she repeats.

I pause at her calling him papaw. I look over at Seth, who just grins.

"Did Mamaw pet one too?" he asks. It doesn't even faze him.

"Sorry about that," Shannon says. "Papaw and Mamaw are easier for her to say than Steve and Shannon. Not to mention, we adore this little angel."

"Did you tell S—" I trip over my words. "Did you say thank you?" These amazing people have accepted us into their lives, into their son's life, and it trips me up. The love and support they offer, it's unlike anything I've ever known.

"Anks," she says, climbing off my lap and rushing to Steve. He lifts her in his arms and gives her a hug.

"You're welcome, sweetheart." He kisses her cheek and she returns the favor—only a lot more sloppy.

"We'll have to go again soon," Shannon tells her.

I watch as my daughter reaches out for her and effortlessly moves from Steve's arms into Shannon's. "Anks," she says again, wrapping her arms around Shannon's neck and giving her a big hug before wiggling to be let down. She reaches into a bag that I didn't notice before and pulls out a stuffed shark. "Sef." Her little legs carry her back to the couch, and she crawls up on Seth's lap. "Sark," she says, holding up the stuffed animal.

"That's pretty cool, Finny. Did you get to see some sharks?"

"Big sarks." She holds her arms out wide to demonstrate.

"Thanks for taking her," he tells his parents.

"How did it go?" Shannon asks.

"It went… not like we hoped." He glances over at me. "She's saying she's not going to get treatment."

"Why on earth?" his mom replies.

"There's no cure for what she has." He goes on to tell them about the statistics of her making it five years.

"You know, I've oftentimes wondered what I'd do in that situation. I've seen far too many succumb to that disease and its treatments. It's her decision and you have to respect that," Steve says.

"Yeah, we know that. It's just hard," he tells them.

"No less difficult for her I'm sure. She may be putting on a strong front, but think about it from her perspective. I can't imagine having to make that choice," Shannon says sadly.

"I'm going to her appointment with her this week. Maybe there will be some new information that will change her mind," I say, hopeful. I know it's selfish of me, but I can't seem to stop it. I'm not ready to lose her. I want her to fight, and maybe, just maybe, there will be a miracle. They happen every day, and if anyone deserves one, it's her. It's Amelia. I won't push her, but deep in my heart, I will her to fight, to kick cancer's ass. Then I'm reminded that there is no cure for small cell carcinoma. Grief hits me deep in my gut as I accept that reality.

There is no cure.

"Well, you let us know what we can do. If you need us to keep an eye on Finley, we'd be more than happy to."

"Thank you. I appreciate that. She's never had… grandparents in her life. Then again, neither have I," I say absentmindedly. I immediately hold my hand over my mouth. I didn't mean to say that.

"Well, now she does. And you, you have us too. All three of you," Steve says. He places his arm around Shannon and she leans into him. "We're going to go. You let us know what we can do." He turns his attention to Finley. "Finley girl, how about giving Papaw a hug goodbye." He looks at me and winks and I feel tears start to well.

She races to him and hugs him and then Shannon. She tells them thank-you again, which is prompted by Seth, and with a big wave, they're off. "I wike sarks," she says as soon as the door is shut.

"Me too," Seth tells her. "In fact, I have something for you." He stands and makes his way to the shelf underneath the TV. He pulls out a DVD and shows it to her. "How about we watch *Shark Tale?*" he asks.

"Yay!" Finley cheers.

She has no idea what it is, but it has shark in the title so she's all-in.

"When did you get that?" I inquire.

"The other day. We stopped at Subway for lunch, which was inside the Walmart. Mark was picking up a princess movie for Daisy, and this one stood out. I thought she might like it after her adventure to the aquarium."

"You're a good man, Seth Jennings."

"Just spoiling my girl," he says fondly, running his hand over her dark curls.

Finley snuggles up to his chest, making my heart skip a beat. He puts his arm around her and pulls her close. Just like a father would do. Her eyes are already heavy as the movie starts to play. She's had a big day and will be out in no time. My phone vibrates in my hand.

Amelia: *It went okay. Lots of tears from all three of us.*

Me: *Do you need me to come over?*

Amelia: *No. Thank you. I'm exhausted.*

Me: *Did they change your mind?*

Amelia: *No.*

Me: *Love you.*

Amelia: *Love you too. We'll talk tomorrow.*

"Amelia?" Seth asks.

"Yeah. She said there were lots of tears. I asked her if they changed her mind. No," I say, shaking my head while fighting off another round of tears.

"There's still time. Maybe the doctors can change her mind at the appointment."

"Maybe." Although I don't think so. Amelia has always been strong-willed. She makes up her mind, and that's that.

Seth and I watch the movie even though Finley has long since passed out. Just as the credits start to roll, his phone rings. "Hello." He pauses. "Hey, man. Really? Okay. Yeah. That works. Sounds good. Let me know if anything changes." He waits and then laughs. "Could be worse, could be snow." Another laugh. "Talk to ya later," he says, ending the call.

"That was Ridge. I guess it's going to rain all day tomorrow. We were supposed to start a demo for a new roof, but we can't be sliding around the roof in the rain, so I get a rain day tomorrow."

"That does sound dangerous. What are you going to do with yourself all day?"

"I don't know. I can keep Finley with me."

"You don't have to do that."

"I want to. Maybe she and I can go to your old place and start packing up her room?"

"You can't move in the rain."

"Dad has an enclosed trailer I can use. He used to be into show cars and hauled them around. He sold the car but kept the trailer. It's come in handy several times."

"I hate for you to use your day off for me and Finley. Go do something fun with the guys."

"Do you not think that getting you both here under this roof, with

126

all of your stuff is going to be a fun day for me?"

"You can't move us on your own in a day, Seth." I know exactly what he's thinking.

"Is that a challenge?"

"No." I laugh. The look in his eyes tells me he would fight to make it happen.

"How about I just bring her bed, some toys, her dresser? Things to start getting her room set up?"

"I'm sure she would love that."

He glances down at my daughter asleep on his lap. "I just want you both here." He gazes up at me, his eyes soft and full of love. "I never want to know what a day of my future looks like without the two of you in it."

That feeling, the want that makes my insides feel like mush returns. It's beginning to be a constant when Seth is around. He makes me feel loved. Wanted. Cherished. I never want this feeling to end.

"Okay. But maybe we should take her to Sonia, so you can get some work done?"

"Nah, she'll be fine with me. This way, I'll be sure to grab what she really loves so I can bring it home first."

Home. I repeat the word in my head as I try to wrap my head around the fact that I agreed to move in with him. Me and my daughter. I've never lived with a man, and the only person other than Finley I've lived with from my choosing is Amelia. I'm excited we're moving forward. If I've learned anything in my life, it's that nothing is guaranteed. Not even how much time we have on this earth. We have to live without fear or regret.

Chapter 13

SETH

Today has been an adventure to say the least. I've watched my friends' kids before, but always with help. Today, I was flying solo with Finley, and let me tell you, little miss thang can wear a man out. However, I enjoyed the day more than I thought I would. We started out by going to Mom and Dad's and getting the trailer. Of course, Mom had us come in for some cookies and milk and then sent some home with us for a snack.

Our second stop was to visit Mara at work. Finley loved that, and she cried when it was time to leave. She perked right up when I told her we were going to visit her toys and to pack them to bring to my house. I'm not really sure she understands the concept of them moving in with me, but she was excited all the same.

Packing was… time-consuming. She'd show me what she wanted to take and I would put it in the box. Only to turn my back and find her playing with it in the middle of her bedroom floor. I managed to pack up two boxes of toys, and all her movies before she took a nap. I set her up on the couch, stacking pillows on the floor in case she rolled off and her fuzzy unicorn blanket that we found in between her bed and the wall. She's been hugging it tightly ever since.

We had some lunch, which consisted of SpaghettiOs and crackers. Grilled cheese would have been better, but Mara brought all the perishables to my place last night. I wanted to make use of what Mara had in her kitchen—fewer items to move over to my place. Besides, who doesn't love SpaghettiOs?

While she was napping, I was able to take her bed apart and load it and the packed boxes in the trailer. I managed to also pack up all her clothes, books, and another box of toys. I have almost her entire room packed, minus her dresser, and some art on the walls. Luckily, I borrowed Dad's dolly so I can move the dresser on my own. I have it on the dolly and am rolling it outside when I hear her start to cry. Shit. Backing up inside the house, I set the dresser by the front door, close the door, and go back to the living room. "Hey, Finny, did you have a good nap?"

"Sef." Her bottom lip juts out, and big ole tears fall down her tiny cheeks. It pulls at my heartstrings.

"What's going on, sweetheart? Are you still tired?" I pick her up and set her on my lap, and that's when I feel the wet soak through. Looking down, she's soaked through her clothes and now mine. Damnit. I forgot to have her use the potty before she crashed. She's in a pull-up, but it looks like it didn't do its job.

"That's got to be uncomfortable, huh?" I ask like a dumbass. Of course it's uncomfortable for her. I stand to take her to her room to change her when I realize all her clothes are packed. I turn to put her down, and she starts to cry, only louder this time. Panicked, I don't want to leave her in here to cry on her own, but I can't take her out in this rainy cold weather wet either. My eyes scan the room, looking for an idea when I spot a small laundry basket. Lifting her in my arms, we go to the basket, and sure enough, there is a sweat outfit in there for her. Remembering Mara told me there were pull-ups in the bathroom, I take her down the hall and into the bathroom.

"Let's get you out of these clothes," I tell her, setting her on her feet. I get her stripped down, and I'm about to redress her when I realize I can't let her walk around the rest of the day smelling like piss. "You ready for a bath?" I ask. Luckily for me, she loves bath time. Mara and I had a talk a few weeks ago when Finley asked for me to give her a bath.

She helped me realize that it's not something she can do on her own, and that as a caregiver, it's my job to do that for her. She went as far as saying that I'm her father figure. That gave me the confidence I needed to put my reservations aside. I've watched Mara do this often enough, so it should be a breeze. I turn on the water, letting it get warm, not hot and set her in. I hand her a mesh bag full of toys and she smiles up at me.

I reach for the bubbles, thinking she'd enjoy that, when I remember Mara told me to never let her sit in bubbles too long. Female anatomy and all that. I guess Finny is prone to infection or something. To be honest, I glazed over in that conversation, not really knowing the rules of men, and little girls who are not their daughters. It felt weird getting that kind of information. However, here I am now using it. That makes me smile. She may not have my blood running through her veins, but I couldn't love her more if she did.

"Okay, kiddo. Let's get you cleaned up." I grab the cup that has a soft side that Mara uses to keep the water out of her eyes. Filling it with water, I place it to her forehead. "Tilt back for me." I explain what I need her to do. Only, she doesn't do it. I try to dump the water anyway and it doesn't begin to get the rest of her hair wet.

"No." Finley shakes her head.

"Finny, we have to wash your hair. What's the point of a bath if you don't?" It's not like she's going to negotiate with me. She's two and a half. That doesn't keep me from trying again. "Hey, how about after bath time, we finish packing up what we can and then go to my place and watch movies and eat popcorn?"

"I want potcorn." She nods.

"Okay. But we have to wash your hair, finish your bath, and I have a few more things to load in the trailer. Can you be a good girl for me while I do that?" Scooping the weird-looking cup full of water again, I repeat the previous process, only this time she tilts her head back for me. I make quick work of washing her hair while talking about movies and popcorn. It works and I feel validated I've got this dad stuff down.

Dad.

I want to be that man for her. I run my hand over the crown of her wet head. "All right, Finny, let's get you dressed." Helping her stand, I wrap a towel around her body and toss one over her head. "Wait, where's Finley? Finley? Where are you, Finley?"

Her giggles go straight to my heart, warming my entire body. She pulls the towel off her head. "I wight hewer." She laughs.

"Oh, there you are," I say dramatically. "I thought I lost you."

"Sef." She laughs even harder.

"Sorry." I raise my hands in the air and grin at her. "Let's get you dressed so I can finish loading up. Then it's movies and popcorn."

"Yay!"

Just like that, she's the most cooperative child on the planet. Sure I might have bribed her a little, but it's not like I offered her unlimited ice cream. In fact, I know popcorn is a snack that Mara won't lecture me about later, and I know it won't keep her bouncing off the walls well into the night.

After she's dressed and her hair is combed, I set her up on the couch with her princess blanket, a sippy cup of milk that we picked up on the way here, and a movie. Eyes glued to the screen, she drinks her milk while I pack up a few more boxes and load them on the trailer. Checking in on her, I see she's still watching the movie, engrossed in the story, so I keep working. This time I go to Mara's room. I make up a few boxes and start emptying her dresser drawers. Her underwear and bras, pajamas, T-shirts, shorts, socks, and scarves. She has an entire drawer full of scarves. Taking the three boxes out to the trailer, I still have room for more. I check in on Finley, and she's still engrossed.

An hour later, I have all of Mara's clothes packed and loaded and everything under the bathroom sink, and in the drawers as well. The trailer is at max capacity, and I don't want to put anything in the bed of the truck because of the rain.

"Sef," Finley calls out and my heart leaps in my chest because she's asking for me. This little girl has her tiny fist around my heart.

"Hey, sweetheart. How was the movie?" I ask, sitting on the couch next to her.

"I want potcorn," she answers.

"You were such a good girl. I'm ready to go when you are."

She crawls into my lap and latches onto me. "Sit tight. I need to get your coat and shoes." Reaching for the remote, I turn off the TV and get to work putting her snow boots on her and her coat. Lifting her into my arms, I hand her the princess blanket she's held onto all day and walk through the house to make sure I have all the lights turned off.

"All right, kiddo, let's go home and get some popcorn."

"Yay!" she cheers.

We make it home, and as promised, I pop up a bag of microwave popcorn. A bottle of water for me and a sippy cup of milk for Finny, and we're posted up on the couch watching *Shark Tale*. That's how Mara finds us.

"Hey, you two look like you're having a good day."

"Mommy, potcorn." Finley points to the half-empty bowl.

"I see that." Mara kicks off her shoes and comes to sit next to us on the couch. "Did you have a good day with Seth?"

"Wook." She holds up her princess blanket.

"I see." Mara kisses her cheek then focuses her attention on me. "How was she?"

"Good. We had a slight pull-up malfunction at naptime, but we took a quick bath and all was good." I go on to tell her everything I got packed up and loaded.

"Wow, on your own?"

"I told you. I'm a man on a mission. I want you both here and the sooner you feel settled, the sooner this place will feel like home to both of you." As I say the words, Finley stretches out on the couch, getting comfortable.

"I think we're good." Mara laughs.

"Perfect. I'm going to start unloading the trailer. You ladies just chill." I lean over and kiss her quickly.

"My want kiss," Finley says, sitting up and kissing my cheek. I return the favor. I watch as she snuggles into Mara. Leaving my girls to cuddle, I get busy unloading the trailer. I back it up to the garage and open the garage door and start unloading into the second bay. This prevents me from having to walk through the cold-ass rain and keeps everything dry. I'll worry about getting it into the house after everything is unloaded.

Half an hour later, the trailer is unloaded and I'm a sweaty mess. I close up the trailer and pull the truck up far enough that I can get the garage door shut. Taking off my shirt, I wipe the sweat from my face and head into the house for a clean one. As soon as I step into the house, the smell of dinner hits me. Dropping my shirt in the laundry room, I enter the kitchen to find Mara standing at the stove, and Finley sitting on the floor over by the refrigerator, coloring.

"That smells delicious."

"Tacos." Mara smiles. She makes zero effort to hide the way her eyes rake over my body.

"What can I do to help?" I ask, coming to stand behind her. My hands land on her hips and I press a kiss to her neck.

"Nothing. It's ready."

"Finny, let's go wash our hands for dinner." I don't give her time to get up before I scoop her up in my arms and race down the hall toward the bathroom. Her laughter trails behind us.

After dinner, Mara pushes me out to the garage to start bringing in boxes while she cleans the kitchen. I start with Finley's bed. It's a princess bed with the headboard being a castle. She loves it, so I want to get that set up first. She and Mara are sitting on the bedroom floor reading a book while I put it back together. It's a simple process. "All right, Finny. You're all set."

"My pwincess bed." She runs and jumps on the mattress.

"No jumping on the bed, missy," Mara warns in her stern mom voice.

Finley flops down on her bottom, her smile still wide. "My woom," she tells us.

"That's right. You ladies hang out, I'm going to go grab your dresser." I head to the garage for another load and that's how the night goes. I bring in the dresser that I left full of clothes, making unpacking a breeze. As I bring in boxes of clothes and toys and the small bookcase, they work on getting it set up. By the time they're finished, I have all the boxes from Mara's room in our bedroom ready to be unpacked.

"It's bedtime," Mara announces. "You're going to Sonia's tomorrow."

"I want Sef."

"I had a great time with you today, Finny, but I have to go back to work tomorrow. How about I read you a story?" Her eyes are drooping and I know it won't be long before she's fast asleep. She nods and climbs into her bed, already having changed into pajamas and taken her bathroom break. I settle in beside her on the floor and hold the book where she can see the pages. Two pages in and Mara stops me with her hand on my arm.

"She's out."

Looking over at Finley, I kiss her forehead before climbing to my feet and placing the book back on her shelf. "She's had a busy day."

"You both have. I can't believe you moved her entire room."

"Well, there are still a few pictures on the walls that we'll need to bring over and hang. She was really good so I kept working."

"Thank you. This is going to make it go so much faster and make her transition smoother."

"She seems to be doing well," I whisper, leading her out of Finley's room after turning on the night light.

"She is. She adores you."

"Good, because I adore her too. You ready to unpack your stuff or do you want to wait until tomorrow night?"

"How much is there?"

"Take a look." I push open our bedroom door and she gasps.

"How did you manage all of this on your own with a toddler?"

"I told you she was good. She helped, took a nap, and watched some TV."

"Is there anything left?"

"Yes, lots of things, but I have all of your clothes and everything that was under the bathroom sink and in the drawers." She's quiet as she looks at the boxes. She peeks inside a few of them. I'm nervous that this is too much too fast. Her silence is killing me. I'm just about to ask what's wrong when she turns to me with a smile on her face.

"I guess I need to unpack."

So that's what we do. I unpack the boxes while she organizes her drawers that I cleaned out for her. This house has two walk-in closets in the master with custom shelving. She gets right to it, hanging up clothes and placing shoes and sweaters on the shelves.

Two hours later, she's unpacked, and the boxes are broken down and in the garage waiting to be packed up again. "I'm going to grab a quick shower," I say, kissing her temple and heading into the master bathroom. I turn on the faucet ready to wash the day away and strip out of my clothes.

I stand under the hot spray letting it beat down on my muscles. I should have asked Mara to get in the hot tub with me. This will have to do for tonight. I'm exhausted. However, when I feel her small hands wrap around my waist and her naked body press into my back, sleep is the last thing on my mind. Turning, I wrap my arms around her and just hold her close.

"This, we need more of this," I say, resting my chin on the top of her head.

"Yeah," she agrees. "You know, I've never done this. I've never showered with anyone."

"No?"

She shakes her head. Her hands move to my chest as her fingers dance over my pecs and down my abs. Her big green eyes lock on mine as her hand grips my cock. The look in her eyes tells me she's hesitant, not sure exactly what she's doing or what she's gotten herself into. I know her experience is limited, and null since the night Finley was conceived. It just might kill me, but this is her show and I'm going to let it play out however she wishes.

"Seth."

"Yeah, baby?" I push her wet hair out of her eyes.

"Tell me what you want."

"I want you."

"No. Tell me what to do. I-I don't know what you like."

I smile down at her. "You, Mara. I like you. I want you. Anytime you want to put your hands on me, be my guest."

"Show me what you like."

"Anything. Everything. As long as it's you." I run the pad of my thumb across her lips. "What do you like, Mara? What do you want?"

"I want to taste you," she whispers, but to my ears, she screams the words.

Raising my hands, I lock them behind my head. "I'm yours, Mara. Take what you need."

Without a word, I see the determination in her eyes with the knowledge she's directing this show. Leaning in, she places a kiss to the center of my chest before taking a step back and dropping to her knees.

I glance down, and the vision before me is enough to send me into orgasmic bliss. Closing my eyes, I focus on taking in deep, even breaths as her hand strokes me faster. When her lips touch the tip of my cock, I have to reach out and brace myself against the shower wall. Tentatively she does it again, swallowing more. Then again, taking more each time, growing braver in taking what she wants. What she needs.

Over and over again, she takes me deep into the back of her throat. I'm so damn close, but I don't want it to end this way. "Mara, babe, I'm close." I tap on her shoulder to get her attention. When she doesn't remove her mouth from my dick, I'm forced to open my eyes and look down. Fuck me. This is a sight I will never forget. "Mara," I grind out.

She stops. My cock's still in her mouth as she stares up at me. Big green eyes filled with lust gaze up at me. I release a groan from deep in the back of my throat when I look further and see her hand between her legs. "Stand up." She must hear it in my voice, the way I'm about to lose my control, lose my fucking mind. "Condom."

I watch as she steps out of our walk-in shower and pulls open the drawer on the vanity. She grabs a small foil packet and comes back to me. Not willing to let her touch me again for fear I'll combust, I take it from her hand, tear it open with my teeth, and slide it over my cock. Tossing the wrapper on the shower floor, I bend down, place my hands on the back of her thighs, and lift her. Instinctively, she wraps her legs around my waist and her arms around my neck.

Turning, I push her back against the wall and kiss her. My tongue fucks her mouth. Her hands grip my hair, and I deepen the kiss. Sliding my hand between us, I press my thumb gently against her clit and begin to rub small circles.

"Oh, shit," she breathes, letting her head tilt back against the tile wall.

"I'm going to come as soon as I slide inside you. I'm at my breaking point, Mara. I need you to get there." I say the words against her lips before my tongue explores her mouth once again. Over and over, I circle her clit. She grinds her hips against me, and when she moans from deep in the back of her throat, I know she's close. Without a word, I remove my hand and align myself at her entrance, pushing inside and feeling her heat surround me. I can't help but wonder what she'd feel like bare. My cock twitches at the thought, and her nails dig into my scalp.

"Seth." She moans my name, and I thrust my hips. That's all it takes. Her body convulses around me, and we're both crying out, flying off into the world of orgasmic paradise. She buries her face in my neck, and I pull her from the wall, holding her close to my chest. Close to my heart. Slowly, she lifts her head and smiles shyly. "A girl could get used to that."

I throw my head back and laugh, smacking her on the ass before carefully setting her on her feet. "Over there, woman, or I can't be held accountable for my actions." I point to the opposite side of the shower to the other showerhead. Sliding off the condom, I step out and toss it in the trash before I finish my shower. I keep my eyes closed and my back turned as I wash away the day. She's too damn tempting.

Fifteen minutes later, we're snuggled up in our bed. Mara is in one of my shirts, and I'm in boxer briefs. I want nothing more than to feel her naked skin against mine, but with Finley in the house, we have to stay covered. Besides, she's here in my arms. They're both here calling this place home. What more could a man really ask for?

Chapter 14

Mara

It's been a long week of worry and constant conversations with Amelia. I want her to fight. I know it's selfish, but I want it all the same. I'm not ready to lose my best friend. Her appointment isn't until eleven, but Ridge told me to take the entire day off. He told me to spend some time with her, so that's exactly what I'm doing. Guilt washes over me. My life is falling into place as hers falls apart. If it were not for Amelia, I wouldn't be here. In Jackson. I wouldn't have interviewed for the job or met Seth.

Seth.

My life suddenly feels like a fairy tale. One I always dreamed of. Finding a man who respects me, loves me for who I am, my past included. When I found out I was pregnant, I was excited and scared, but I knew in my heart Blake would do the right thing. I wish he would have had that chance. My fairy tale turned into something different, something better, and all because of Finley. And now, Seth. I never imagined I would find a man who would treat my daughter with so much love and affection. Sure, I know there are men out there, but I never thought I would find one, and I'd been okay with that. I'd been okay with it being me and Finley against the world.

Then Seth came into our lives. Like a slow-burning flame, we got to know each other, and now, I feel like that flame is burning out of control. My heart speeds up whenever he's near, and when I watch him with Finley, it melts into a puddle at my feet.

I've never known this kind of love. Never had this kind of bond with a man. It's unexpected, but I wouldn't change it. No, I want to relish it. I want to shout from the rooftops how much I love him. How much *we* love him. It's no longer me and Finley against the world. It's me, Finley, and Seth, and I love it.

So much.

A knock sounds at my window and causes me to jump. My hand flies to my chest as I look over and see Amelia standing there. I roll down my window and wave. "Hi."

"Hi." She laughs. "What are you doing sitting in my driveway at nine in the morning like a damn creeper?"

"I'm taking you to breakfast, then your appointment."

"Mara," she says with a sigh, "I told you. I'm a big girl. I can take myself to my appointment. I've already had this conversation with my parents."

"You're also stubborn as hell. Go grab your purse as I'm starving." I stare her down. I'm not willing to budge on this. She can try to push all of us out all she wants, but I'm not letting it happen. I know damn good and well the others are not going to either. She may try to act all tough and closed off like she doesn't need a shoulder to cry on, but I know better. I'm going to be there for her every step of the way. Maybe, just maybe, I'll be able to convince her to change her mind.

"So, how are things going with Seth? How's the new living arrangement?" she asks twenty minutes later. We're sitting at a local diner sipping coffee as we wait for our breakfast.

"Great."

"Great, huh?" She smiles. "You're welcome," she teases.

"Thank you, Amelia," I say, overly sweet.

"I expect a wedding invitation," she says with a smile, and then she immediately sobers.

Reaching across the table, I gather her hand in mine. "I don't know if there will be a wedding or invitations, but I know that I love him. I know that he treats me as if I'm the light in his life, and Finley, you would think she was his with the way he dotes on her."

"He's a good man."

"He is. We're not there yet, but it sure would be nice to have my best friend by my side when we do get there."

"Mara, we've been over this."

"I know we have. I know it's selfish of me. Hell, we all want you to fight this thing, but you're young, and cures are found every day. Even if there is no cure, five years is a long time, and you can break those odds, Amelia."

"Maybe." She shrugs. "But I don't want to. I've researched this. I've talked to three different oncologists. I know what to expect. I know that the drugs they give me to slow the cancer alter my quality of life. I know that there is no guarantee that the drugs will even work. I don't want to pump that poison into my body and become even sicker. I want to do this." She uses the hand that's not held tightly in mine to motion between the two of us. "I want to go to breakfast with you. I want to live my life. I understand that the cancer is going to spread. I understand that when that happens, the end of life will not be a fucking walk in the park. I get all of that. I also get that I feel fine. I have a cough, I get tired easier, but other than that, I feel good. I want to hold onto that feeling for as long as I possibly can."

"I'm not okay with that," I say, fighting back my tears. "I need you."

"You have Seth."

"He doesn't replace you, Amelia." I let go of her hand and sit back in the booth, crossing my arms over my chest. Now she's just pissing me off.

"I didn't mean it like that."

"Then you better spell it out for me." How dare she compare my relationship with Seth to our friendship. It's altogether different.

"What I meant to say is that you have a shoulder to lean on. He's going to be there for you, for both of you."

"Are you sure surgery isn't possible? Maybe we can look into treatment overseas?"

"Mara." She sighs my name as if I'm exhausting her. Good. Maybe that means I'm wearing her down. "No, it's not possible. I've reached out. I've researched. I've cried. I've gone through it all since the day I found out it might be possible. I've talked to families whose loved ones have this cancer. No matter how hard the fight, it never ends the way you want it to."

"How do you know unless you try?" I don't know what else I can do to change her mind. She's set in her decision no matter how many times I beg, or the others beg. Seth told me that Kent called her last night and tried to talk her into it, but it was no use. She's made up her mind and I hate it. I hate that she's not fighting, but at the end of the day, I know it's her choice. I just can't help but think she's making the wrong one.

"Mara, I love you. You were there for me during the most traumatic time of my life in college. You're my best friend and I need you here with me now. Not just here sitting across the booth with me, but I need you here in the moment. I need you to respect my decision, and I want to live." She stops and swallows hard. "I want to live each day as if it could be my last. Can you do that for me? Can you please respect that I've made up my mind?"

"H-How can I do that? How can I accept that you're d-dying? How can I accept that you're not willing to fight for your life?"

"Don't you see? I am fighting for my life. I'm fighting for the good days. For the memories I can make while I'm healthy. If I'm sick all the time, that won't happen. Regardless of what I do, Mara, I'm going to die."

I watch as she swipes at a tear that's rolling down her cheek. Closing my eyes, I try to block it out. The tears. Her words. I want this all to be a bad dream. I swallow the lump forming in my throat, but it does nothing to stop the tears that begin to fall. Slowly, I open my eyes to find her watching me. Her lone tear has, like mine, turned into streams coating her cheeks.

"Please, Mara," she pleads. "I need my best friend. I need you to respect my choice. You don't have to understand it, but please, I need you to respect it."

Defeat. It washes over me, as well as acceptance. This is her choice, and it's my job to be there for her through good times and bad. "Every step, Amelia. Do you hear me? Every single step I'm going to be there.

You want memories? We're going to make memories." Reaching into my purse, I pull out an envelope from a bill and a pen and slide it across the table. "Make a list."

"What?" She wipes at her face and looks at me like I've lost my mind.

Maybe I have.

"Make a list of things you want to do. We're going to make them happen."

She smiles across the table. "There are a few things you can't make happen," she says, her voice cracking. "Things I'll never get to experience, but with you and Finley, I got pretty close."

"Write it all down, Amelia. All of it. Anything and everything, no matter how far out of reach. Write it down." I don't know how I'm going to make this list happen for her, but I'm going to try my hardest. I'll get Seth in on it as well. He can rally the guys, and I'll call the girls, and we'll see to it that as many items as possible are crossed off her list.

Fifteen minutes later, she sets the pen down and slides the envelope across the table. With a deep breath, I pick it up and read it.

1. Visit the Grand Canyon
2. Get a tattoo
3. Fly on a plane
4. Be in two places at once
5. Watch the sunrise and sunset in the same day
6. Take lots of pictures
7. Spend time with those I love
8. See Niagara Falls
9. Swim in the ocean
10. Fall in love
11. Get married
12. Have a baby

My heart feels as though it's going to beat its way out of my chest. I expected bungee jumping or skydiving. Not… this. Basic everyday living. I choke back a sob as what's happening settles deep in my bones. My best friend is dying. There are things on this list that she will never be able to accomplish, and my heart breaks for her.

"Amelia." I look up to find her watching me.

"I'm sure I can think of more, but you know I don't really know how much time I have."

It's on the tip of my tongue to tell her to fight, but we've been down that road. Her mind is made up, and I told her I would respect that. I do respect that it's her decision, but I hate it. I hate that I'm losing her. It feels as though she's giving up. I know that's not the case. She's grabbing life—what little she has left—by the horns.

"This is a start." I manage to push the words past my lips.

"We better get moving." She takes a sip of her coffee then stands and saunters off to pay the bill, all while I sit frozen, her list gripped tightly in my hands. Some of these she'll never make happen, but for the ones that I can control, I'll see to it she gets to mark them off her list.

My best friend wants memories. I'm going to give them to her.

"Would you stop fidgeting? We know the results. This isn't some life-altering appointment. I'll get the numbers from my bloodwork, tell them I'm not taking treatment, and then we're out of here," Amelia says, reaching over to take my hand in hers.

She's trying to comfort me. I need to get out of my own head, my own grief, and be there for her. "I'm sorry. I'm still adjusting to all of this."

"Knock knock," a female voice says. "Amelia." The woman holds her hand out and Amelia shakes it.

"Hi, Dr. Hampton. This is Mara, my best friend."

"Nice to meet you, Mara." She holds her hand out for me and I take it as well. "How are you feeling?" she asks Amelia.

"Good. Still have the lingering cough. I get tired easier. Then again, that could just be my mind playing tricks on me. Other than that, I feel great."

I watch the two as they talk back and forth. "Being that tired is to be expected as your body tries to fight off the cancer. Expect more of that along with nausea, vomiting, and headaches when you start treatment."

"About that." Amelia glances over at me. "I'm not taking treatments. I want to live what time I have left not being sick."

"Amelia, you do realize that without treatment, the disease will steadily progress. With treatment we can hope that it slows down. Giving you more time."

"I do. I also know that the chemo and the radiation will make me sick, and there is no guarantee it will slow the growth." She glances over at me. "I took everything we talked about, and this is my decision. I don't want treatment."

"Okay." Dr. Hampton nods and looks down at the folder in front of her. "There are some results I need to discuss with you. Is it okay to speak freely?" She nods at me.

"Yes. I've told my friends and family. Everyone knows. Is it worse than we thought?" Amelia's voice is strong, but her hand that's holding mine is shaking.

"No, but we did find something new in your bloodwork."

"Okay," Amelia says slowly.

The silence in the room is deafening as time ticks by as we wait for the doctor to tell us what they found. My heart thumps in my chest, my palms are sweaty, and I want to scream at her to spit it out already. I'm so afraid it's worse than what they thought. That we have even less time than we had hoped to have.

"Amelia." Dr. Hampton closes the folder and focuses on my best friend. "You're pregnant."

I'm not sure whose grip is tighter, hers or mine. I do know it's tight as we each try to process the bomb that was just dropped on us.

"W-What? I think I heard you wrong. Can you repeat that?" Amelia asks.

"You're pregnant."

No. No. This is not happening. Please, God, no. I don't need her to tell me to know that her baby is Seth's. The man I love. She's having his baby. I don't know how to process this. I'm at a loss for what to say or do or think.

"Pregnant? That's not possible. I've—Oh, God." She glances over at me and I see remorse flash across her face. "Mara," she whispers.

"Considering your current circumstances, I would suggest you terminate the pregnancy."

"What?" Amelia's head whips around to face the doctor. "Have you lost your damn mind? I'm not taking treatments, so I can have this baby. My mind was made up before, but now, now I know why. I mean, I didn't know then, but it makes sense to me now. My gut was telling me no treatments. This is why. I'm keeping this baby."

I close my eyes and focus on breathing. This can't be happening right now. Why? Why, when things were starting to turn around for me, does life have to twist my new reality?

"Mara." Amelia's voice is soft and pained. "Talk to me."

Slowly, I open my eyes to find Amelia and Dr. Hampton watching me. "I-I don't know what to say."

"I'm sorry," she whispers.

"Amelia—" Dr. Hampton starts, but she cuts her off.

"No. I'm keeping this baby. You're not going to talk me out of it. What you can do is send my records to my obstetrician, Dr. Hatfield." She stands and holds her hand out for me. "Let's get out of here."

I don't take her hand, but I stand and robotically follow her out of the office, down the hall, out of the building, and to my parked SUV. I stop next to the driver's side door and focus on getting my emotions in check.

"Mara, I'm so sorry. I know we used protection. I—Please just talk to me."

I stare at her over the roof of my car. "Seth, you need to call Seth."

"I will. I'll tell him. Right now, I'm worried about you. Why don't you let me drive?"

"No." I shake my head and it wakes me out of this fog I've been in since the doctor dropped the news. "No, I can drive. Call him. We'll go back to o-our place." I stutter over my words. Will he still want it to be our place? So many unanswered questions now that this new development has been revealed. Does he want us to stay? Do I want to stay? Does he want this baby? Question after question runs through my mind as I drive us home.

Chapter 15

SETH

I've checked my phone for what feels like a thousand times. I told Mara to call me if they needed me today. The guys have all been quiet as we wait to hear how Amelia's appointment went today.

"Hear anything?" Ridge asks as I'm sliding my phone back into my pocket.

"No. Not yet."

"She's not going to change her mind," Tyler speaks up.

"We might as well accept that," Mark adds.

"Remember when we were in high school and she was determined to drink us under the table after prom? She drank until she made herself sick. She's never been one to be swayed once she makes up her mind about something," Kent recalls.

"Yeah," I agree. "I hate it, but it's her choice. We just have to be there for her and support her through this."

"How do you support someone through death?" Mark asks. "I mean, I was there for Dawn, but it wasn't her who was dying. How are we supposed to stand back and watch it happen?" He shakes his head.

"We don't have a choice. This is her decision," Ridge comments.

"You." Tyler points at me. "You're the one who is going to get the worst of it. She and Mara are close. That's double for you."

"I know." I run my hands through my hair. Our families have been through so much these past few years. Would it be too much to ask for some good news for once? Before I can voice my thoughts out loud, my phone rings. Rushing to grab it out of my pocket, I see Amelia's name on the screen. "Hey," I answer, mouthing her name to the guys.

"Hey, Seth. We're back at your place. You think boss man would let you come home early? Mara needs you."

"I'm on my way." I end the call, shoving my phone back in my pocket. "That was Amelia. They're back at my place. She asked me to come home. Says Mara needs me."

"Go." Ridge reaches out and takes the hammer I was using out of my hand. "You need us, you call."

"Thanks." I barely have the words out before I'm rushing out to my truck. I don't bother to wait for it to heat up. Instead, I put it in Drive and crank up the heater. Mara needs me. I have to get to her.

I break more traffic laws than I care to admit on the way to my place. We're working on a job that's about a half hour away, but I make it in just under twenty minutes. The truck is barely in Park when I'm pushing open the door and jogging up to the front porch. "Mara!" I call out as I enter the house.

"In here," Amelia calls back.

I make my way to the living room following her voice and find Mara curled up on one corner of the couch, a blanket thrown over her legs, and Amelia on the loveseat in the same position. I get to Mara and drop to my knees in front of her. "Hey, baby. What's wrong?" I ask like a dumbass. I know she's upset about Amelia, but this is not what I was expecting. Sure, I expected her to be sad, but this… this is more than sad. Her face is streaked with tears. Her eyes are full of pain and red from crying. She's curled into herself.

"Seth, maybe you should sit down," Amelia suggests.

I turn to look at her over my shoulder. "What happened?"

"Sit." Amelia nods to the couch.

Standing to my full height, I sit next to Mara on the couch, pulling her legs onto my lap. She doesn't even acknowledge me. "Hey." I lean into her, kissing her on her forehead. "I'm right here." I place my arm around her shoulders and pull her into me. She comes willingly, sliding onto my lap, but she's still not speaking. "Tell me what's going on here." I look across the room at Amelia. She looks tired, and I can tell she too has been crying, but she doesn't look as though the world is coming to an end, not like Mara does.

"We got some unexpected news today at my appointment."

I wrap my arms around Mara and hold her close to my chest. "Okay. Are you going to fill me in or do I have to guess?" I'm getting irritated that she won't just tell me what's going on.

"There's really no easy way to say this, so I'm just going to blurt it out. You know, like pulling off a Band-Aid."

"Amelia." My voice is low, a warning that my patience is wearing very thin.

"I'm pregnant."

Pregnant. Oh, shit! I squeeze Mara tighter as she begins to cry. "P-Pregnant?" I ask, even though I know I heard her.

"Yes."

"What does that mean?" That's a stupid fucking question. I know exactly what it means. My palms sweat and I'm sure if I were standing, my knees would be knocking. This is the last thing I expected to hear today. Is it safe for the baby? Is it safe for her? A million questions filter through my mind. I can't believe this is happening.

"Seth, do you really need me to explain the birds and the bees to you?" Amelia asks, her tone playful. She's hiding behind humor.

"Stop." Again, my voice is firm. "Stop with the kidding around. You know what I meant. What does that mean for you? For the baby?" I'm trying to remain calm and ask the right questions. I'm trying like hell not to show her that I'm freaking out.

I'm going to be a father.

Amelia is pregnant.

She's dying.

Holy fuck!

"It means that I'm having a baby. It means that you're going to be a father. It means that I'm dying, and this baby is going to be your responsibility. It means that you're not going to change my mind. No matter what you say, I'm keeping this baby." She wipes at her eyes and continues. "I never thought I would get to be a mom, to know what it's like to feel my baby growing inside me. You gave me that. Our one drunken reckless night gave me that. I'm a strong believer in everything happens for a reason, and I believe that's why we got trashed and ended up in the same bed together. I was meant to know this… love. This bond between mother and child. I already feel it, Seth. That's why I felt so strongly about not getting treatment. I feel it deep in my soul. This was meant to be."

Mara is holding onto me as if I might disappear. Then again, maybe that's me holding onto her. I can't believe this is happening. I love Amelia; we've been friends for as long as I can remember, but that love, it's nothing like the love I feel for Mara. For Finley. I will love this baby with everything in me. Will Mara? Will one night destroy the future we are building? I pray to God that it doesn't.

"How are you feeling? How is the baby?" I keep my eyes locked on her looking for signs she might be hiding the truth about how she's feeling, while my arms are locked tight around Mara, holding her close. She's my lifeline in this sea of unexpected events.

Amelia's smile, although tired, it lights up her face. "I feel good. I'm drained and have this stupid cough that comes and goes, but I feel good. Great in fact. I want this, Seth." She reaches for the table and grabs an envelope with writing on it. "Earlier today Mara asked me to make a list of things I wanted to do before this disease takes me. I thought it was silly, but she was finally accepting my decision to not take treatments, so I obliged her. Right here, on this list I wrote become a mom. I knew it would never happen, but it was something I wanted regardless. Wishes do come true. I want this, Seth. This baby. I need you to tell me that you're on board with this. That you are going to love this baby for both of us when I'm gone." Her voice cracks and she clears her throat. Amelia, always the strong one, never wanting to show emotion.

"What kind of question is that? This is my child we're talking about. Of course I'm going to love and care for him or her. How can you even ask me that?"

"I know this is a lot to take on. I know I'm blindsiding you with this, but, Seth… I love this baby." Her hands cover her still flat belly.

"Is this safe for you?"

"I'd already decided I wasn't getting treatments."

"Did you know? Is that why you've been so adamant? Did you know you were having my baby and didn't tell me?" Mara flinches in my arms when I say my baby, but I hold tight to her, needing her close.

"No. I didn't know. I promise you. I did, however, have this gut-wrenching feeling that I didn't want treatment. I meant it when I said I didn't want to be sick, and I want to make memories. I mean that with all that I am, but this… this baby is a bonus. I get to be a mom. I get to feel my child growing inside me. I get to witness the miracle of life, and most of all, I get to leave a piece of me behind. I may be dying but this baby, he or she will live for me. I know it sounds crazy, but it makes it all a little easier. To know that when I leave this world, part of me, not just my memory, but part of me, my blood, my heart, will still be here."

"We have to get you checked out. Get the baby checked out."

"I'm way ahead of you. My oncologist is sending my file to Dr. Hatfield. I'm going to call when I leave here to make an appointment." She stands and wipes at her eyes. "I know the two of you need some time. I didn't want to leave her alone." She walks over to the couch and takes a seat on the coffee table facing us. "Mara," she whispers and waits for Mara to look at her. "I love you. I'm sorry. I know this has to hurt you and be confusing for you. When I told you that I don't have feelings for Seth, I didn't lie to you. He's one of my best friends. I'm happy it is him, because that means I know this baby will be loved and cared for after I'm gone. I'm sorry this is happening to us, but I'm not sorry about this baby. He or she is my blessing." Reaching out, she gives Mara's shoulder a gentle squeeze. "I'll give you two time to talk. Call me if you need anything. I'll let you know when my appointment is." She stands and grabs her coat, slides into her boots, and walks toward the door.

"Amelia, wait. Are you okay to drive? Where's your car?"

"I'm fine." Her hand rests on her belly. "Mara drove. I'll have Mom or Dad drive me back later and drop off Mara's car. I'll text you before I come." With that, she walks out the door.

My mind is a mess. Jumbled full of the information that Amelia just dumped on me. First and foremost, I'm going to be a father. Mara tries to pull away, but I hold tight. "Talk to me," I whisper.

"I'm afraid to," she says through her tears.

"Hey." I lift her chin with my index finger and turn her to face me. "What do you mean you're afraid to? There is nothing you can't say to me. I know you're upset, but I promise you that night meant nothing. But this is my baby."

"I know that. I would never ask you to walk away from your child. I just…. Where does this leave us? Do you want Finley and me to leave? This is a huge change for you, Seth. One that you're not ready for."

"No," I say firmly. "You're not leaving. This is your home. You're my home. You and Finley."

"But, Amelia?" she says, letting the unspoken question hang in the air.

"She's having my kid, but she's not the love of my life. I hate it. I hate that it's not you. However, I don't hate her or my unborn child. This is a clusterfuck of epic proportions, but that doesn't change how I feel about you. I love you, Mara. You and Finley, you're my family. We're just adding to it."

I wait. Holding my breath for her to tell me what's on her mind. Her eyes well with tears as they begin to slip over her cheeks. "I love you. I've never known a love like what I feel for you. I don't want to lose you, but I will step back. I would understand if you needed to focus more on Amelia and the baby. She's my best friend, and you… you're the love of my life, and this is so messed up. I'm losing her, and now I'm so afraid that I'm losing you too."

"What? Baby, no. You're not losing me. Never. I know this mess is twisted and complicated, but we'll make it through this." Please, God, let us make it through this. I send up the silent prayer, but then it hits me. What if she doesn't want to do this with me? "Mara?" I cradle her cheek in the palm of my hand, her tears soaking into my skin. "Tell me you're in this with me. That you're not going anywhere." I pause and try to find the words I need to say. "Tell me." I swallow the lump that is lodged in my throat. "Tell me you're willing to raise this baby with me?" I ask, choking on my own emotions. Tears burn my eyes as I wait with bated breath for her reply.

"What?" she whispers.

"The mother of my unborn child has terminal cancer. You are my heart, my whole heart. Tell me I'm not going to lose you over this."

"No. Of course not. I just don't want to keep you from—" she starts, but I kiss her.

A quick, chaste kiss.

"I need you in my life, Mara. This is a surreal twist of fate, but I want you by my side as we make our way through this rocky sea."

"Okay."

"Okay?"

She nods. "I was so scared of losing you. That maybe feelings you didn't know you had would surface."

"Not at all. I love her as a friend and now as the mother of my child, but that love doesn't come close to the love I have for you. We're going to fight through this."

"She has a list." Mara wipes at her eyes and hands it to me. "I want to make it happen for her. All of it."

I skim through the list. "Marriage?" I ask, eyebrows raised.

"Well, maybe not that one, but the baby part, you did that, so who knows. It's not entirely impossible."

My eyes read through the list one more time. "I need to call the guys. We're going to make this list happen for her."

"Are you going to tell them? About the baby I mean?"

"Shit." I rake my fingers through my hair. "Yeah, they don't know about that night. This is going to be a shock to all of them."

"Amelia should be here for that conversation."

"I agree. How long until we have to pick up Finny?"

She glances at the clock. "I told Sonia I would be there by four."

"Good. We have some time. I want to hold you." Standing with her in my arms, I make my way to our bedroom and carefully set her on the bed. Stripping out of my jeans and hoodie, I climb in bed behind her, pulling her to my chest. "I love you, Mara."

"I love you too."

I don't sleep, but she does, just like I knew she would. Exhaustion was written all over her face. There are too many things bouncing around in my head to rest properly. I have a baby on the way, and I'm going to be a dad. I've got some things to work out.

After I tell the guys.

Chapter 16

Mara

I wake to the sound of laughter that I know is my daughter. Glancing at the clock, I see it's after five. I didn't mean to sleep that long. The emotional roller coaster of the day took it out of me. Throwing off the covers, I make a quick stop to the restroom before making my way down the hall toward the sound of my daughter's laughter.

"Sef." Finley giggles.

"Look," he says, spotting me and pointing over her shoulder. "Mommy's awake."

"Mommy!" Finley scrambles to her feet and comes rushing toward me.

I bend down to catch her. "Hey, sweetie. Did you have fun at Sonia's today?"

"Nugs." She points to the Chick-fil-A bag on the table.

"I called the guys. They're going to be here at seven. My parents are taking her out for ice cream, so I thought I should feed her first."

"Dinner before dessert is always a good idea," I say, walking into the living room with Finley in my arms. I sit on the couch, and she slides off my lap and settles onto the floor beside Seth. "Did you tell them?"

"No. Not yet. I wanted to do it in person. I asked Kent to stay a little while once my parents bring her back so I can sit them down and tell them. I wanted you to be there with me. He didn't ask questions, but considering everything that's been going on, he probably just thinks we need some time together."

"Okay."

"You get rested?"

"I did. I'm sorry I crashed like that."

"Nah, we're a team. Besides, I needed some Finny time."

"Bite." Finley holds up a chicken nugget that she bit into.

"How are you going to grow big and strong if I eat your chicken nuggets?"

"I eat," she says, taking a big bite.

"Good girl. You have to eat it all if you want ice cream."

She nods, swallows, and takes another bite. "I do," she says with her mouth full of chicken. I know I should correct her, but I let it go.

"You should try to eat something." Seth hands me a small package that I know contains my favorite chicken sandwich before taking one for himself.

Finley chatters as she eats, filling the silence between us. Seth watches her intently like she's the most precious gift in his life. Soon, there will be another baby for us to love. My heart squeezes painfully in my chest. I can't believe my best friend is dying of cancer, and she's pregnant with my boyfriend's baby. Talk about a cruel twist of fate. But that's life. It's unexpected and unpredictable. You have to learn to roll with the punches and take it one day at a time.

"I done," Finley says, the same time there's a knock at the door.

"I think that might be Mamaw and Papaw. Think we should let them in?" Seth asks Finley.

"Yay!" She scrambles to her feet and races for the door.

"Hold up, Finny. Don't open that door until I get there!" Seth yells, climbing to his feet and following her. "Hey, come on in." He greets his parents.

Slowly, I stand, and I know there is no use fretting over how I look. It's been a long, emotionally exhausting day. So instead, I meet them in the foyer and paste on my best smile, which isn't hard when Finley's sitting on Steve's hip talking his ear off about ice cream.

"Hi." I wave, and Seth immediately comes to me and slides his arm around my waist.

"It's nice to see you, dear." Shannon greets me with a smile that could warm the darkest of souls.

Finley and I are so lucky to have them in our lives. We have Amelia to thank for that. I swallow hard, fighting back the emotions that threaten to break free. "You too. Thank you for taking her." I manage to speak past the tears that are threatening to fall.

"We enjoy our time with her. We'll be back in a little while." Shannon steps in and wraps her arms around me. "We're here for you," she whispers.

"Thank you." I give her a sad smile. She thinks I'm upset about Amelia, and I am. I'm also sad for her. I'm not mad about the baby. How could I be? It was before Seth and I were more than just two people who met one time and shared a few messages. Okay, more than a few, but I was there, he was here, and neither one of us ever expressed that we were interested in taking things further than just friendly conversation. Now, here we are and although I'm glad that it's me, because I know I will never let a day go by that this baby doesn't know how amazing his or her mother is, my heart is breaking that my best friend won't get to see her baby grow up. She'll miss all the firsts. I'm having a hard time dealing with that.

"Mara." Seth bends his knees to look me in the eyes. "You okay?"

I blink hard and realize it's now just the two of us standing by the front door. "Yeah, sorry, I just kind of spaced out."

"It's fine. I know this is a lot to ask of you." He runs his fingers through his locks. "Fuck, I hate that this is happening, that we're in this situation, but what she said makes sense. Right? I mean, I've been thinking about it, and a baby is a miracle no matter what, and as unconventional as this might be, this gives her something to live for."

"No, I agree. As soon as the doctor told her, it was like she changed. She was defeated and lost in her grief. I can't explain it, but this is something she never thought she would have, and you gave her that."

"I can't help but think that she's right. Everything happens for a reason. She invited you here, you took the interview. We got to know each other slowly, as friends, then that one night," he says quickly. "Now her cancer, and her refusing treatment and then the baby. You being the love of my life, her best friend, but I can't help but agree with her. Everything happens for a reason."

Before I can reply, there's a knock at the door. "I'm going to go clean up dinner." I slide from his embrace and shuffle to the living room to clean up our wrappers and napkins. I take my time to throw away the trash, not wanting to face this. Taking a deep breath, I make my way back to the living room, following the voices of Seth's friends... no, his family. They're in for the surprise of their lives.

"Hey," Amelia says as soon as I walk into the room. She steps toward me and wraps me in a hug. "I love you, Mara. Please tell me that you're okay with all of this, that you and Seth are working things out?"

"We're good," I assure her. She pulls back and wipes the corner of her eye. "Good, because there is no one else in this world I want to be the mother of my baby." Her voice cracks as her hand covers her belly.

"What are you two gossiping about over there?" Kent calls out.

Amelia gives me a watery smile as we turn to face the crowd. "Oh, hush," she says, looping her arms through mine and leading us to the couch. Seth is sitting on the left side, I take a seat next to him, and Amelia next to me. My eyes scan the room and I see worried faces. They all know Amelia had an appointment today, and the guys, and I'm sure the wives, know by now as well that Seth left work because I needed him. They're in for a shock.

Amelia moves to where she's sitting on the edge of the couch. "Thanks for coming. Before I tell you about today's appointment, I want you to know what all of you mean to me. Most people are lucky to have one or two close friends, but I have all of you. Every one of you means the world to me, and I can't thank you enough. To know that you're here supporting me and my choices, even though you don't agree with them, well, I don't really have the words to tell you what it does to my heart."

"We love you," Kendall speaks up. "It's not our choice, it's yours. As your family, it's our job to love you through this."

"That's what we're going to do," Tyler speaks up.

"You tell us what you need," Mark adds.

"You were there for me," Dawn tells her. "I'll never forget that."

"I hate this so much," Reagan says, fighting back her tears.

Amelia gives her a forced smile. "Me too, but everything happens for a reason." Amelia looks over at me and then at Seth. I hold my hand out for her, and she takes it, her grip firm. She moves her gaze to Seth, and he must give her what she's looking for. Taking a deep breath, she faces everyone and lets the two words that none of us ever expected to hear settle in the room around us. "I'm pregnant."

Silence.

"From the very beginning, something has told me deep in my gut to not take treatments. This is why. My baby."

More silence.

"The father?" Ridge finally speaks up. His voice is heavy with emotion, and I'm sure this is bringing back some painful thoughts for him. I don't know all the details, but I know Knox's mom died soon after giving birth.

Amelia turns to look at Seth.

"No," Kent says in shock.

"I'm the father," Seth says, his voice barely audible, but in the silence of the room, it sounds like he's screaming.

"What?" Tyler asks.

"When?" Mark asks.

"How?" Kent adds.

"Come on, Kenton. You really need me to explain it to you?" Amelia teases, just as she did with Seth.

"New Year's Eve," Seth speaks up. "We were both beyond wasted and woke up the next day, and yeah." He stumbles over his explanation while running his hands through his hair.

"Wow," Reagan breathes.

"We agreed to keep it between us because it was a night that neither one of us really even remember, but the evidence was there. We're friends. Neither of us have those," Amelia wrinkles her nose, "kind of feelings for each other."

"Mara?" Dawn's attention is focused on me.

"Mara and I have been through a lot together. She's my best friend, outside of all of you. There is no one else in this world I'd rather have helping Seth raise our baby."

I try to hold it in, but I can't. A sob rips from my chest as tears begin to fall. Seth wraps his arm around me and pulls me closer, but it does nothing to keep the pain away. The pain of losing my best friend. She has had everyone in this room her entire life, as well as her parents. She's been my only true family and I'm losing her. The pain, I can't describe it, this heavy crushing feeling to my chest. Amelia reaches over and takes my hand in hers, giving it a squeeze. Her silent way of telling me she's right here.

"I don't expect any of you to understand it, or even agree with it, but I'm going to be a mom." Amelia's voice is wistful. "I'm going to leave a piece of me behind in this world, and that makes it okay. I just——" For the first time tonight, her voice wobbles, and she has to stop to compose herself. "I just hope that all of you will be there, you know? For the baby? I want my child to grow up with this... this love and support that you all have given me, and I know it's asking a lot, but I need you to promise me that you can make that happen." I hand her the box of tissues that Seth grabbed for me. "Seth and Mara, they're going to need your help."

"Of course," Ridge says, the others murmuring their agreement.

"I love you. All of you. It makes my heart happy to know that not only will my baby have an amazing dad, but a mom who will love him or her unconditionally." She turns to face me. "Mara, I've seen you with Finley. I was there the day you found out. I was there with you when she was born." She takes a minute to wipe her eyes. "I'm glad it's you. You're an incredible mother, and I couldn't ask for more."

Beside me, Seth shudders, and I know he's lost the control on his emotions as well. "Amelia," he whispers. "Are you sure this is what you want? This is an impossible situation to be in, and I hate——" He stops, unable to go on.

"There is no choice for me, Seth. I knew from the very beginning I didn't want the poison pumped into my body for what? Maybe a few extra months? There is no cure for the type of cancer I have. I'm going to die. There is nothing that any of you or any of the doctors can do to change that. It's the hand I've been dealt, but someone up there"—she points toward the ceiling—"they've been watching over me. This baby is a gift. A chance to leave a piece of me behind with you." She looks around the room. "With all of you."

Kendall stands and walks toward us. She stops in front of Amelia and gives her a hug. Pulling away, she does the same to me, then to Seth before taking her seat next to Ridge. "Okay," she says. "What now?"

"This." I pull the piece of paper from my pocket that we made at the diner earlier today. It seems like a lifetime ago. "I had Amelia make a list, things she wants to do, things she wants to see."

Ridge reaches out and takes the list, his eyes skimming over it before passing it on. Each one of them takes their time reading over it.

Dawn stands. "What are you doing tomorrow?" she asks Amelia.

"Uh, nothing. I'm waiting to hear when my OB appointment is going to be."

"Good, you and I are taking a road trip."

"A road trip?" Amelia asks, confused.

"Yep, we're going to drive to the state line. There's an overlook, and we're going to stop, take in the sights. Then you're going to straddle that line, one foot in Tennessee, one foot in Kentucky."

Amelia grins. "Why have I never thought of that?"

"I don't know, but that's what you're doing tomorrow. Be ready around ten, and I'll stop by and pick you up."

"Wait, don't you have to work?"

"It's my day off."

"Daisy."

"Will be with her grandma," Mark chimes in. "You ladies go and have a good time."

Amelia hesitates then nods. "Okay. Thank you. I'm excited. I can't believe I've never thought of that before."

"As for the rest of this," Ridge says, handing the paper back to Seth after taking a picture of it with his phone. "We can make it all happen, but two. Those are all up to you," he tells Amelia.

"There is only one," she tells him. "I've already fallen in love." She glances down where her hands cover her still flat belly. "This baby…" She rubs her hand over her belly. "This little miracle is more than I could ever ask for. In fact, we should forget the silly list. As far as marriage, sure it would have been nice, but I skipped that step and I get to be a mom. For how long, I don't know, but I get to experience life growing inside me. There is nothing more that I want than that."

"Nope," Ridge says as he stands. "We're going to get out of your hair, but if you need us, you call. Any of you." He looks at the three of us sitting on the couch.

After a round of hugs and a tearful goodbye, it's just the three of us. "You want me to stay while you tell your parents?" Amelia asks.

"Nah, I got it. What about you? You want me there?"

"I told them earlier. They're sad, but they understood. I'm going to head home to them now."

"Be safe," I tell her, wrapping her in a hug.

"Always." With a wave, she's out the door.

"How are you?" I ask Seth.

"I'm okay. Still in shock, I guess. Processing that she's dying and now having… my baby." He swallows hard. His arms pull me in close, offering comfort in his embrace.

"It's a lot to take on."

"Hey," Kent says, breaking up our hug when he returns from starting Amelia's car. "Your parents just pulled in."

"Thank you for staying."

"Anytime. Finley needs to see how much cooler I am than you." He tries to lighten the situation.

"Twenty bucks says she has you joining a tea party or wearing makeup before the night is over."

Kent shrugs. "That makes me the cool uncle."

"Mommy, I's got ice cweam." Finley runs into the house like the tiny tornado that she is.

I can't help but laugh at her. "I can see that. Hey, you remember Kent, right?" She nods. "He's Seth's friend. Well, he wants to read you a couple of stories."

"Weally? I wuv stowies. Wet's go." She grabs his hand and pulls him off to her room.

"Sorry about that," I tell Steve and Shannon. "Thank you for taking her. I normally would make her thank you as well, but…." My voice trails off.

"Oh." Shannon waves me off. "She's the sweetest little thing. She thanked us already. She's such a joy."

"Mom, Dad, we need to talk." Seth goes right for it. He waits until his parents are sitting to start telling them about Amelia and the baby. His mom cries and his dad looks as though he could. They listen as he tells them what's been going on.

"Wow," Shannon says. I think she's going to be upset, but a slow smile spreads across her face. "Another grandbaby to love." She beams.

I want to hug the hell out of her for claiming my daughter as her own. They've welcomed us both with open arms, given us love and family that we've never had before. I will forever be grateful. Then again, I guess I have Seth to thank for that. He made me fall in love with him. By extension, we get his large family. His support system. We need them now more than ever.

"What do you need?" his dad asks.

"I don't know." He runs his fingers through his hair. "This is a crazy situation, but in a few short months, I'm going to have a son or daughter." He swallows hard. "I'm going to need you."

"Anything," Shannon says. "Mara, honey, what about you? What do you need?"

"Me?"

"Yes, you," she says with conviction. "She's your best friend, and you're going to be helping my son raise this baby. You are as much a part of this as Seth and Amelia."

"I—Nothing that I can think of."

"Well, when you do, you know how to get ahold of us. We love you." She stands, as do Steve and Seth, and they all hug. I remain sitting until I see her hand held out for me. I take it, standing as well, and she hugs me tight. "I'm so happy he has you," she whispers. "You call me if you need anything at all." Pulling away, she moves, and Steve steps in her place and hugs me as well.

"We're going to get out of your hair," he tells us, stepping back. "You need us, you call." His dad gives us both a pointed look that has us nodding our agreement.

"Give Finley a kiss for us," Shannon says as she waves over her shoulder. A moment later, they are out the front door.

"That went well," I say. It's lame, but what else is there to say in this situation?

"Yeah." Seth pulls me into his arms and rests his chin on top of my head. "This is all kinds of crazy, Mara. I don't know how to act or how to feel." He whispers his confession.

"Sef!" Finley comes racing into the foyer. She grabs onto Seth's hand and pulls him down the hall. I trail along behind them, anxious to see what the fuss is all about. "Wook," Finley points from the doorway of her bedroom inside with a giggle.

Sneaking my head under Seth's arm, I peek in and see Kent sitting in the middle of her bedroom floor. He has a pink ribbon in his spiky dark hair and bright purple eyeshadow on his eyes. I love Seth, and all these guys, and admittedly, they're hot, Kent included. I can't stop the laugh that escapes me, not only at my daughter's delight but at this man, beautifully ripped and covered in ink, wearing ribbons and eye shadow.

"Unca Kent is pwetty." Finley giggles.

"Come here, you little bugger." Kent crawls to his feet and scoops her up in his arms. He tickles her side until she's gasping for air through her laughter.

I feel her joy in my soul. Seth wraps his arms around me, pulling me back to his chest, and I know he's thinking the same thing. Amelia is going to miss this. All of it. My heart breaks for my best friend, for my boyfriend, and for their baby. I vow here and now to always be here for him or her. No matter what happens between Seth and me. I will always be here.

Chapter 17

SETH

This last week has been a blur. I'm still struggling to wrap my head around the fact that I got one of my best friends pregnant, and she's dying. What kind of messed-up shit is that? Is this the universe trying to punish me for something? No, it can't be. Being a father, this baby is a blessing, not a punishment, but Amelia and her cancer, that feels like a whole lot of fucking punishment.

Our family has proven yet again that we take on life's obstacles together. Together we rally, and that's exactly what we're doing this weekend. The women in our group have taken it upon themselves to mark off every item on Amelia's bucket list. Specifically spending time with those Amelia loves and taking lots of pictures. That brings us to today.

It's Saturday night, and we're all at Mark and Dawn's for dinner. All five of the ladies have cameras and have been snapping pictures all night. I know Mara has also informed Amelia that she's taking a picture of her weekly, front, back and side angle to show the baby when he or she gets older.

That shit rips my gut into shreds when I think about it. My child will never know his momma, and I fucking hate it. I'm smiling and laughing because that's what Amelia needs from me, but on the inside, I'm a fucking hurricane of emotions. It's not fair; she deserves to be here to see our child grow up.

"So, I've been thinking," Reagan says. "About this tattoo."

"What about it?" Kendall asks her.

"Wait," Amelia speaks up. "We have to take that one off the list." She glances down to where her hand rests over the baby. "Precious cargo and all that."

"Oh, I know. I'm just planning ahead. We can get these after you deliver the baby."

"I-I don't know how I'll be," Amelia confesses.

"We'll cross that bridge when we come to it. Anyway, I thought we could all get matching tattoos," Reagan says. "I think we should all look for a design and then choose from there. We can get them in the same spot, or anywhere really."

"I'm in," Kendall says.

"Me too," Dawn tells her.

"Me three," Mara agrees.

Tipping back my bottle, I drain my beer and head to the small kitchen in the basement for another. I pass the door to the small bedroom, and that morning comes rushing back to me. It was a mistake. I was so drunk, and I seriously still don't remember that night. I remember being torn up about liking Mara and the fact she lived so far away. I remember thinking if things were different I would make her mine. That led to drinking. I remember pounding back beer after beer, chased with shot after shot. That next morning, we were both mortified at what we'd done, and now here we are, a few months later, and that night resulted in a baby. My unborn son or daughter.

"Hey." Ridge's hand lands on my shoulder. "You good?"

I nod. I want to scream and yell and tell him no, I'm not good. How could I possibly be good? But I hold it in. Ridge has been through his own hell and was able to make it to the other side. I can do this. I can be strong for both of them. All of them.

"You want to answer that question again?"

"Not tonight." My voice heeds a warning that my friend takes.

"It's been a while since I've seen her smile like this," he comments, pointing to where the women in our lives are gathered on the section couch with their phones looking for tattoos.

"Yeah," I agree. He's right. Amelia has been carrying her illness with her, not letting us in, and even after she told us, she was tight-lipped, but the minute she told me she was pregnant, there was a change in her. As if she has something to live for. To fight for.

"This isn't going to turn out all sunshine and roses," I tell him, taking a swig of my beer.

"No," he agrees.

"I don't know how to do this," I say quietly.

"One day at a time, brother." Ridge rests his hand on my shoulder, giving it a tight squeeze.

I swallow back the lump of emotion forming in my throat. I know I have to be strong for Amelia, for Mara, hell, for all of them, but fuck this is hard. I want my baby, but what kind of bastard does that make me? For her to give up her life for our child's. I'm struggling with that. I know that's not really what's happening. I know there is no cure for her cancer, I know that she's not choosing the baby's life over her own, but it feels that way. I can't seem to make my brain understand that she's dying.

"This a private meeting?" Tyler asks, joining us. Mark and Kent follow along behind him.

"Nope, just taking it all in," Ridge says, saving me from my pity party for one.

"They're excited." Mark looks at his wife and smiles.

"About what?" I manage to ask, fighting back the anger and sadness.

"They're planning a trip, a long weekend to Niagara Falls. Marking another item off the list," Kent tells us.

"Should she be traveling?" I ask.

"Her OB said it was safe," Tyler explains. I turn to look at him, eyebrows raised, and he laughs. "Hey, I listen to my wife." He chuckles.

"Sounds like my little sister has you trained," Ridge jokes.

Tyler shrugs. "My wife talks, I listen. Simple as that."

"What about you? How are things with Mara?" Mark asks.

"Great. She's incredible, and Finley, that little girl." I can't hide the smile that pulls at my lips when I think about her. "I just wish... fuck, I don't know what I wish."

"Whatever you need," Tyler announces.

What I need is for this to be a bad dream. Not the baby. I'm okay with the baby. Sure, it's complicated with Mara, Amelia, and me, but it's a baby. What I'm not okay with is the cancer. The fact that it's silently eating away at her, and she's letting it. I want her here on this earth for as long as possible, but I want my baby. This situation is fucked and my head is fucked because of it.

"Do you think Sonia and your mom would mind helping out with Finley for a few days?" Mara asks.

We've just gotten home from Mark's and are lying in bed. The room is dark, all except for the moonlight. Her back is to my chest, and my arms are locked around her. Having her close. Moments like this, holding her while there is a storm raging inside me, almost seems as if it's under control.

Almost.

"What do you mean?"

"The Niagara trip."

"Is there a reason I need help?"

She turns to look at me over her shoulder even though the room is dark. "You want to keep her?" There's surprise in her voice.

"Why wouldn't I? She's our daughter." I can't see her, but I can sense her surprise from her body language and her tone of voice.

"Seth," she whispers. She rolls over, and her hand lands on my cheek.

I pull her close and just breathe her in. I'm trying really hard not to get pissed off that she wouldn't think that I would watch her. I know it's my anger at life in general, not Mara. "What do you think we're doing here, Mara? When I asked you to move in, I meant to share your life with me, and that includes Finley. I know she had a dad, but he's not here, but I am, and damn it, I want to be that person for her. For both of you. Why can't you see that?" Pissed that I'm getting frustrated, I release my hold on her and slide out of bed. Feeling my way through the dark, I exit the bedroom and make my way to the kitchen. Reaching into the fridge, I grab a bottle of water and down it. Once finished, I toss the empty bottle in the trash, then brace my hands on the counter, and slowly count backward from ten. When that doesn't work, I start at a hundred. I focus on deep, even breaths. I have to get my shit in order. I can't go snapping at her. Finley is her daughter, not mine. I have no claim to her whatsoever. No matter how badly I wish that were not the case.

"Seth." Her soft hand lands on my bare back. "I'm sorry."

Standing, I pull her into my arms and bury my face in her neck. I love this woman. I'm being a dick, and she's still here. Still standing beside me. "No, I'm sorry. It's all just… getting to me I guess."

"We've never really talked about Finley. I know you love her."

"I do. You two are my entire world. It's as if my heart has two strings, one for each of you, and the two of you are tugging on them, pulling me closer."

"We love you too." She rests her head against my chest as we stand in the darkness of our kitchen holding on to one another. "You want to be her dad?" she finally asks.

"More than anything."

"Okay."

My heart stills in my chest, and I have to suck in a deep breath to remind myself to keep breathing. "Yeah?"

"She's a lucky little girl."

"I'm the lucky one."

"We'll tell her tomorrow when we pick her up from your parents' place."

"I want you both to have my last name."

"Okay."

"Just like that?"

"Life's too short. I know she loves you, you're the only father she's ever known. I know that I love you, and that's not going to change. With everything with Amelia, it makes you look at life differently. At least it does me. I know in my heart you're the best thing that's ever happened to us."

I swallow hard, trying like hell to hold in my emotions that are threatening to take over. "I—" I cough to clear my throat yet again. "I love you both. So much."

"We love you too."

I hold her tight, letting our conversation sink in. My life is in pieces, my happiness with Mara and Finley. Not only am I gaining a daughter in Finley, but gaining mine and Amelia's baby too. Then there's Amelia. I feel bittersweet joy at the prospect of what my future holds when hers has a time limit. None of us know when that might be, but we know it will be sooner rather than later. I have so many things to be thankful for. Then there's the sadness, the anger, and the pain for Amelia.

Mara's words play on repeat in my mind. *"Life's too short."* No truer words have ever been spoken. One breath, one second, one minute, one hour, hell, I'm not sure how much time passes as we stand in the middle of our kitchen, bathed in darkness holding onto one another as if the other might disappear. What I do know is that even through the sadness that threatens to choke me, I have to keep moving toward the light.

My light is Mara.

Finley.

My unborn child.

Suddenly everything is clear. Mara, Finley, Amelia, our baby... they're all counting on me, and I'm not going to let them down. I have to pull myself out of this pity party and chase the light. Starting now.

Dropping to one knee, I capture her hands with mine. "I can't do this. Life... I can't do it without you. I don't want to. I know I come with some baggage, and our situation is fucked up, but, Mara, I love you. I love Finley, and I want you to be my family. You said okay when I told you I wanted you both to have my last name. So here I am on one knee, pledging to love you both until I take my last breath. I promise to be the man she can look up to, to guide her through life. I promise to love and cherish you both. Mara Reyes, will you do me the incredible honor of becoming my wife? Will you marry me?"

I can't see her, and I'm kicking myself in the ass for doing this in the middle of the night in the dark in our kitchen, but fuck, the moment felt right to me. Standing, I reach out and flip the light over the sink. We both squint with the new light in the room. When my eyes finally focus, they're on her tears. The ones that are rolling silently over her cheeks. I begin to panic, worrying this isn't what she wants after all… until I see her smile. She's smiling through her tears, and it lights up her face.

I drop back to my knees. I need to do this where she can see me. "Mara, will you marry me?"

She begins to nod, and I'm on my feet. Lifting her in my arms, I twirl us around in the kitchen. Her laughter rings out and it soothes my soul. Stopping us, I set her on the counter and settle between her legs. My hands cradle each side of her face. "I can't believe you're mine, Mrs. Jennings," I say before pressing my lips to hers. I keep it slow as my tongue traces her bottom lip. I have a lifetime of kisses. Right now, I need to show her what she means to me.

She's the first to pull back, and this time, it's her turn to cradle my face in the palms of her tiny hands. "You've changed my life. You've changed Finley's life. We're so lucky to have you. "

"We need a ring."

Her smile is blinding. "I don't need a ring. I have your heart, Seth. That's more than enough."

"Nope. We're getting you a ring. In fact, we're going to go shopping in the morning. We can pick it out together before we go pick Finny up from my parents."

"Seth." She tries to argue.

"You're getting a ring, baby." Turning, I give her my back. "Hop on." She chuckles and wraps her arms and legs around me. "Hit the light." I lean in close so she can reach the switch and slowly make my way back to our room. When I place my back to the bed, she releases her hold and falls back, laughing. Grabbing my phone from the nightstand, I pull up the website of the jeweler I know the guys have used for their wives' rings. "Let's take a look. See what you like."

"Seth, this isn't necessary."

"Fine, I'll just pick it out on my own. I'm thinking what, like five or six carats?" I ask.

"No." She takes my phone from me and begins scrolling. "That's too much. I'd be afraid to lose it."

I smile. I know she's not flashy, but I also know that would get her to tell me what she really wanted. We'll see how big a stone she chooses. I might still insist on an upgrade. Nothing but the best for my future wife.

Chapter 18

Mara

Girls' trip weekend. I'm excited and nervous all at the same time. I waved goodbye to Seth and Finley this morning, and my daughter didn't have a care in the world as she waved from her daddy's arms. Daddy. She doesn't call him that all the time. I don't think she really understands at her age, but when she does, I swear I see him light up. One day when she's old enough, I'll sit her down and tell her how we both fell in love with her father.

"How do you think the guys are going to do with the kids?" Dawn asks.

"I'm not worried," Kendall replies.

"I'm a little worried." Reagan laughs. "The boys are a lot to handle sometimes."

"Yeah, but they're older. It's not like they're both taking bottles. Tyler has it under control," Dawn comments.

"What about Mark?" Kendall asks.

"Pft, I doubt they even miss me. Daisy and Mark are like two peas in a pod. They've had this special bond since the day she was born."

"They'll miss you," I tell her.

"What about you?" Amelia speaks up. "You think Seth is going to be calling his parents begging for help?" she says with a laugh.

"Honestly, I doubt it. He's great with her."

"Ladies, we're lucky," Reagan says. "Our men, our babies, each other." She reaches over and rests her hand over Amelia's.

"That we are," Kendall agrees.

"So…" I speak up from the seat in the back of the minivan that we rented. "I think this trip is going to mark two items off the list."

"How so?" Kendall asks, glancing at me in the rearview mirror. She's taking the first leg of driving.

"Well, I booked a suite in the hotel. It has three bedrooms, two with double beds and one king. It looks out over the falls. It has a balcony that shows us both the east and west. That means we can watch the sunrise and the sunset in the same day, over the falls."

"And of course we're taking a ton of pictures," Dawn says.

"We're making memories," Reagan agrees.

"Right, so we're ticking these items off. What's left?" Kendall asks, this time keeping her eyes on the road.

"Get a tattoo, which we're waiting for. Fly in a plane, swim in the ocean, fall in love, and get married. The others, we either have planned or are in the process of completing. You know, baby needs to cook and all that," I say. I'm trying to keep my voice cheery and void of the heartache I feel.

"I was thinking," Amelia says. "I'd like to make a scrapbook for the baby. Take these pictures, these memories, and put them to good use. I've been researching, and I could journal each moment so he or she knows what I was feeling. What that moment meant to me."

I lose my composure as a sob breaks free from my chest. Surveying the car, everyone is wiping at their eyes. We're all affected by this, by her life, and this battle she's facing. We're affected by the love she has for her baby, and the memories she wants to make and leave behind.

"Let's do it," I say through my tears.

"Count me in," Reagan says.

"Me too," Dawn and Kendall say.

"We can set up at my place, in the basement. I'll have Seth get us some tables and we can leave it all out. Maybe get together as often as we can and do it together?"

Amelia turns to look at me over her shoulder, tears in her eyes. "I love that idea, Mara."

"Good. I'll text Seth now, letting him know our plan." I don't need to tell him now, but it's a good excuse to check in and remove myself from the sadness that's causing my chest to feel as though it's cracking open.

> **Me:** *Hey, handsome. Do you mind if the girls and I set up scrapbook central in the basement?*
>
> **Seth:** *Hello, future wife. This is your house too, Mara.*
>
> **Me:** *I love you. How's our girl?*

He replies with a picture of him and Finley sitting on the living room floor coloring.

> **Seth:** *We miss you already so we're drawing you a picture.*
>
> **Me:** *I miss you too.*
>
> **Seth:** *So what's up with scrapbook central?*
>
> **Me:** *Making memories and preserving them.*
>
> **Seth:** *You're an amazing woman, Mara.*
>
> **Me:** *Because I have the love of an amazing man.*

"Mara," Dawn says, and I look up to find them laughing. All eyes, except for a quick glance from Kendall, are on me. "We're not even an hour in and he has you all mushy."

"Hey!" I say, not even a little bit offended. "I was telling him about scrapbook central at our place."

"Let me see that ring again." Reagan turns in her seat, and I waste no time thrusting my arm in the middle of the third-row seat to show her.

"Mara," Amelia says softly. The van is suddenly quiet except for the heavy rhythm of my heart beating in my chest. "I'm glad it's you. I know that when I'm gone, you'll be there for them. All three of them."

"Amelia." I choke out her name.

"It makes this easier, you know? To know that my baby has you." She glances around the van. "All of you. I don't have to worry about a mother being in his or her life. He or she has four amazing women to look up to. I have no regrets."

A sob breaks from my chest and I lose all composure. I try to hold it in, but there's no use. My body shakes with the overwhelming grief of losing my best friend. "I hate this," I say, my voice muffled through my pain. "This isn't fair."

"Life isn't fair, Mara. It's unexpected and it's messy. It's oftentimes unkind, but how you push through… how you hold your head up high and remember those who leave this earth before you, that's what's important. Keeping the memories alive."

"I'd rather have you," I mumble, wiping at my eyes.

"You will have me," Amelia says. She looks down at her belly, her hand resting over her baby. "You will forever have a piece of me with you."

Kendall pulls over to the side of the road and puts the van in Park. Even through my blurred vision from my tears, I see her rest her head against the steering wheel as her shoulders shake. All five of us are lost in our grief.

"I love you guys so much. I can't ever thank you enough for doing this for me. This trip, the list, the baby. I'm not scared." Amelia wipes at her eyes.

Silence surrounds us as we get ourselves together. Without a word, Kendall puts the van in Drive and just like that, we're back on the road. I know moments like this are going to be plentiful in the coming months. I just hope that I can survive them.

"I look like a drowned rat." Amelia laughs as she flips through someone's camera. I'm not sure who's she has because we all brought them. Kendall, Reagan, and Dawn all have these fancy SLR cameras that take like a billion pictures in a minute. Mine is just a small digital that I bought when I found out I was pregnant. It takes great pictures, but it's nothing fancy. Amelia actually has the same one. We were roommates at the time and got them on sale.

"That was pretty cool to be that close to the falls," Dawn says, looking through what I assume is her camera too.

"The lights at night." Amelia tears her eyes away from the pictures. "It was unlike anything. I've always heard it was beautiful. It's definitely something to see."

"I'm glad we did this. I love my husband and my boys, but it's nice to get girl time," Reagan says, tossing herself back on the bed with a sigh.

"It really has been fun. We should plan our next trip," Dawn says at the same time I get a text.

> **Seth:** *Hey, babe. We just wanted to say hi.*

It's a picture of Seth and Finley sitting out on the back deck. She's wearing sunglasses that I've never seen before and a big pink floppy hat. The smile on her face tells me she's having a blast with Seth. I turn my phone around so the girls can see. "Looks like she's having fun."

"Are you kidding? He's spoiling her rotten." Amelia laughs.

"I have no doubt."

> **Me:** *Looks like you two are having a good time.*

> **Seth:** *We are, but we miss Mommy.*

> **Me:** *I'll be home tomorrow afternoon.*

> **Seth:** *We'll be here.*

"What do you say we head down to the hotel restaurant and grab a bite to eat? I'm exhausted," Amelia says.

"Yes." We are all in agreeance. This trip has taken a lot out of her, but she's never stopped smiling. Well, unless you count on the way here in the van, but even through her sadness, you could tell she's at peace with her decision.

"Okay, I'm ready to see my babies. All three of them." Reagan laughs.

We all murmur our agreement. It was nice to get away, but I've missed Seth and Finley something fierce. Speaking of, my phone vibrates with a text message.

Seth: *Are you almost home? Finley and I have a surprise for you.*

Me: *About 30 more minutes.*

Seth: *Have the girls drop you off first.*

Me: *Oookay??*

Seth: *Humor me, future Mrs. Jennings. Have them come inside with you.*

"Well, ladies, I think Seth is up to something. In fact, I know he is. He says that he and Finley have a surprise for me, and to have you drop me off first, but you all have to come inside with me."

"Do you have any idea what it is?" Reagan asks from her place behind the wheel.

I look over at her. "No, I have no idea. I know better than to ask. He's not going to tell me either."

"Sounds like Ridge," Kendall comments from her seat in the third row.

"Y'all are lucky. You have a man in your life who cares enough to surprise you." This from Amelia.

"Shh, don't let them hear you say that." Dawn shushes her. We all laugh, but in the back of our minds, we're all thinking the same thing. Number ten and number eleven on her list will never happen for her. She's never going to fall in love and get married... nor live happily ever after. But she does get to be a mom. Speaking from experience being a mom, that outweighs a fancy wedding, and it's an all-new kind of love. One only a parent knows. I'm happy for my friend that she'll have at least that.

"Thank you for this. Watching the sun rise and set at the Falls was truly magical," Amelia says as we pull into my driveway.

"It really was. I can't wait to print some of these pictures," Reagan says, turning the ignition off in the van. She looks over at me. "Ready for your surprise?"

"Wait? Do you know what it is?" I ask her.

"Nope, but I know these guys and whatever it is, it's going to be sweet. I don't think they have it in them to be anything else."

"You know, when I first met them all, they were rather intimidating with the ink and the bad-boy vibes they have going on," I admit.

"Pft, a bunch of teddy bears." Reagan chuckles.

"Okay, let's go see what the surprise is." One by one, we climb out of the van and make our way to the front door. Before I can turn the knob, the door is pulled open and my heart, both halves, are there smiling at me.

"Mommy!" Finley cheers and rushes toward me. I scoop her up in my arms and hug her tight before kissing her cheek.

"Hey, sweetie. Did you have fun with Seth?" I feel weird calling him dad in front of our friends. It's not something we've done, and for some reason, I haven't told them about that conversation. Well, not all of it. I told them about the proposal and how he wants to adopt her. They didn't ask and I didn't tell.

"Hey, baby." Seth steps forward, slides his arm around my waist, and kisses my lips. "Missed you," he mumbles.

"Daddy, no, my kisses," she says, reaching for him.

"I'm sorry, baby girl. Daddy missed Mommy." He easily takes her from my arms and settles her on his hip.

My heart, it's doubled in size; at least it feels as if it is at their easy banter. "This is new," Amelia leans in and whispers. She doesn't say anything else, but I know I'm in for it later for not telling her.

"So, where's this surprise you're teasing us with? We have some husbands and babies to kiss." Reagan grins at Seth.

"Of course." He smiles. "Right this way, ladies. Finny and I worked on this all weekend. Didn't we, Finny?"

"I's go shopping."

"You were Daddy's big helper," Seth praises, bouncing her in his arms.

We follow him through the house and to the steps for the basement. One by one, we make our way downstairs, and my eyes scan the room.

Nothing looks out of place. "What am I missing?" I ask.

"Nothing yet. But in there." Seth points to one of the doors that leads to an extra room. There are two of them down here, along with a full bathroom, a kitchenette, and a huge entertaining area. There are french doors that walk out to a patio, which is where the hot tub sits. Above the walkout, is a huge deck that leads to the backyard where Seth has informed me will be Finley's new swing set he wants to build her for her birthday.

With each step I take, I can feel the girls behind me. Slowly, I turn the knob and push open the door. Flipping the light switch, my mouth drops open when I take in the room. There are two large white tables with drawer units on each end. There are a couple of bookshelves with what looks like organizing bins. Another table that sits against the wall holds a Cricut box and a printer box.

"You said scrapbook central, right? I didn't know what that meant exactly, but Finny and I went to the local craft store and bought a few things. The lady there suggested IKEA for tables. So after we made our purchase there, we headed to get furniture. I started out just picking up a few supplies to get you started, but then well, it turned into this."

He steps next to me, and with our daughter still in his arms, kisses my temple. "You said a long time ago, when we were just messaging, that one day you'd like to get into scrapbooking with all of Finley's pictures she's drawn and the ones that you've taken. When you said that all of you were going to start making it happen, I wanted to get you started."

"Seth, this is… incredible. How did you manage this with an almost-three-year-old?"

"Finny's my big-girl helper."

"I's am." She nods her little head up and down.

"Seth," Amelia speaks up, but her voice cracks and all she can get out is his name.

Reagan walks up to him and wraps her arms around his waist. "You did good," she whispers, but we all hear her.

"I can't believe you did all of this." I survey the room.

Finley wiggles in his arms, so he lets her down, and she rushes toward Kendall and Dawn to tell them all about how she helped. "This is your home, Mara. This is something you told me that one day you'd love to find the time to do, and when you messaged, I figured I'd help make that happen. We have the space, and now that we're a team, you'll have time to come down here and do your thing. Finny and I can hang out, and who knows, when she gets a little older, she might want to start helping."

"I love you." I stare up at him, my eyes wet with tears, but I don't move to wipe them away. "Thank you, Seth."

He opens his arms, and I don't hesitate to walk into his embrace. Wrapping me in a hug, he buries his face in my neck. "Making memories, baby."

Making memories.

I've been dwelling on the time I'm not going to get with her. The time that Seth and their baby isn't going to get with her. Hating the fact that Finley is losing such an amazing woman in her life, the one who has been there from the start. However, what I need to be worrying about is making the most of what time we do have. I can't change the outcome, but I can make a memory, lots of them. And that's what I plan to do.

Chapter 19

SETH

Sliding my phone in my pocket after checking it for the tenth time in the last five minutes, I try to keep my cool. Amelia and her parents flew to see the Grand Canyon, marking two more items off her bucket list. They're supposed to be coming home tomorrow, but I haven't heard from her since yesterday. Her parents are in their seventies. They tried for years to get pregnant, and then one day, after years of accepting they would never have a baby, her mom found out she was pregnant.

I was uneasy about her visit with them. They're both older, and she's fragile, no matter if she wants to admit it or not. However, in the end, I know they needed this. All three of them needed this time together. I made her promise to check in every day and here it is, almost four in the afternoon, and nothing. I've called her twice, and sent three text messages and still no reply.

"What's with you today?" Tyler asks as I toss the tools into the toolbox.

"Nothing."

"Yeah, right," Mark scoffs. "It's not just nothing. You've been a

183

moody dick all day. What gives?"

"I said nothing," I say through gritted teeth.

"Might as well tell us." Kent keeps the jabs coming.

My anger is building, but not really. I've been a spark, just waiting for the wind to turn me into a blazing inferno for weeks. "Fuck off."

"Oh, I think we hit a nerve," Ridge chants.

"You know what, fuck you. Fuck all of you."

"You're not really my type." Tyler shrugs as if I'm letting him down easy.

"FUCK OFF!" I roar. They don't bother to jump or move or even look pissed off. "She's not answering her phone, and she checks in every day. What if something happened to her or the baby? Huh? What the fuck am I supposed to do for them from here? Even worse, how will I know?" I begin to pace back and forth, running my hands through my hair.

"I'm sure she's fine," Mark says gently.

"Keep going," Kent says.

"What?" I stop pacing and look up at him.

"That all you got?" he taunts.

"Fuck you," I spit. "Until you're in my shoes, fuck you," I say as I begin to pace again. "I mean, this is so messed up. Our best friend is having my baby, and she's dying. *Dying*. How the fuck am I supposed to handle that? What's worse is I'm madly in love with her best friend, and I'm fucking scared as hell I'm going to lose her over this. Sure, she says she's with me, and all is good, but what happens when things get tough? Huh? What happens when the baby gets here, and I'm raising it in the house we share? What happens when..." I swallow hard. "What happens when Amelia dies? What will she do then? Can she raise this baby with me? Will she?" I stop and crouch to my knees, letting them hit the plywood floor we just installed. Hunched over, I can't stop the onslaught of emotions that take over. A sob breaks free from my chest and my shoulders begin to shake. Lifting my hands to cover my face, they're shaking too.

I'm fucking losing it.

My heart can't handle this.

The baby.

Losing Amelia.

Loving Mara.

"I don't know if I can do this," I stutter through my confession.

I feel a strong hand land on my shoulder. "You can and you will," Kent assures me.

"You're right," Ridge adds. "This is fucked up, but our family will rally. That's what we do."

"Let us help you," Tyler says.

"Don't hold that shit in, Seth," Mark scolds.

"The worst part about it all? I'm a selfish bastard. I want Amelia to live for our baby, for all of us, for her. I want the baby, because well, he or she is my blood. I want Mara and Finley to have my last name, and I want to know that it's all going to be okay." Lifting my head, I see my four best friends sitting on the floor gathered around me.

"It's not going to be okay. Not at first. It's going to hurt, and you're going to ask yourself why," Ridge says. "My situation was similar, but I didn't know my time with her was limited. I didn't know that the one and only time she held our son was going to be her last. I didn't get to ask her how she wanted to raise him. If there were any special family moments he should know about. You have the chance for all of that, Seth. It sucks, cancer fucking sucks, but you have some time. Time to take those pictures and make those memories that you will share with your son or daughter for years to come. He or she may never remember their mother, but they will know her through you."

"We're in the same situation with Daisy," Mark adds. "To watch Dawn lose her sister and become a mom to a tiny little girl the same day, a little girl who will never know who her father was? We have no idea. So what happens if she gets sick and needs something that Dawn or I can't give her? Sure, Dawn is her aunt, but we're not her biological parents. What if she needs something and we can't help her? That is a real fear that my wife and I live with every day. However, we don't let that stop us from loving her. She's our daughter in every way that matters."

"Mara, she's one of the good ones, Seth. Can you really see her leaving you because of this baby? Amelia is her best friend. Chances are even if you were not in the picture, Mara would have been Amelia's first choice. We all know her parents are too old to care for the baby," Tyler points out.

"Can nothing we do be easy?" I ask.

They all laugh. "Brother," Tyler says, "if it was easy, would it be worth it? Fight for love, fight for the bond that the three of you have."

"Life has a way of working out. It's not always how we planned, but in the end, things are how they are supposed to be."

"You sound like Amelia with all the 'everything happens for a reason' shit she's been spouting." I've heard her say that more times than I can count.

"She's not wrong," Kent speaks up. "I've watched each of you fall, and although the road has been rocky, I believe that we are all where we are supposed to be."

"Yeah, and what about you?" I ask him.

He shrugs. "I might have missed my shot. Then again, maybe I've yet to meet her, but I do know that seeing the four of you all happy and in love, it makes a man want to reevaluate where his life is going."

"Take it one day at a time, Seth. Learn to deal with this unexpected bond. Embrace it. In the end, that's what's going to get you and Mara through this." Ridge offers his words of wisdom.

I think about what they're saying, and I know it's true. I just needed to have some sense talked into me. "I'm sorry I've been a dick."

"No need to apologize. You've been holding this shit in, and that's not good for you or them," Tyler explains.

I nod. There is no use in denying the fact that I have indeed been holding it all in. Trying to keep myself in check to stay strong for Mara, Amelia, and Finny. That little girl. She transitioned to living at my place as if it was the most natural thing in the world. She definitely has my heart by a string just like her mama.

"You gonna get that?" Kent chuckles.

I break out of my thoughts to hear my phone ringing. Scrambling, I pull it from my pocket and swipe at the screen. "Hello?"

"Hi." Amelia's tired voice is like music to my fucking ears.

"Are you okay? The baby?"

"We're fine. I've been at the hospital all day."

"What?"

"I'm fine, it's my mom. She fell. Luckily it was at the hotel. We had just come home from a day at the canyon."

"Is she okay?"

"Yeah, just sore. They were worried about a broken hip, but luckily she's okay."

"What do you need?" I can feel the guys' eyes on me as I talk to her.

"Nothing. Just checking in. We're still flying home tomorrow."

"Okay, good. What about their place? Anything she needs?"

"No, I don't think so. They already have the wheelchair ramp since neither of them are the best at stairs these days." She's quiet, and I wait for her to keep going. I've known her long enough to know that there is something on her mind. "Seth," she says quietly.

"Yeah?"

"They can't take care of a baby."

"They won't have to." I'm confident in that. This baby is my son or daughter, and I will be raising him or her. This is something we've already discussed, but I guess she feels it's worth repeating.

She releases a heavy breath. "Thank you. I know this is weird, and it puts us in this crazy situation as friends who are going to be parents. I know that after I'm gone, our baby will be loved. Just promise me you will take the baby to see them? I don't know how much time they have left, but... can you promise me that?" Her voice is soft.

"Done."

I hear her sniffle. "You're a good man, Seth Jennings." I let her words wash over me. I want to do right by both Amelia and our baby, and Mara and Finley. I feel like I'm being torn in two worrying about all of them. To hear her say this calms some of my anxiety that I'm not doing enough.

"Safe flight. Call if you need anything." I end the call and take a deep breath—what feels like the first of the day. Quickly I explain what happened to the guys.

"Go home, get some snuggles from your daughter and loving from your fiancée," Ridge tells me.

"Thanks, man." I feel myself getting choked up again. "You don't know what a relief it is to have you all in my corner, even when I'm being a dick."

"Oh, we know," Tyler says. "We've all needed to lean on the others at one point or another. That's what friends and family are for. You call us if you need anything."

Standing, we quickly finish packing up the tools, and I wave and beep as I pull out of the site first.

I need to see my girls.

☀☀☀

As soon as I walk into the house, something that smells amazing greets me. After washing my hands in the utility sink in the laundry room, I make my way toward the kitchen, following the smell.

"Daddy!" Finley cheers. She's sitting at the kitchen island coloring while Mara makes dinner. I will never get tired of her calling me that. The love that shines through her eyes, it's for me, and I'm honored to be able to fill this spot in her life. Biologically she's not mine, but she's the first of my kids to make me a daddy, and it's the best damn feeling.

"Hey, Finny." Stopping next to her, I bend to kiss the top of her head. "Were you a good girl for Sonia today?" I ask her.

"My was."

"I was," I correct her with a smile. I make my way to the stove and wrap my arms around Mara and kiss her neck. "Hey, beautiful. That smells amazing."

"Better than you," she teases. "You've got about ten minutes to shower before dinner." She turns to face me and places a kiss on my lips. "Welcome home."

Home.

"How was your day?" I ask.

"Uneventful, now go." She shoves at me and I laugh. Leaning in, I kiss her one more time before jogging down the hall to shower.

Five minutes later, I'm in a pair of sweatpants and a T-shirt. "Just in time," Mara says as she makes Finley a plate.

"What is this?" The smell is making my mouth water.

"Nothing special. Just homemade beef barbecue and french fries."

"French fries." Finley claps, making us both laugh.

"You have to eat your sandwich too, and your applesauce," I remind her.

"I do's, Daddy," she sasses. It's too damn cute to correct her.

"I will," Mara does it for me.

All through dinner, Finley keeps us entertained. She chatters about Sonia and coloring, I think. She'll be three in about six weeks, and she talks well, but when she gets to talking fast, it's hard to keep up with everything she's telling us.

"Okay, kiddo, time for a bath." Mara stands to clear the table.

"Bath or dishes?" I ask her.

"I get a choice?"

"You can sit on the couch and I can do both, but that cuts into our family cuddle time, so…." I shrug.

"Bath." She scoops Finley up in her arms and their laughter follows them down the hall.

Twenty minutes later, the three of us are snuggled on the couch watching the Disney channel. Finley is sitting still, which means we're close to losing her to sleep. Her head is on my chest, my arm around her, while Mara's head is leaning on the opposite shoulder. I don't even remember what life was like without them.

"So I've been thinking. There are only two items left on Amelia's list that we can make happen."

"Okay."

"Finny turns three soon. What if we took a short vacation to the beach? It's about a seven-hour drive to Pensacola. I was thinking break it up in two days driving, giving Amelia breaks. Unless she's doing well, then we can drive straight through?"

"Finley would love that," Mara agrees.

"I think so too. What if we get married while we're there?" I toss it out there. It's something I've been thinking about a lot lately. I need her to know she's the love of my life. That I want the future we're building together to be everlasting.

"What?" This time she sits up and looks at me. Her eyes dart to Finley, and they soften, telling me she's fallen asleep in my arms.

Keeping one arm around our daughter, the other reaches up and cradles her cheek in my palm. "I love you, Mara. I love Finley, and I want this to be permanent. Nights like tonight. Marry me on the beach in Florida."

Her eyes well with tears, and I start to worry that I'm pushing this too fast when a slow smile graces her lips. "You really want to do this?"

"Yes." Simple answer, no hesitation.

She nods. "Okay."

"Yeah?"

Another nod. "Yes."

"Pick a date. You tell me when and I'll take care of everything."

"Are the others going to join us?"

"They're family so they're invited. I don't know if they'll be able to make it work with jobs and kids, but I'll try like hell to get them all there. My parents too."

She glances down at Finley. "I want you both to have my last name, Mara."

"I love you, Seth Jennings."

"Oh, baby." Sliding my hand behind her neck, I bring her closer. "You have no idea how much I love you."

"I think you should show me."

"I'm going to put our daughter to bed, and come find you." The words are barely out of my mouth before she scrambles from the couch and races down the hall. Carefully, trying not to wake her, I lift Finley into my arms and carry her to her room. Once I have her in her bed, I cover her with her princess blanket and turn on her stars nightlight before closing the door. I leave it cracked so we can hear her. Just in case.

Across the hall, I push open our bedroom door, closing it and turning the lock. It's time to show Mara with my body what my mind sometimes can't find the words to say. I'm going to cherish her, love her with all that I am.

Chapter 20

Mara

I left the small bedside lamp on because I want to see him. Seth's eyes are so expressive. He can tell me everything he's feeling with just one look. And tonight, I don't want to miss it. These past few months have taken us by storm, but we're fighting our way through it.

When the bedroom door opens, then closes, and I hear the tick of the lock, I know he's taking his job of "showing" me seriously.

"Fuck," he murmurs when he sees me lying naked on our bed. Lifting his arms, he reaches behind his head, grabbing the neck of his T-shirt, pulling it off before dropping it on the floor.

He's standing before me in low-hung gray sweatpants. They hang at the V of his hips, exposing the intricate work of his dragon tattoo. It starts at his hip and ends on his thigh. It's sexy, and I'm ready for him to drop his pants and show me the goods.

"Mara." My name is a growl from deep in his throat.

My eyes snap up to his. "Keep going," I encourage.

"You keep looking at me like that, it's going to be over before it starts."

"Like what?"

"Like you want to trace every inch of my skin with your tongue."

"Mmm," I agree. "That tattoo, and well…" I drop my eyes to his hard length, lick my lips, and then give him my full attention once again. "Among other things."

"Your eyes look like emeralds." On either side of his hips, he slides an index finger under the waistband of his sweats and tugs. I watch as he pulls the elastic out and around his dick. He's hard and ready, and if I had known he wasn't wearing underwear… well, it would have been torture.

Beautiful torture.

I watch him as he steps out of his sweatpants that are pooled at his ankles. I'm riveted on the show before me as he fists his dick and begins to stroke. "Seth," I choke out. I want to be the one touching him.

"I can't right now, baby." He makes his way to the side of the bed and reaches for a strip of condoms, only to find an empty box. "Fuck," he says under his breath.

"Seth," I moan, my eyes are back on his fist and each gentle glide from root to tip. I can't take it, watching him has me more turned on than I've ever been in my entire life. Cupping my left breast and tweaking my nipple, my right hand travels over my navel, and I don't stop until I reach my clit. Two fingers repeating a circular pattern has me arching off the bed.

"Mara, baby, you can't do that. I—Fuck." He drops his hand and marches to the bathroom. I hear drawers being opened and doors being slammed on the vanity. His grumbling comes next, but I can't make out what he's saying. My mind is clogged with the pleasure I'm giving myself. "Fuck me." His deep rasp has me turning to look at him.

He's standing in the doorway of the attached bathroom, his hands above his head gripping the doorframe. His dick is hard and ready, and his eyes looked pained. "No condoms," he rasps.

"Come here." My voice is not my own. It's deep and husky. Sexy. His eyes flash to mine, then to where my hand is taking control of my pending orgasm. Slowly, he sits beside me on the bed, and his hand lands over mine, mimicking my movements.

"Let me," he croons.

Reluctantly, I pull my hand away and let him have control. His thumb takes over as he slides two long digits inside me. I squeeze my legs together on instinct. "That won't do," he says, standing from the bed. His hand is suddenly gone, and so is he, but not for long. His calloused hands clamp around my ankles and pulls me to the edge of the bed. Before my brain can catch up to what's happening, he drops to his knees, throws my legs over his shoulders, and his mouth is attached to my clit.

"Seth." I cry out his name because his tongue... it's worlds apart from his hands or mine. Burying my hands in his hair, all I can do is hang on for the ride as he devours me, his fingers working in tandem with his tongue as he wrings every ounce of pleasure from my body.

Slowly, I feel it. The fire that builds. The hot liquid desire coursing through my veins. My legs clamp around his head, my back arches off the bed, and I pull him closer with my hands gripping his hair. My body is stiff as I feel it racing faster and faster and faster. The fire flames until complete euphoria crashes into me. I cry out as my body convulses underneath him.

When I finally fall back to the mattress, my grip on his hair long forgotten, and my legs limp over his shoulders, he kisses my inner thigh and works his way from under my legs and stands. With extreme effort, I force myself to open my eyes, and I will be forever grateful that I did. Standing at the end of the bed is Seth standing, feet apart, eyes closed, head tilted back as he strokes his cock. Not the slow languid strokes from earlier. No, these are hard and fast and the absolute sexiest thing I've ever seen in my life.

His legs begin to quiver as his strokes become faster, harder, and suddenly, I need him. Regardless of the epic orgasm I had just moments ago, I need him. I'm greedy when it comes to Seth.

"Seth," I manage to croak when a low moan from somewhere deep inside him tumbles from his lips. He doesn't stop, chasing that sweet oblivion he just gifted me. "Seth," I say again, louder this time. Slowly, his eyes peel open, and he lifts his head. He doesn't stop stroking. His eyes, dark molten chocolate, lock onto mine, and I can see everything he's feeling.

Lust.

Desire.

Love.

So much love in the depths of his gaze.

"I need you."

"Mara," he chokes.

"We're getting married. You promised to love me forever. We don't need condoms."

Finally, I have his attention and his stroking stops. His eyes are laser-focused on mine as he steps forward. "What are you telling me, Mara?"

"I'm saying I'm on the pill, have been for a while. It regulates my cycle, which I know you don't care about and I can't believe I'm saying this right now." Stopping, I close my eyes and take a deep breath. Slowly, I open them. "I'm saying that I love you, and I trust you. I don't want anything between us."

"Baby." He caresses my cheek, tracing it with his thumb. Bending, he presses his lips to mine and I can taste myself on him. I always thought that would gross me out, but not when it's Seth. I'll take him any way I can have him, and to be honest, it's a turn on. To know he just gave me pleasure, and now I get to taste mine and his.

He pulls back from the kiss and I see the indecision on his face. He's a good man. One who will always put mine and my daughter's needs before his own. I know this, and it's with that knowledge, I voice the one thing that can sway things my way. "Fuck me, Seth. I need to feel you inside me. Nothing but you and me."

He growls, gently pushes me back on the bed, and lifts my legs to rest on his shoulders. Stepping between us, he grips his cock and aligns himself at my entrance. "I'm so close already, and you had to bring out that sexy fucking mouth of yours." He traces my pussy with the head of his cock, coating himself in me. "Say it again." His hand falls away as just the tip is poised.

Ready.

Waiting.

"Fuck me, Seth." The words are barely out of my mouth when he presses forward and gives us what we both want. He places a hand on each of my legs and pushes them back, leaning in close, his lips a breath from mine.

"Hold on." Two words in his low sexy growl are the only warning I get before he's pounding into me. Over and over and over again. Thrust after thrust, he chases his orgasm while my second of the night builds.

"So fucking hot and wet." He grinds his hips into mine. "So tight."

I grip the bedsheets as I take everything he's willing to give. I want it all.

"Mara, I'm c-close," he pants. "Where do you want me, baby? Where do you want me to come?" he grits out.

There is no decision here. "Inside. I want to feel you lose control." As if my words are a trigger for his orgasm, he stills, and I feel him releasing inside me. Something about the act, the intimacy has me following him over the edge.

Carefully, he releases my legs and lets them fall to the bed. His hands hold his weight on either side of my head so he doesn't crush me. "I love you."

"I love you too." He kisses me, long and slow, a complete contrast to the way our bodies just came together. This is us together, slow and sweet, fast and hard, dirty talk or sweet nothings. I have it all with Seth, and I can't imagine a day in this world without him.

Two days later, Seth and I are sitting at the dining room table booking rooms for early June for our wedding in Pensacola, Florida. Between the two of us, we've talked to everyone, and they're making it happen. Everyone is coming with us, including my future in-laws.

"You excited?" Seth asks.

"I am actually. I can't wait to be your wife." He leans over and presses a kiss to my temple. "Oh, I almost forgot. I have something for you." Reaching down into the bag that I carry back and forth to work, I pull out a manila envelope. I slide it to him.

"What's this?"

"Open it." I smile, letting him know it's not bad news. We've had enough of that to last a lifetime.

Cautiously, he removes the packet of paperwork inside and begins to read. I watch him carefully, and I see it. The moment it dawns on him what it is he's reading. His head pops up, and his jaw is slack. "Mara?"

"I called Kendall the day after you proposed. I was nervous to ask her, but I wanted a good attorney. She gave me the name and number of the man they used, who is also the same attorney that Mark and Dawn used to adopt Daisy. There is no contest because I didn't list a father on her birth certificate. All you have to do is sign. He'll file the petition with the court."

He's frozen still. The only part of his body moving is the rise and fall of his chest as his eyes scan the papers in his hands. "This is real?" he asks again.

"Hey." I place my hand on his arm, pulling his attention back to me. "You don't have to sign them. I just thought—"

He cuts me off by kissing me hard.

"I'm signing them. Hell, I might frame them. You're really doing this? You're going to share your daughter with me?" The awe in his voice warms my heart.

"In her heart, she's already just as much your daughter as she is mine." Speaking of said daughter, she comes rushing into the dining room and climbs up on Seth's lap.

"Daddy, I'm firsty."

Seth swallows hard, his eyes wet with unshed tears. He wraps her in a hug, then sets her on the table in front of him. Carefully, he takes her two tiny hands in his larger ones. "Finley, I love you. I love being your daddy."

"Do you wuv getting me juice?" she asks, making us both laugh.

"Daddy will get you some juice, but I need you to sit in my lap for a minute. Can you do that?"

"Otay," she says, letting him place her back in his lap.

Reaching for a pen, he flips to each page he needs to sign and initial and makes quick work of it. Once he's done, he slides the packet back into the envelope and hands it to me. "I'll always love you," he whispers in her ear.

"I wuv you too, Daddy. Now juice?"

He smiles at her. "Yeah, Finny, now we can get you some juice." She climbs off his lap and races to the kitchen. "Wait for me," he calls out, then reaches over and takes my hands in his. "Mara, I will never forget this moment as long as I live. Thank you for loving me, for sharing that perfect piece of you with me. I promise I will love you both until the end of time." His words have tears welling in my eyes, but he's not there to see it. No, he's already off and heading to the kitchen to grab our girl some juice. I sit and listen to him talk to her, and in that interaction, I can hear how much they love each other. Their bond was fast and it's strong. I love that I'm no longer the only person she can rely on. The only one she trusts to get her juice or read her bedtime stories. I love our family.

A few minutes later, Finley is set with a cup of juice and her crayons on the living room coffee table, and my fiancé is back and we're in full-wedding-planning mode.

"I love that it's Finny's birthday that week, as well as our wedding. We get to celebrate all month."

"All month, huh?"

"Yeah, I mean, we're getting married on Friday and her birthday is the following Friday. I say that counts for a month of celebration."

"What am I going to do with you?" I ask, laughing.

"Love me."

"Done."

"Thank you, Mara. I'll never be able to give you a gift like you've given me with Finley."

"Your love is all we need."

He grins. "Look at us, all sappy and domesticated."

I just shake my head and go back to work. There is one thing for certain, there will never be a dull moment in our household. I smile at that. Even though there is sadness and pain looming in our future, I'm excited about what's left to come. We'll carry the loss of Amelia with us daily, but I know we have to keep moving on, that's what she wants, and that's how life happens. If you don't move with it, you'll be left in the dust. The memories of those you love will always linger in your heart and in your mind.

Chapter 21

SETH

I've become a master at hiding my worry. I mask it with smiles and laughter when inside I'm a tornado of worry and sadness. Today is one of those days that even though I try, the mask I try to slip firmly in place just isn't sitting where it's supposed to.

"Hey." Mara places her hand on my bouncing knee.

We're sitting in the waiting room at the doctor's office. They called Amelia back a few minutes ago, and since our relationship is not... intimate, except for that one drunken night, I opted to stay out here until the doctor finishes her exam. Then, she'll call me back for questions if I have any, and then the ultrasound. No matter how many times I've sat in this waiting room, my nerves are still shot. I still worry that there might be something wrong with the baby, that the cancer that's eating at one of my oldest friends is somehow going to affect our unborn child. The doctors have assured me that although not impossible, it's highly unlikely. That admission does nothing to calm my nerves or the constant worry over my child. Over my friend.

"Mr. Jennings," the nurse calls. I stand, bringing Mara with me.

Usually she goes back with Amelia, but for some reason, today she stayed with me. Maybe I'm not as good at hiding my worry as I thought I was. With her having cancer, they want to keep a close eye on the baby, so she comes twice a week instead of once a month like other women at the same stage of pregnancy.

"Hi," I say as soon as we step into Amelia's small exam room. She's sitting up on the table, fully dressed. I take in the dark circles under her eyes, and I know despite what the doctors tell her, she's not gaining weight as she should be.

"Come on in, guys. Dr. Hatfield will be right back." As soon as she says it, the door pushes open and in walks Dr. Hatfield.

"Seth, Mara, how are you?" she greets us. We exchange pleasantries and wait. "Well, let's get to it, shall we? Amelia is doing well. The baby is measuring correctly. You only gained a pound, but that's progress from the loss that we've seen." She looks up from her computer to face Amelia. "However, as the pregnancy progresses, it may be that we have to admit her to ensure that both she and the baby are getting the nutrients that they both need."

"What should we watch for?" Mara asks.

"Extreme fatigue. If she has any cramping or Braxton Hicks." She rattles off a list of other signs we should watch for. "This isn't meant to scare you, but I want the three of you to be prepared for what could be right around the corner."

"Is it safe for them to travel?"

"Yes, take breaks so she can stretch her legs, just eat small meals multiple times per day, and stay hydrated. She's taking her prenatal vitamins, and I know they make her nauseous, but as long as they are staying down, they are vital for the baby. I've already explained this to Amelia."

"Thank you," I say, not really knowing what else to say to all of that. My worry is ramped up by one thousand.

"You're welcome. Now onto the fun stuff. Are you ready to see your baby?"

"Yes," Amelia and I say at the same time.

"Follow me."

I help Amelia off the exam table and we follow Dr. Hatfield down the hall and into another exam room. It's dark, and the tech is there waiting for us. "All right, let's take a look. Amelia, if you'll have a seat on the table and lie back, we'll get started."

I hold my breath as I wait for the tech to get everything set up, and then she presses the wand to Amelia's growing belly. She moves it around the gel she placed on her abdomen and clicks on her screen. "I'm just taking measurements for the doctor," she says, explaining why she's being so quiet. "All right, so are we wanting to know the gender? Or are we sealing it for a gender reveal party?" she asks.

Amelia looks at me and then to Mara with tears in her eyes. "I-I don't know how much time I'll have after, so I'd like to know now. Seth?"

I can't speak, so I nod my approval. Mara, who is holding Amelia's hand, reaches the other out for me, and just like that, the three of us are linked together, more than just by our hands, but by the bond of friendship, and the life of the baby on the screen.

"Okay, well, this right here—" The tech points to the screen. "—this is your son. Congratulations, it's a boy."

A boy.

I'm going to have a son and a daughter.

"Seth?" Mara squeezes my hand and I give her my attention. "Congratulations, Daddy." She smiles despite the tears that coat her cheeks. I nod.

"A little boy," Amelia says wistfully, her eyes glued to the monitor. She then turns to me and smiles. "Thank you, Seth. I know we didn't plan this and it's unconventional, and it puts pressure on the two of you and your relationship, but this little miracle…" She chokes on her words. "This little miracle," she tries again, "he's the best thing I've ever done. He will always be my greatest accomplishment in life."

Mara leans down and offers her a hug, then steps back, allowing me to do the same. "He'll never go a day without knowing how much you love him. I promise you that."

The tech clears her throat, and I step back. "Here are some pictures. I printed a lot so that each of you could have a set." I love that they know our situation and don't offer any judgment. Not that we've done anything wrong. We were all handed this scrambled hand in life that we're just trying to make sense of.

"Thank you so much." Amelia sits up once the gel is wiped off her growing belly and slides the pictures in her purse.

As a trio, we exit the room, make Amelia's follow-up appointment and ensure it works with all our schedules, and exit the building. The warm May sun beats down on us, and I smile. It's the little things like sunshine that I have to remember to stop and enjoy. With so much bad, sometimes the good can be overshadowed.

"How about lunch?" Mara asks.

"Yes. Then I was thinking maybe we could go shopping, I want to buy a few things for him." Affectionately, Amelia rubs her belly where our son is growing. "A little boy," she squeals, and it's been a long damn time since I've seen a smile that big light up her face.

"You ladies have fun. I need to get back to the job site." I pull Mara into a kiss. "I'll see you at home." Pulling away, I hug Amelia and then bend down to talk to my son. "Take care of your mommy," I whisper. With that, I give my fiancée one more quick kiss and I rush off to my truck.

✶✷✶

Pulling into the job site, I grab the blue box of cigars off the seat. I couldn't resist when I drove past the local party supply store. I stopped on a whim and they had these. I had to buy them. They're not really cigars—they're blue bubble gum—but they get the point across all the same. I'm having a little boy.

"Well?" Tyler asks as I walk into the house we're in the middle of remodeling.

"Care for a cigar?" I ask in my most pretentious voice.

"No shit?" he asks. "Congrats, man."

"A boy!" Mark cheers, which is followed by words of congratulations from Ridge and Kent.

"Finley gets a little brother," I tell them.

"How is Amelia?" Ridge asks.

"Not gaining weight like she should, but she didn't lose any." I go on to tell them the details of the appointment and the ultrasound. "Oh, I have pictures." Reaching into my back pocket, I hand them to Kent and explain what he's looking at before doing the same with the other two.

"You know, I never can tell what they're looking at on these things, but it's cool as hell to see the heartbeat and the baby moving around," Tyler says.

"We missed all that," Mark comments. "Definitely going to be there for all of it with the next one."

"You trying?" Ridge asks.

"Not officially, but we're taking practicing really serious." He grins.

"I can't wait for another one. I just have to convince my wife." Tyler laughs.

"Really?" Kent asks. "I thought it would have been the other way around."

"Nah, she wants more, but wants the boys to be out of diapers first. We're potty training."

"Yeah, we're doing that with Everly too. She's not taking to it as fast as Knox did."

"That's because with Knox, he could sink the Cheerios," I say with a laugh. "And we taught him to pee outside like a man."

"A fact that got me in trouble with my wife." Ridge chuckles.

"Man, if you would have told me three years ago that one day we'd be standing on the job shooting the shit about potty training instead of going out and finding our entertainment for the night, I would have laughed my ass off," Mark says.

"Yeah, if we only knew then what we know now." This comes from Kent. He's not being sarcastic or malicious in any way. It makes me think there is more that he's not telling us. He keeps dropping these cryptic lines. One day soon, I'm going to have to sit him down and pull it out of him. There will be beer involved. Alcohol always helps loosen the inhibitions.

"Life changes," Tyler says. "I must say as much as I loved those days with you guys, nothing compares to a night at home with my wife and kids."

We murmur our agreements, and I notice Kent is quiet. Interesting. Normally he would spout off about not drinking the water or something similar. There is something he's not telling us. Then again, maybe he's just envious. I know I was.

My phone vibrates in my pocket. Pulling it out, I see Mara's smiling face on the screen. "Hey, babe. Miss me already?" I ask. The guys chuckle.

"Seth, don't freak out." Mara's voice comes through the line calm as can be, but hesitant.

"Mara, you cannot call me and tell me not to freak out and not tell me what I'm not freaking out about. What's going on? Are you okay? Finley? Amelia? The baby?"

"Everything is okay. Amelia and I were shopping, and she started coughing and couldn't catch her breath. I insisted she go to her primary care to be checked out. Her oxygen levels are low, so they're having her wear oxygen."

"All the time?"

"Well, she'll always have a small portable tank with her. That way, if she needs it, she can use it like today. But no, not all that time. Not yet."

"The baby?"

"He's fine, but it's important for her to have enough oxygen for both of them."

"Where are you now?"

"I'm taking her back to our place. She's going to put her feet up and relax. We might work in the scrapbook room a little."

"Do you need me to come home?"

"No, we're all good here. I just wanted you to know what was going on."

"Thanks," I say, running my hand through my hair.

"I love you, Seth. I promise everything is okay. If it wasn't, I would tell you. I just wanted you to know. I felt like, you know, with the baby and all, you just needed to be aware."

"Call me if anything changes. I'll swing by Sonia's on my way home and pick up Finny. Oh, and, Mara?" I wait for her to reply.

"Yeah?"

"I love you too." Ending the call, I slide my phone back in my pocket and am met with the concerned eyes of my brothers. "Amelia started coughing and couldn't stop. I guess she wasn't getting enough oxygen. They have her on portable oxygen, and she'll have it with her from here on out for when she needs it."

"Fucking cancer," Kent mutters.

I hate this disease and what it's doing to her. I hate the constant worry for her and our unborn child. I'm scared that she needs oxygen at just nineteen weeks into her pregnancy. What will the next twenty-one look like? Will she make it to full-term? I've done some reading, and I know the closer to her due date that she delivers, the safer it is for the baby, but is it safe for her?

This is an absolutely impossible situation, and I would never wish this on anyone. I know we're not the only people to have cancer alter our lives, and we won't be the last. We can put a man on the moon... how can we not cure this fucking disease?

Chapter 22

Mara

I'm standing in the living room looking over the list in my hands to make sure I have everything. Today we're leaving for Florida. In three days, Seth and I will be married at a private ceremony on the beach. All our friends, our family will be there. Last weekend at Daisy's birthday party, Knox informed us he was in charge of rings at the wedding. At four years old, and the oldest of the kids, he's a fierce protector. Not that I'm surprised by that; he's like his dad and his uncles. The kid doesn't have a choice but to grow up loving and protective; he's surrounded by it.

Daisy smiled her way through wrapping paper and gifts, and then she enjoyed the hell out of her little pink birthday cake. It was a sad moment for all of us. No one voiced it, but we were all thinking the same thing: Will Amelia live to see their baby boy see his first birthday? I don't speculate, and I try not to think about it. She's declining fast, wearing her oxygen more and more. I tried to cancel this trip, but she refused to let me. She wants to swim in the ocean, and she wants to be there when Seth and I pledge our love for one another.

So we move forward. We keep living our lives as if everything is okay when we all know that's not the case. We put on our happy faces, take lots of pictures, and involve her in everything. Capturing and making those memories that we'll have for years to come, for when she's no longer physically here with us.

"Momma," Finley says, pulling on my shirt to get my attention. I look down at her and smile. "I go Mamaw and Papaw?" she asks.

"No, sweetie. We're going on vacation. Mommy and Daddy are getting married."

"I's get mawied?"

"Definitely," Seth tells her, joining us. He lifts her into his arms and rubs his beard across her cheek, making her giggle. "We're going to be a family, remember, and you get to change your last name just like Mommy. All three of us will be Jennings."

"Yay!" she cheers, but I don't think she truly understands. What she does understand is the smile that lights up her daddy's face and the excitement that comes off him in waves.

"Go grab your princess blanket," Seth tells her, placing her back on her feet. "Babe, you've checked that list a hundred times."

"I know, I just… we've never been on vacation. Our trip here last summer was our first trip ever. What if we get all the way there, and I find out that I forgot something that she needs?"

"Then we'll go to the store and buy it. All you need to worry about is that in three days, you're going to be Mara Jennings—Mrs. Seth Jennings. Everything else will work itself out."

"You're right." I nod. "Amelia should be here any minute."

"Good. I'm going to start loading these things into the SUV." With a quick kiss, he grabs a few bags and heads outside to load up the Tahoe that we rented.

Fifteen minutes later, Seth has everything loaded up. I have a bag of snacks and a small cooler. I run back to the bathroom and grab a few more pull-ups just in case. I know we can buy more, but you can never be too prepared.

"Did you bring extra oxygen?" I ask Amelia when she arrives.

"Yes, Mom." She rolls her eyes, but a smile plays on her lips. "Mara?" She waits for me to look at her. "This is what you want, right? To marry

Seth?"

"Yes." My answer is immediate and spoken with zero hesitation.

"Then why the nerves?"

"I don't know. I guess because I'm getting married. My life suddenly feels like a dream coming true, and I don't know how to handle that. For so long, it was me, and then it was me and you, then me and you and Finley. Now—" I pause, collecting myself. I refuse to break down on her. "Now, it's me and Finley, and Seth, and you and the baby, and his parents, and your group of friends that are really family. I've never had any of this, and if this is a dream, I don't ever want to wake up."

"You're not dreaming, Mara. Seth loves you. He loves Finley. This is your real-life fairy tale and I couldn't be happier for you."

"You brought me here. You're responsible for bringing us together. You've always been there for me from the day we met." I close my eyes and take a deep breath. "I don't know what I'm going to do without you."

I watch as she blinks away her own tears. "You're going to lean on your husband, your in-laws, and your new family. All of them. You're not just marrying Seth. You have a huge support system behind you. And on those days when you need me, just talk. I promise you I'll always be listening." Reaching up, she wipes under her eyes. "Now, let that brain of yours rest, and get your ass in the car. We've got a road trip to get to and a wedding to attend." With that, she grabs her oxygen tank and heads outside.

I don't bounce back as quickly as she does; instead, I lose my battle with my tears. I'm not ready to say goodbye, and I know just by looking at her that the disease is taking its toll. Not to mention the pregnancy, which is draining to a woman who is fully healthy. Hearing the door open, I turn my back and quickly wipe away my tears.

"Mara?" Seth asks. He walks up to me and turns me to face him. He sees my tears and his face softens. "I figured when I saw Amelia wiping her eyes, this is how I would find you." He doesn't say anything else. Instead, he wraps me in his strong arms and lets his warmth seep into me. I feel safe here, like nothing else in the world can get to us, but we both know that's not true.

"Okay, are we all loaded up?" I pull back and look up at him.

"Yes, Finley is already strapped in, and Amelia is too. You ready to go get married?"

"Yes."

"Then get your fine ass in the car, Mrs. Jennings." He grins.

That's exactly what I do. Within minutes of locking up the house, we're on the road, and in just a few short days, we'll be married. Glancing over at Seth from his spot behind the wheel, I can't help but dream about our future and everything it might hold. Whatever comes our way, I'm glad it's him who will be by my side.

We allowed ourselves two days to make the drive. We figured it would be easier on both Amelia and Finley. We arrived at the beach house late yesterday afternoon and discovered that everyone else had beaten us here. Not that we minded. We made lots of stops to stretch our legs and just took our time. We knew we had three days. Last night, Ridge, Tyler, Mark, and Kent had the grill going when we pulled in, and we all relaxed around a small fire and had dinner. We had a small birthday party for Finley as she turns three next week. We wanted this to feel like a celebration to her. Kendall and Ridge stopped and picked up a cake when they got here yesterday, and my daughter loved every minute of the attention she was given. After presents, Amelia was exhausted, so she went to bed early, as did the kids. It was a long day of fun in the sun, and then birthday activities once we got here. I couldn't have asked for more.

That brings us to now. It's early morning, and I'm about to marry my best friend. Seth and I decided to marry at sunrise instead of sunset, with the hopes that we would all still be going at sunset. Sure, Amelia has already marked it off her list, but we thought why not have her witness it again? Finley and I are dressed in white thin-flowing dresses. Our hair is braided intricately thanks to Reagan, and our feet are bare. We had to get up rather early, but it's worth it. We're making memories after all.

"We get mawied now?" she asks.

"Yes." I smile down at her, and slowly, she and I walk down the small aisle of chairs that the wedding planner we hired set up for us. Down in front is Seth, and Kent is standing beside him. He's officiating the wedding just like he did for Mark and Dawn. It's fitting considering how close these guys are.

My husband is wearing khaki shorts, and a white button-up with the sleeves rolled to his elbows. He's handsome, and I can't believe he's mine. As if he's thinking the same thing, his eyes watch my every move until we are almost to the end of the aisle.

"Daddy, we get mawied!" Finley yells and races toward him.

He bends down to catch her and scoops her up in his arms. He kisses her cheek as she settles on his hip. I take the few remaining steps until I'm standing before them.

"Both of my girls are beautiful." He leans in and kisses my cheek.

I expect him to put Finley down—she's supposed to be sitting with Seth's parents—but he doesn't even attempt to let her go. Instead, he tells her to take my hand. She reaches out for me, and I take it, smiling at her. Then with his free hand, he takes mine, and the three of us stand in a circle, a family, one unit as Kent proceeds to walk us through our vows.

Seth's eyes hold my gaze the entire time. Finley rests her head on his shoulder as we speak of love and forever. It's the perfect ceremony; I couldn't have asked for more.

"Seth," Kent says, drawing my attention.

Seth smiles at me, and then turns his attention to our daughter. "Finny," he says, getting her attention. She raises her head and looks at him. "Today, I not only marry your mommy, but I marry you," he says, and she grins, nodding her little head. "I vow to love you and be there for you. I promise to kiss your skinned knees and read you all the bedtime stories you want. I'll be there when the boys come knocking to scare them away," he says, and everyone laughs. "I love you, my daughter. For now, for always." He kisses her cheek.

I'm bawling. The tears are falling at a rapid speed, and I'm sure I look a hot mess. Finley places her tiny hands on his cheeks and turns him to face her.

"I wuv you, Daddy."

Seth swallows hard as his eyes well with tears. He turns his attention back to me and gives me a watery smile.

"You may kiss your bride," Kent says.

Seth releases his hold on my hand and kisses Finley on the cheek.

"Come here, baby girl. Daddy has work to do," Kent says, reaching for our daughter as everyone laughs. She goes to him easily, something she would not have done a year ago.

Seth steps into me, frames my face in the palm of his hands, and whispers, "I love you, Mrs. Jennings," against my lips and then presses his to mine.

"Yay! We mawied." Finley cheers, which causes him to chuckle and pull away with a smile I've never seen from him before. It can only be rivaled by mine and our daughter's.

She knows today is a special day, that getting married is a big deal. We've explained that to her, but I know she doesn't understand what really happened here today as the sun rose over the ocean. A man, a wonderful man, pledged his heart to us, to both of us. One day when she's older, I'll make sure she knows how special he is and what he's brought to our lives. Not that she'll need me to tell her. Her daddy will do that all on his own. But still, I want her to hear it from me. The way he came into our lives and loved us both unapologetically.

"Let's eat!" Tyler calls out, and that's that. I married the man of my dreams, and he wants to be a father to my daughter. He *is* a father to my daughter, and I thank God, and Amelia, every day for bringing him into our lives.

We head back to the house where we have a huge breakfast buffet catered. The kids loved the mouse pancakes, while the adults indulged in biscuits and gravy, french toast, eggs, and fresh fruit. You name it, we had it.

"I don't think I can eat another bite," Seth says, pushing away from the table.

"Well, now that the most important meal of the day is out of the way, you two need to get moving," Amelia says.

"What? Where are we going?" I ask her.

"The two of you have plans," she says vaguely.

"Go on, we're keeping Finley," my mother-in-law informs us.

"I don't understand." I'm confused as to what's happening.

"Today is a special day," Amelia states. "It's the first day of your forever, and you've been amazing these past few months. Both of you have been there with me through this, all of you have." Her eyes scan our friends and family. "However, today it's about the two of you, and the love you share. So we're taking Finley." She waves at everyone in attendance. "And you two have a reservation here." She slides a plain white envelope toward us. "While I appreciate the sentiment of the early sunrise wedding, I won't be watching the sunset, at least not with the two of you. Go, enjoy this mini honeymoon of sorts."

"We've got this," Kendall speaks up. I know it's because she's a nurse and that will ease our minds. "You're going to be five miles down the road. If we need you, if Finley needs you, we'll call."

"Mrs. Jennings?" Seth whispers in my ear. I turn to look at him and his lips press to mine.

"Go." This from Ridge.

Standing from our seats, we hug Finley, telling her we have a special trip and to hang out with Mamaw and Papaw. She hugs us and sends us on our way. Not a worry in sight.

An hour later, I stand behind Seth as he slides the room key into the door of our beachfront room. We're on the fifteenth floor, and I can imagine the views are breathtaking. Seth pushes open the door, stepping back and letting me enter the room, pulling our small suitcase behind me.

"Mara."

Releasing the suitcase, I turn to him. He smiles and stalks toward me. "Mr. Jennings."

"Mrs. Jennings," he replies. "Turn around." I do as he says. He traces his finger over my exposed back. "I've thought about stripping you out of this dress at least a hundred times today." I not only hear the zipper, but feel the cool air of the air conditioning hit my exposed back. "So soft," he murmurs.

"Seth," I moan as his lips trail up my back.

"Yeah, baby?"

I turn in his arms and wiggle my hips until my dress pools around my ankles. I'm standing before him in nothing but a white thong that has *Mrs. Jennings* embroidered on it. "You're taking too long." I reach for his shorts, and manage to get the button undone before he's stepping back and removing them himself. I watch as his shorts and boxer briefs are kicked to the side. His thick cock juts out like a beacon; he doesn't bother with the buttons of his white shirt; instead, he rips it open. Buttons fly around the room, but we're so lost in one another, in this moment, we don't even care.

"Fuck, you're gorgeous." Reaching out, he traces the swell of my breasts with his index finger, running his thumb over my pebbled nipples. "I want to devour you and I don't know where to start first."

"How about here?" I fist his cock in the palm of my hand and stroke him.

"You're going to have to stop that. This will be over before it starts."

"Then you better step up your game, Mr. Jennings."

"I want to cherish you, take my time loving every inch of you, Mrs. Jennings."

"We have the rest of our lives for that. I need you inside me. I need to feel connected to you, to my husband." His eyes soften and I know I've got him.

He drops to his knees and slips his fingers under either side of my thong, carefully removing it. He peers up at me and grins. "I'm keeping these," he says as I step out of them. I watch as he holds them up and grins when he reads *Mrs. Jennings*. Reaching behind him, he places them on the suitcase before turning back to me. "On the bed, wife."

"Oh, is that how it's going to be? What if I said I wanted you on the bed?"

He stands, and with his hand on mine, he guides us to the bed. He climbs on and moves to the middle, placing his hands behind his head. "Well, you got me here, now what are you going to do with me?"

He makes me feel brazen and bold, something I've never felt in my life. To know that this man is mine for eternity, it does something to me. It gives me a confidence like I've never known before. Slowly, I climb on the bed, settling on my knees beside him. I run my hands over the ridges of his abs and find my way to his cock. I grip him, causing him to moan. Lazily, I stroke him.

"Mara, baby, I thought you said we didn't have time for this?" he pants.

"Did I?"

"Tease," he grumbles good-naturedly.

"What do you want, husband? Tell me what you need."

He sits up, slides his hand behind my neck, and pulls me close. "I want you, Mara. All of you, and preferably coming all over my cock."

"Like this?" I move to straddle him.

"You're getting close," he says, wrapping his arms around me. My breasts press against his chest as his lips make themselves at home in the crook of my neck. "Let me help you." He breathes the words into my ear.

Lifting to my knees, I wait for him to align himself at my entrance. When I feel him, I lower myself, painfully slow until he's deep inside me. "Now what?"

"Fuck me."

"Like this?" I swivel my hips and lift myself off him only to have his hands settle on my hips, pulling me back down.

"Like this." His lips crash to mine as he lifts me and then pulls me back down. We easily find a rhythm as we make love for the first time as husband and wife. Fast, slow, intimate, or wild, it's still love.

"Mara," he growls as his hand slides from my hip to settle between us. As soon as his thumb brushes across my clit, I explode. Light flashes behind my eyes, as an electric current courses through my veins.

Together, we cry out before collapsing onto the bed. Our bodies are slick with sweat, but neither one of us seem to care. We're celebrating.

"I never thought that sex with you could get any better. I was wrong."

"Yeah?" I ask, barely able to form words.

"Yeah. Must be the new title and the new last name." He pats my ass and we both laugh. "Come on, wife, let's take a shower and then do that again."

"We're not getting any sleep tonight, are we?"

"Nope."

The night is magical, and one I'm sure neither of us will ever forget. Although it was nice to get away from it all, we miss our girl and head back to the beach house the next morning.

***

"You ready for this?" I ask the girls. We're all standing hand in hand in our bathing suits staring at the ocean.

"I'm not really a fan of swimming with fish, or sharks, or snakes, or…

creatures," Dawn admits.

"The water's warm. We already know that," I say as it laps at our feet. This is one of the final items on Amelia's bucket list, and we wanted to be there with her to mark it off, not just to watch, but to make the memory. Our husbands—it's not even been forty-eight hours, and I've already said it a dozen times; I can't seem to help myself—anyway, our husbands and Seth's dad are on the beach with the kids. Seth's mom is on one side of Amelia while I'm on the other. Ladies unite as we stand tall beside an amazing woman, who is fighting to bring a healthy baby boy into this world. Fighting to leave a piece of her behind after she takes her last breath.

"Okay, on the count of three," Kendall says.

"One," Reagan counts.

"Two," Dawn calls out.

"Three!" Amelia cheers, and we move forward into the water.

We walk until we're about waist deep and stop. Amelia stands still with her eyes frozen on the horizon. I can't begin to imagine what's going through her head right now. We've successfully marked off everything that we're capable of making happen but the tattoo and having a baby, which she's working on. The tattoo, we have picked out. We decided on a heart that also appears to be two hands that are locked together. We know where we're going to get it and have already made arrangements that if Amelia is too sick to go there, the guy is willing to come to us.

"It's beautiful," Amelia whispers as I wrap my arm around her shoulders.

"It really is."

"Hey, what are you two gabbing about over there?" Kendall calls out.

"I thought we were swimming?" Dawn asks.

I love her for pulling us out of this sadness that is threatening to take over the moment. Instead, Amelia turns to her and splashes, and just like that, the water fight is on. We move closer into shore, where the water is just at our ankles, and the kids join us. The guys stay back and snap pictures. Every single one of them has a camera in their hands, and it's a moment that touches deep in my soul. They're capturing this, savoring the little things in life to be shared with our kids later. They probably won't remember it since they're all under the age of four, but they'll see it. They'll hear the stories and know about this day. The day Amelia got to swim in the ocean for the first and more than likely, last time.

After frolicking in the water with the kids, we head back up to the house where the guys again man the grill, and with full bellies, and the kids snuggled in their beds, we watch the sunset. Dawn, Amelia, and I are huddled together on a blanket on the beach, while Kendall, Reagan, and Shannon are on another right beside us. I can hear the guys chatting, and the echo of their laughter fading into the dusk of the day.

"Thank you," Amelia says quietly. "Thank you for today, for this trip, for all of it."

Before I can form words through the lump in my throat, Kendall, Reagan, and Shannon are surrounding us, and we're all in one giant group hug. No words are spoken, but we don't need them. She knows we're here for her and we love her. She knows that today will be forever in our memory and in our hearts.

Chapter 23

SETH

"If you don't stop staring at me, I'm going to have them put you on the 'not allowed to visit' list," Amelia says. Her eyes are closed, but she can feel my stare.

"Do you have one of those?" I ask, not fazed by her threat.

Slowly her eyes open, and I can see the exhaustion plain as day. "No, but you're first on the list." She sighs heavily. "Seth, I'm fine."

"You're in the hospital. You're not fine," I fire back.

"I'm dying, Seth. What do you expect?"

"Stop."

"No. I won't stop. It's my reality. No matter how unexpected this diagnosis is, it's my truth, and you have to face that. Our son needs you to face that. I'm going to be here until he's born, maybe longer. Who knows if I'll ever get to leave, but you know what? I'm okay with that. I'm okay with it because these tubes are giving him what he needs since my body seems to be revolting at anything I put into my mouth. You sitting here staring at me is not going to work for me. Go home to your wife and your daughter."

"They're on their way here."

"Of course they are. Let me visit with Finley, and then you can go. Leave Mara. She doesn't stare."

I can't hide my grin. If she's feisty, she's feeling better. Last week was the Fourth of July and the twenty-five-week mark of her pregnancy. We had a get together at our place, and the girls surprised her with a baby shower. It's early on, but they wanted her to be in good health to participate, and we can all see this disease and the pregnancy are taking a toll on her.

The guys helped me paint the nursery, and together, she and Mara set it up. Mara and I needed to be ready for when he's born, for raising him, and we wanted her to be as involved as possible. It was a tearful day for all of us, but together as a family, we got through it.

"Have you thought of anymore names?"

She sighs, and I know I have her. "Yeah, what do you think about Ryder?"

"Ryder Jennings," I repeat aloud. "Sounds badass." I grin at her.

"Yeah?" Her eyes, although tired, light up at my acceptance.

"Yeah, I'm digging it. Middle name?" I ask.

"You can say no, but I was thinking my last name for his middle name. You know, something of me that's always with him."

I nod. I have to fight hard to not show her my pain, knowing that she's not going to see him grow up. "Ryder Anderson Jennings." Standing from my chair, I walk to stand beside her bed and place my hand on her belly. Leaning in close, I whisper—my words only for my son, "I love you, buddy. Daddy can't wait to meet you."

When I look up, Amelia has streams of tears covering her cheeks. "I'm glad it was you, Seth. I know I sound like a broken record, but it's true. I need you to know that. I'm glad someone up there was looking out for me and had the stars align to make it you. I can't imagine what I would be feeling right now if this baby, if his father was some stranger or a random hook-up. I can't imagine the fear of not knowing that he will always be loved and taken care of."

"We would have never let that happen, any of us."

"I know that." She gives me a half smile. "But it sure makes it a hell of a lot easier not having to worry. I know he's going to be safe, loved, and, most of all, that you'll never let him forget me. That eases my soul, Seth. I know you think that this cancer has hardened me and, in a way, it has, but in others, it's brought me peace." She closes her eyes, and I think she's going to nap like she should be when she continues to speak.

"In college, I went to this party and had too much to drink. Mara, she didn't want to go as she had to work that night and said she was too tired. I begged her to come after she got off work, and because she's the amazing friend that she is, she agreed." She pauses for a long time, then starts again. "I remember being hot, so hot from a combination of too much alcohol and all the bodies that were at the frat party. I knew she was on her way, so I made my way to the porch for some air. Only when I got there, I wasn't the first with that idea, so I kept walking, down the steps and around the side of the house. It was dark and cool, and the sound of the music from inside seeped outside, filling the night air. That's why I didn't hear him coming. Some guy—I'd never met him before—he came on fast and strong, pushing me up against the house, smashing his body into mine. The alcohol slowed my reflexes, and he had me pinned before I realized what was happening."

"No," I breathe. Her eyes open and she shakes her head.

"No. Mara, she saved me. Somehow over the music and the noise of the party, she heard me scream as she was approaching the house. She yelled for help, and a couple of the guys who were on the porch came running. They pulled him off me, and I slid to the ground. I remember Mara dropping to her knees next to me and pulling me into her. Later she told me the guys beat the hell out of him."

"Thank God," I murmur.

"You see, Mara and I, we've been through a lot. Not two months later, she found out she was pregnant with Finley. I was her roommate and volunteered my help until Blake came back, only he never came back. He never knew about the incredible little girl. We've been through it all, Mara and I, and to know she's the one who will be helping you raise our son, that makes my heart smile, Seth. I know I keep repeating myself, but life, the timeline of events, they happen for a reason, and here we are full circle. You're one of my oldest and dearest friends; we're having a baby. A night neither of us remember resulted in a miracle I never thought would happen. Then you marry my best friend. It's fate, and I need you to understand that I'm at peace with it. Does it suck? Absolutely, but the knowledge that he's going to be safe, happy, and loved, that a part of me will live on with my family, that's a rare gift that many in my situation never receive. I look at it as a blessing in disguise."

I wipe at my eyes. What am I supposed to say to all that? Thankfully, my phone rings and I don't have to, at least not right away.

"Hey, babe."

"Hi, are you still at the hospital?" Mara asks.

"Yeah."

"I'm on my way. I'm picking up a milkshake. Hopefully she can drink some of it. Do you want one?"

"No, I'm good. Thanks, though."

"I packed up some scrapbook stuff we can work on for a few hours if she feels up to it. She's making one for the baby."

I'd assumed that was the case. "Be safe. Do you have Finny?"

"No." She chuckles. "Your mom called and said she was trying to make cookies but couldn't do it without Finley's help. I just dropped her off."

"Sounds like Mom. All right, I'll see you in a few. Love you."

"Love you too."

I wait for the line to go dead before sliding my phone back into my pocket. Looking up, I find Amelia with a dopey smile on her face. "I'll make sure he never forgets you."

She nods. "Make sure he sees that love you have for Mara. I want him to be a man who's not afraid of love but runs toward it. Make sure he's one of the good ones, just like his daddy and his uncles."

"This sucks," I say, taking in a deep breath as tears threaten to fall.

"It does," she agrees, closing her eyes. We're both quiet as we let ourselves get lost in our thoughts. "Seth," she whispers.

"Yeah?"

"Stop staring."

I can't help but laugh at her. It wasn't my intention to stare, but I'd been lost in thought. Since it was in her direction, I have no argument. "Nah, I'm good." I chuckle, and if her eyes were open, I know she'd be rolling them.

"Knock, knock," Mara says a few minutes later. She pushes open the door holding two milkshakes in her hands. "Peanut butter," she says, setting the milkshake in front of Amelia before coming to sit next to me. Leaning in, I kiss her lips because if my wife is near, I need to be as close to her as I can get.

"What's in the bag?" Amelia asks, taking a small sip of her milkshake.

That makes Mara smile. "I brought some stuff to work on."

"You don't have to sit with me. You have a little girl and a husband who's annoying as hell." Amelia tries to give me a stern look but fails, making us all laugh.

"Finley is with Steve and Shannon making cookies, and my husband has somewhere to be."

"Where?" I ask.

She shrugs. "Not here."

"I see how it is. We're married now, you have my last name, and you no longer need me around," I tease.

"Meh." She laughs, and I lean in to kiss her again.

"Fine. I'm going. This one kept yelling at me anyway." I stand and go to Amelia, kissing her forehead. "Call if you need anything, and don't be corrupting my wife telling her stories about me."

"No promises," Amelia sings.

"Trouble. You two are nothing but trouble." Bending, I whisper to her belly, "Take care of your mommy." Then I go to Mara and bend to kiss her softly. "I love you. I'll see you at home."

"Be careful." She smiles up at me. I can see the joy of the life we're building clouded with sadness and pain for our friend. They say life doesn't give you more than you can handle, but sometimes I think that "they," whoever that may be, was living in some kind of alternate universe. Our family has been through enough. We need some good. Maybe even a miracle.

I drove around for a while after leaving the hospital. I didn't want to go home to an empty house. I hate when Finny and Mara are gone. It's too quiet. So I drove until I ended up at the high school. I walk the football field and remember back when the five of us used to tear up this field. Those were the days. Not a care in the world. Although I don't want to go back, I miss the times when life seemed to be simpler. I'm sitting in the middle of the field at the fifty-yard line when my phone rings.

"Hey," I greet Kent.

"What's up?"

"Oh, you know, reliving the glory days."

"Yeah? How exactly are you doing that?"

"I'm at the high school field. Just… needed to clear my head."

"Want some company?"

I think about his question. Do I? Yeah, if it's one of my best friends, one of my brothers, then yes, I'll always take their company. "Sure."

"Be there in ten," he says as the line goes dead.

Lying back on the grass, I stare up at the blue-lit skies. It won't be long and the colors will begin to change as the sun sets and night falls. I let the past few years play out in my mind. It seems as though we've taken hit after hit, and although everything works out in the end and life moves on, it's still a lot to take on. Closing my eyes, I send up a silent prayer that I can make it through these next few months. Becoming a father for the second time… Amelia… everything is so uncertain, except for the fact that we know our time with her is fading fast.

"What are we looking at?" Kent asks.

Slowly, I open my eyes and turn to where his voice came from. He's lying on the ground next to me looking up at the clouds. "Nothing."

"You doing okay?"

"Nope." I turn back to the sky.

"Figured as much. How is she?"

"Feisty."

He chuckles. "That's good. Means she's feeling better. I haven't been there to see her today."

"I left when Mara got there. They basically kicked me out."

"I see who wears the pants in your marriage," he teases.

I laugh, but he's got it all wrong. "It's not that she wears the pants as

224

much as I'd do anything for her. When she smiles and those green eyes of hers light up, yeah, I'd do anything to see that happen."

"Yeah," he says like he knows.

Now's my chance to see what's going on with him. "Want to talk about it? About her?"

His entire body freezes. "Not really."

"When you do, you know where to find me."

"It was a long time ago," he admits.

"How did we not know about this?"

"Because I was a dick, kept her quiet. She moved on."

"You sure about that?" I ask him. "Seems to me if you're this torn up, she might be too. And fuck you for not telling us."

He laughs. "What's that saying? I wish I knew then what I know now?"

"You didn't know then that you loved her?"

"I never said I loved her."

"You didn't have to. It's written all over you. More so the last few months."

"It's hard not to think about her when I see all of you happy, getting married, starting families. Makes me wish for what might have been."

"Call her."

"That ship has sailed," he says with a heavy sigh. "Now, I thought I said I didn't want to talk about it?"

"Right." I laugh. My phone rings, and I pull it out of my pocket seeing my mom's face on the screen. "Hey, Mom."

"Hi, honey. Finley wants to talk to you."

I sit up. "Okay. Is everything all right?"

"Yes, dear, everything is fine. Here she is."

"Hi, Daddy."

Her tiny little fist squeezes at my heart just hearing her voice alone, but when she calls me Daddy, I doubt I'll ever stop feeling pure joy when she says it. "Hi, Finny. Are you having fun with Mamaw?"

"I's maked cookies."

"You did? Did you save one for Daddy?"

"He can't see you nod, sweetie." I hear my mom whisper.

"My did," she answers. "I take some to Auntie A?" she asks.

My little girl has her momma's heart. "Yes. I'll be there to get you in just a little while, okay?"

"'Kay, Daddy." She hands the phone back to my mom.

"It was her idea. She said the baby needed cookies."

"She hasn't been eating much, but I know for Finley she'll try. Might not be the most nutritious, but it's food all the same. I'm leaving the field now and heading your way."

"The field?"

"Yeah, Kent and I were just catching up."

"Oh, well, you be safe." I know she wants to say more, wants me to open up to her, but there's nothing to say. This situation is beyond normal, and we're just taking it all one day at a time.

"I'm going to head over to the hospital. I'll see you there?" Kent asks, standing.

"Yeah. I'll be right behind you." With that, we leave the field and the memories of our youth behind us. During the drive to my parents, I vow that my kids will be kids for as long as possible. I want them to live happily and as carefree for as long as they can. They'll have adult problems and the challenges that life brings their way soon enough.

Chapter 24

Mara

I'm in the hospital reading on my Kindle while Amelia sleeps peacefully. She had a rough night last night, so I'm glad she's getting some rest. She's thirty-three weeks today, and she's still here. Her team of doctors, both for her and the baby, thought the sterile environment was best. She's on oxygen all the time now, and her body is weak. She's all belly as baby Ryder grows stronger every day. They do daily ultrasounds, which all three of us have come to look forward to. She has another one scheduled this afternoon, and Seth asked her if we could bring Finley.

Amelia was all for it, and my heart melted at his thoughtfulness. It's going to be hard to explain to a three-year-old she has a baby brother that wasn't in her mommy's belly. Thankfully she's too young to really understand. One day we'll have to explain it all to her. But Seth, my husband, he's amazing. He's always putting me, Finley, and Amelia first. Sure, it's not the ideal situation, but the three of us, we have this… bond. It's deep, and instead of brooding or being pissed off, we've embraced this unexpected turn of events and are focusing on the here and now.

"Hey," Amelia croaks.

I hit the Off button on my Kindle and place it on the table beside me. I wasn't really reading anyway. I was too lost in my thoughts. Standing, I offer her a drink of water.

"Thank you."

"You get rested?" I ask.

"I did, actually. What time is it?"

"Just after three."

"Seth is supposed to be here with Finley. He didn't forget, did he? You better call him. I want her to see this. I don't know why I didn't think of it earlier," she rasps.

"No, he didn't forget. He left work about ten minutes ago. He's picking her up from his mom's and heading this way. He'll be here."

"Good, that gives us some time. I've been meaning to talk to you." She takes a deep breath and coughs. I stand close in case she needs… I don't know what, but I'm here for whatever it might be.

"Okay," I say once her coughing subsides.

"I want you to be Ryder's mom."

My heart falls to my feet as I brace myself on her bed to keep from falling. "Amelia—" I start, but she cuts me off by holding up her hand.

"Let me say this." She waits for me to nod that I'm going to stay quiet and listen. "I know you, Mara. I know the person you are and the love you have for your daughter. I want my son to have that love, to feel it."

"Amelia," I whisper as pain slices through me for my best friend. For my husband and their unborn child.

"I want him to call you Mom. You are and will be his mother for the rest of his life. I want you to adopt him," she says, wiping a tear from her eye. "I want you to love him for both of us."

My heart stalls in my chest. "I love him already," I confess.

She nods. "I know you do. I know this is a forgone conclusion since you and Seth are married, but I felt like I needed to say it. I don't want there to be any regrets or feelings of guilt after I'm gone." She pauses, catching her breath. She loses it so quickly these days. "I want you to love him freely with the knowledge I'm smiling down on you. Every time he calls you Mom, my heart will be full because I know that you are the one person on this earth, other than his daddy, who will love him like only I could."

I reach for her hand as tears flood my cheeks. I don't think I can speak for the lump in my throat. Instead, I let her words play in my mind. My free hand rests on her belly, careful of the fetal monitors. I look up to find her watching me, tears that match my own tracking down her cheeks.

"Promise me, Mara. Promise me you will love him with no regrets. That there will be zero guilt. Love him for both of us."

I nod. "I promise. With all that I am, I promise you he will be loved enough for both of us, and I will never ever let a day pass that he doesn't know how truly amazing you are. I'll tell him how you fought for him, loved him the minute you knew he was growing inside you."

She nods, her tears now preventing her from speaking. She begins to cough, so I help her sit up a little higher. Once she's calmed down, she whispers, "Thank you. Now clear up your face before Finley comes in here and sees you like this."

"This is all your fault," I tell her, smiling through the pain and sadness that's circling us, threatening to swallow us whole.

"Knock, knock," Seth says, pushing open the door fifteen minutes later. He eyes me suspiciously, but I give him a smile, letting him know I'm okay.

"Auntie A, I's makes more cookies," Finley says, holding up a baggie of cookies and handing them to Amelia.

"Oh my goodness, I think you've grown since I last saw you."

Finley giggles. "I'm a big girl," she says proudly.

"That you are." Seth lifts her to the bed to snuggle next to Amelia.

"So, I have a surprise for you," Amelia says. "You're going to get to see Ryder today."

"I's do?" Finley's eyes are wide with excitement. She stares at Amelia's belly as if the baby is just going to jump out at her.

"You do."

Seth and I have yet to tell her that baby Ryder is going to be her brother. Officially, as her adoption should be final in a few weeks. Seth finds my eyes over Finley's head, and I nod my approval. I'm just too emotionally drained to try and make her understand, but her daddy, my husband, the man who loves us both unconditionally, I trust him to do it.

"Come here, Finny." Seth holds his arms out for her and she carefully climbs into them. "So, Mommy, Daddy, and Auntie A, we have something to tell you."

Her little head nods and he has her full attention. "You wuv me." She says it with absolute certainty, and I can see my husband melt at her conviction.

"We do, baby girl. So much. We also love baby Ryder. We love him so much that he's going to be your baby brother."

She gasps, and her little hand flies to cover her mouth. We've been working on her inside voice, especially when in the hospital. "A baby brover?" she asks with awe in her voice.

Seth nods. "Yes. He's going to live with us, and as his big sister, you have to look out for him, teach him things once he gets older."

"I's a big siser?" Again, nothing but pure joy in her reply.

"You are."

"Ryder's room by my room," she says like it all makes sense now.

She asked what we were doing while painting the room. We told her we're painting Auntie A's baby's room and that was enough to appease her. Besides, it was blue, so that wasn't something she was interested in. She's a girly-girl. Pink and purple all the way.

"That's right. So, what do you think, Finny? You ready to be a big sister?" he asks her.

Her little head bobs up and down. "I's can do it."

"Good girl," he praises, hugging her tight to his chest. Her little arms are around his neck, squeezing with all she's got.

"Are we ready to see how Ryder's doing today?" an ultrasound tech asks. She wheels a portable ultrasound machine into the room. Seth, with Finley in his arms, steps back, as do I, giving her room to settle in. I make my way to the opposite side of the room, and he opens his arm that's not holding our daughter for me. I waste no time snuggling into him. One arm's around his waist, the other's resting on his chest over his heart. I feel his lips press to the top of my head.

"There he is," the tech says.

"Me see," Finley says, craning her neck.

"Come lay with Auntie A," Amelia says, speaking up for the first time since we broke the news that Ryder was going to be Finley's baby brother. "Put your hand right here." Amelia guides her hand to the side and Ryder kicks, which is visible on the screen.

"He kickeded me," Finley says excitedly.

Reaching out, I place my hand on Amelia's belly, feeling little Ryder move around. Seth steps up behind me and places his hand over mine. It's a moment I will never forget.

The bond.

The love.

The trust.

I will cherish all three as long as I live, just like I will the memory of my best friend. Stepping back, Seth does as well, wrapping his arms around my waist. I pull my phone from my back pocket and snap a few pictures, not that I need them, but it will be a nice visual for Ryder when I tell him the day his big sister found out she was going to be just that, his big sister.

"Everything looks great." The ultrasound tech wipes the gel off Amelia's belly and packs up her equipment. "I'll see you tomorrow, Momma," she tells Amelia.

Amelia bursts into tears.

"Auntie A." Finley soothes her, her tiny palm resting against Amelia's cheek. "Don't cwy."

"I'm happy," Amelia assures her. "These are happy tears."

I have a feeling this is going to be a good moment, so I hit Record on the camera on my phone and hold it, so they don't realize I'm recording.

"I love baby Ryder so much," Amelia manages to tell her. "I'm so honored to be his mommy, but your mommy is going to be his mommy too."

"Hims has two mommies?"

Amelia's lip quivers. "He does, and I'm so happy that it's your mommy and daddy and that you're his big sister. I couldn't have picked a better family for him."

"I's love him, Auntie A."

More tears fall, but Amelia smiles through them. "I know you do, sweet girl. I'm counting on it."

"Okay, munchkin, Auntie A needs some rest." I hold my arms out for Finley, and she comes to me without complaint. "We're going to go, but I'll be back later," I tell Amelia.

"No. Stay home. You three need a normal night home. My parents are stopping by later and so is Reagan. I promise if anything happens, I'll call you."

"Amelia." Seth's tone of voice is stern and full of concern at the same time.

"I'm still here," she says with certainty. "Go, have a family night. I'll be here tomorrow."

Seth nods, gives her hand a gentle squeeze, and the three of us head home. The drive home is quiet. I was expecting lots of questions from Finley, but she's quiet. I pull into the garage, and she unbuckles herself and waits for me to open the door for her. She goes straight down the hall; I assume to her room.

Seth looks up from where he's making grilled cheese at the stove. "What's up with that?" he asks.

"I'm not sure." I walk down the hall and peek in Finley's room, but she's not there. I see the door to the nursery is open and I peek inside. She's standing next to the crib with her princess blanket. "Finley, sweetheart, what are you doing?"

"Baby brover?" she asks.

"Oh, honey, he's not here yet. He's still in Amelia's tummy."

"I luv him, Mommy."

"You girls ready to eat?" Seth asks.

"Daddy." Finley rushes to him, latching onto his leg.

Seth helps her detach and drops to his knees in front of her. "What's going on, Finny?"

"I wuv my brover. You daddy."

I think I know what she's trying to say. She just got Seth as her daddy.

I think she's worried we're going to lose him. "Baby girl," Seth whispers. It's with that I know he gets it too. He knows her so well. "I'm always going to be your daddy. Nothing will ever change that. Ryder is my son and you are my daughter. I love you both with all of my heart."

"And Mommy?"

He looks up, his eyes soft as they land on me. "Mommy is the love of my life. You, Mommy, and Ryder are my entire world. I promise you that will never change."

"I wuv you, Daddy."

I wipe a tear from my eye. I love this man with everything that I am.

"Finny, I love you too. So much. You're always going to be my little girl. You are the first to make me a daddy. That's special," he tells her.

"I's special?" she asks.

"More than you'll ever know." He stands, lifting her with him. He opens his arm for me and I go to them. My heart. My family.

The rest of the night, we stay close together, snuggled on the couch. Seth reads Finley three stories as we lie in her little princess castle twin bed. It's another one of those moments, those memories I'll never forget.

Chapter 25

SETH

"Welcome to the world, Ryder Anderson Jennings," I whisper to my newborn son in my arms. He's so damn tiny at thirty-seven weeks, but he's a fighter, just like his mother. He's doing great, eating and breathing on his own. Weighing in at six pounds and one ounce, he's nineteen inches long. The doctors gave Amelia shots to strengthen his lungs, and the nutrients she was receiving through her IV also helped him grow. The doctors administered it as a precaution in case he delivered early.

We got the call in the middle of the night that Amelia was in labor—this time for real; we've had a few close calls, but they were able to stop it over the last few weeks. It was rough for her. She was exhausted, the pushing too much for her lungs, but she fought it. She fought hard and delivered our son into the world. I hate this, the fact that I know she's fading fast, and that delivering Ryder took a lot out of her.

I haven't left her side since early this morning. Mara and I have been stuck to her like glue, and my wife... she's incredible. She was there for Amelia, coaching her, reminding her of the details of Finley's delivery.

Mara's now sitting next to me, head resting on my shoulder as she sleeps. Amelia is sleeping peacefully. She'll cough in her sleep, but it subsides and she falls right back to sleep. Me, I can't seem to shut my eyes. I can't stop looking at my son. I've been holding him for the last two hours, and I'm good to continue to do so.

My phone vibrates in my pocket, and I know it's my parents. We dropped Finley off to them in the middle of the night. I texted them to let them know Ryder was here and healthy, along with a picture. They sent their love with the promise to stop by after we've had the chance to catch a couple hours of sleep.

A soft knock against the door and it's pushing open. I hear my dad making a shushing sound, reminding Finley to be quiet because her baby brother might be sleeping.

"Daddy!" she whisper shouts. Her little feet rush to me.

"Shh, everyone is sleeping," I say in a hushed whisper.

"Is dat my brover?" she asks. She's wearing a pink T-shirt that says *I'm the big sister.* My parents must have stopped at the gift shop on the way up.

I hear a sniffle, but I don't have to look up to know it's my mom. "Yeah, sweetie. This is your little brother. Ryder."

"I wuv him." She leans in and kisses his tiny head.

"Be easy," Mara whispers, and suddenly her head is no longer on my shoulder.

"Hey," Amelia says groggily.

"How are you feeling, dear?" my mom asks.

"Okay. Tired," she admits.

"Childbirth takes a lot out of you. Can we get you anything?" Mom asks.

"No, thank you."

"Ryder, look who's awake." I stand and carry him to the bed. Mara is on her feet and helping me raise the bed for Amelia to sit up. "Go see Mommy," I say, handing him off to Amelia.

"Hey, handsome," Amelia coos. Her eyes are glued to our son. My eyes find Mara's, and she's watching Amelia with tears in her eyes. Glancing at my parents, they have the same.

"I wuv my bruver," Finley announces proudly.

"Come here you." Amelia pats the space beside her.

"Careful, Finley," Mara warns her.

Slowly, slower than I've ever seen my daughter move, she settles in next to her aunt and her baby brother. "Hims needs to wake up."

Amelia laughs softly. "Babies sleep a lot. He won't be able to play with you for a few months at least."

"Oh," Finley says, dejected, and we all chuckle at her.

"It's almost time for him to eat," I tell Amelia. "I was hoping you would wake up in time to feed him."

"Would you like to hold him?" Amelia asks my mom.

She nods, tears in her eyes. "More than anything." Mom steps next to the bed and takes Ryder from Amelia. She gets comfortable in a seat next to my dad, and together, they take in their new grandson. Finley climbs off the bed and races to my dad. He doesn't hesitate to pull her onto his lap. He snuggles her close, and for about the one-millionth time in my life, I'm grateful for my parents. Shannon and Steve Jennings are the most loving, caring parents a kid could ask for. I'm damn lucky to call them mine.

Mom trades Dad. He takes Ryder while she snuggles Finley to her chest. Mom chatters with Finley about making cookies when they get home, giving my girl her full attention. Something Finley needs. I don't want her to get jealous of Ryder. I mean, I get it. She just got us, and now there's this new baby taking what she just got used to having. I make a mental note to make sure we have some daddy-daughter time. I never want her to question how much I love her.

Mara reaches for her camera and starts taking pictures. I sit back and take it all in. My family. My heart feels full while it's breaking at the same time. When Ryder starts to fuss, I know it's past time for him to eat. By the looks of it, Amelia is ready to crash, so we need to get this moving for both of them.

"All right, buddy, time for a bottle." I take him from my dad, snuggle him, and hand him off to Amelia. Mara places a nipple on one of the premade bottles and hands it to Amelia with a small receiving blanket.

"We're going to go. We've got cookies to make," Dad says, and Finley cheers. "Give Mommy and Daddy a kiss."

We give hugs and kisses, and they're gone. A few minutes later, Amelia's parents are knocking on the door. They both look frail, and I know their health is fading, and Amelia's disease is taking a toll on them. The stress and worry over your daughter and grandchild must take a lot out of you.

"Hey." Amelia lights up when she sees her parents. Her mom breaks down sobbing when she sees them.

"Harold, Ethel, it's good to see you," I greet them.

"He's beautiful," her mom says between sobs, never taking her eyes off Ryder.

"You want to hold him?" Amelia asks her mom.

"Oh, he's eating."

"It's fine. It's time to burp him anyway," Amelia assures her.

Mara is there. She takes Ryder from Amelia, places him on her shoulder, and whispers to him, rubbing his back. He burps, and she smiles, kissing his tiny hat-covered head. Ethel takes a seat, Harold sitting next to her, and Mara hands him off to her.

"Here's his bottle," Mara tells her.

"We're going to step out. You need anything?" I ask Amelia. She shakes her head. "Ethel, Harold?"

"No, thank you," Harold answers, never taking his eyes off his wife and his grandson.

Mara follows me and we give them some time. "You hungry?" I ask my wife.

"No, but I'll go with you."

"I'm not really either. The doctor came in and said that Ryder is doing great. He's going to be released tomorrow."

"That's excellent news."

"Yeah, except they're not releasing Amelia. The delivery took a lot out of her. She's weak and needs constant oxygen. I know she's going to fight it."

"She's tired."

"I know." I pull her into me and hold her close. Everything boiling inside me seems to calm when Mara is in my arms. "She's going to force them to let her go home."

"Her room is ready."

I nod, unable to form words for the emotion clogging my throat.

"She wants as much time with him as she can get."

"Yeah. It's getting close, Mara."

"I-I know." She stumbles over her words. "I've been trying to pretend that's not the case, but the delivery took all she had. She's a fighter," Mara states. I don't reply because she knows that I know. We've both been there through it all, day in and day out, the appointments, all of it. We've watched Amelia decline, but still when she holds our son, it's... her dream's coming true before our eyes.

"The girls and I still need to take her to get that tattoo."

"I got a guy. Does great work. I trust him to be in our home with our kids. I'm certain he'll come to us. I was going to call him earlier, but time just got away from me."

"I'm glad. That's going to be so much easier on her."

"Yeah. He lives a few hours away. We all got some ink from him on a job we were on a few years back. Great guy, he and his brother own the business. They're legit."

"You're a good man, Seth Jennings."

"Just trying to make it easier on her. She wants this, and I'll be damned if I don't do everything I can to make it happen. After she's given me.... Yeah, I'm going to make it happen."

***

Three hours later, I'm back in the waiting room. Mara went home to shower and visit with Finley at my parents' place. She's coming back to spend the night. Kendall and Ridge are visiting, so I stepped out to call Blaise Richards. It rings twice before he picks up.

"Blaise."

"Hey, man, it's Seth Jennings."

"Seth, how the hell are you, man? It's been too damn long," Blaise says.

"Taking it day by day. Listen, I have a huge favor and will make it worth your while."

"Shoot."

"A good friend of ours, the guys and I, she's d-dying." I choke on the word. "She made a bucket list of sorts and getting a tattoo was on the list. She can't travel, and well, I was hoping you or Asher or hell, both of you could come up and do it. My wife, and the guys' wives, are all getting one too. The ladies want the same thing."

"Damn," he murmurs. "That's some heavy shit, Jennings."

"Yeah, it's a little heavier. She just had a baby. My baby."

"You said your wife wants a tattoo too?"

He's confused, which is understandable. I go on to give him the CliffsNotes. "So, there you have it."

"Wow. All right, so yeah, I'd be happy to. I'm sure Asher is up for it as well. When are you thinking?"

"Sooner than later. I-I d-don't know how much longer…." I trail off, not able to finish the sentence.

"You got it. Let me talk to Tatum and Asher. I'll give you a call once we have a time set up. I've got you."

My shoulders sag in relief. "Thanks, Blaise."

"Don't mention it. I'll be in touch." The line goes dead.

I'm glad it's going to be him. I trust them. They do great work, and I know they're not going to be hitting on our wives. They're madly in love with their own. Heading back to the room, I see that Ridge and Kendall are gone, but Tyler and Reagan have taken their place.

"He's such a cutie," Reagan coos.

"You need another one of those," I say in greeting.

She looks up and smiles.

"Go ahead," Tyler tells her.

"We're pregnant," she blurts, making Amelia and me laugh. "Sheesh, I've been holding that in."

"Congratulations."

"Thanks," she and Tyler reply at the same time.

"The twins are two and a half, and potty training is going great, so yeah, we're hoping they will be at least just in nighttime pull-ups, but if not…." She shrugs.

"It will all work out," Amelia tells her. "I'm so excited that they all get to grow up together like we did."

"Amelia," Reagan says, and you can hear the regret in her voice.

"No." Amelia waves her off. "We all know it's happening. I want you to keep going. I want you all to keep living. Having adorable babies. Lifetime friends for Ryder. It brings me peace."

"We're due mid-July," Reagan tells her.

"We're getting so many kiddos, I need to make sure I put all these birthdays in my phone. I don't want to forget them," I joke, trying to lighten the mood.

"Well, you two are the first to know."

"Is it a secret?" I ask. If so, I need to make sure I don't slip in front of the guys or worse, the twins.

"Not anymore," Tyler answers.

We talk for a while longer. Tyler holds Ryder, and when Mark and Dawn come in, they leave, letting them have their turn to visit with us and Ryder. Mara comes back while they're still here, and like my wife, she's always prepared and has more than enough food for everyone, so we all sit and eat together in Amelia's room. I keep an eye on Amelia, and she barely picks at her food, but that's to be expected. That's what landed her here all those weeks ago.

"I'm not staying here," Amelia announces once Mark and Dawn have left, and the remnants of dinner have long since been forgotten.

I nod. I don't bother to argue; I knew this was coming. "Okay."

"We've got you all set up at our place. We've turned the dining room into your room, and we made up the spare bedroom for your parents. They're more than welcome to stay too, anytime they want." This has been the plan, but we never told her how we were going to execute it.

"The dining room is set off from the kitchen and the living room. We hardly ever use it with the island as we eat in the kitchen. It will be the easiest for your hospital bed and equipment. We moved the loveseat and a few chairs in there so that when you have visitors, they'll be comfortable."

She shakes her head as tears well in her eyes. "I love you both. So much. I don't know how I could do this without you both. Thank you for all that you've done for me, and for loving Ryder the way that you do."

"He's my son," I tell her.

"And mine," Mara says, choking on the admission as tears fall unchecked. "W-We love him. We 1-1 -love you too."

"You better get some sleep. This little guy"—I point to Ryder, who is snuggled up on my chest—"is going to be hungry again soon." It's not that I can't feed him, but I know she wants to. And we don't know how many more chances she's going to have to do so.

I watch as Amelia smiles before her eyes flutter closed as exhaustion takes over. Mara snuggles up to me in the lounge chair that unfolds into a bed. Amelia is breathing hard, but I know she's asleep even as she struggles to breathe evenly. Mara relaxes against me, and Ryder, he's snoozing his fast little baby breaths against my neck. I don't sleep, afraid that one of them will need me. I'll try for a few hours after Ryder eats. Right now, I'm just taking in the moment where we're all together. My gut tells me we don't have many more of these.

Chapter 26

Amelia

I was discharged from the hospital two days ago. Mara and Seth set me up with a hospital bed, and we have a homecare nurse who comes in every day and helps me do simple tasks like take a bath. I can't seem to do anything without running out of air and feeling light-headed. Mara offered to do it, but I refused to let her. I don't want her to have to take care of me. She has a husband and two kids to take care of. Ryder is her son just as much as he is mine. And although it might sound strange, I'm happy about that. When this disease does take me, he will never lack the love of a mother from a woman who will treat him as if he's part of her in every way.

Glancing over at my son who is sleeping in his bassinet, I smile. I can't seem to help myself. I feel like shit, my body is weak, and I'm on oxygen all the time, but my heart is happy. Sure, it's heart breaking to know I'm leaving him, but I've known all along that I wasn't going to have much time. That's why I'm writing these letters.

I have cards for the big birthdays: one, five, ten, thirteen, sixteen, eighteen, and twenty-one. I wish I could give him a card every year for the rest of his life, but I don't have that in me. The letters, those are for big days like graduating high school, getting married, and having a baby. I want him to know I'm going to be there with him in spirit no matter where life takes him. Mara also helped me make him a scrapbook. We took weekly pictures of my baby bump as he grew and documented his kicks, each doctor's appointment, sonogram pictures. You name it, we documented it.

I hate that this is how my son will know me, but at the same time, it's more than what most people get. Look at Mara, she has nothing of her parents, no memories, no pictures, nothing to document her family.

Speaking of Mara, she's been fantastic through all of this. I am so glad that things have worked out the way they have. Seth needed a good woman, and Mara, well, she and Finley needed a man to stand by them. They needed to be part of a family, and ours, well, it's huge, and once you're in, the bond is everlasting.

Ryder starts to fuss and Seth appears in the doorway. "I think someone's hungry," he says, holding up a bottle. Stepping into the room, he pulls the table away, and hands me the bottle. He then goes to the bassinet and lifts our son to his chest. He kisses his little head before placing him in my arms. "You need anything?" he asks.

"No. We're all set. Thanks, Daddy."

He grins. "You're welcome. Just ring the bell when you're done or call me." He disappears out of the room before I can say anything else. He's been great about giving me time with Ryder. Mara has taken what feels like thousands of pictures. During the day, I take care of his needs, and at night, they take over. I've gotten pretty good at changing diapers on my lap. There have only been a few incidents where he peed on me and one dirty diaper that was out of control. I had to call for backup as it was everywhere. Seth came to my rescue while Mara captured the moment with her camera. I'm not sure that's how I want my son to remember me, but then again, I want him to know that I did what I could for him, while I was still here.

"You better slow down, piglet," I tell my son as he sucks greedily on his bottle. "You know Mommy's going to have to take that from you to burp."

His dark eyes stare up at me without a care in the world. "I love you so much, baby boy. I've been meaning to talk to you about something. Mommy has to go away. It's not because I don't love you, I love you so much my heart is bursting. Sometimes mommies and even daddies have to leave those they love behind. It's not fair, but you'll find out that there are a lot of things in life that are not fair. There are going to be times when you have to be the bigger person and just walk away. Trust your dad and Mara. She's your mom too and they will always want what's best for you."

I pause, pulling the bottle from his mouth. He grunts and whines, but he needs to burp. Careful of my oxygen tube, I place him on my shoulder and start to rub and lightly tap his back. "Whenever you need to talk, just start talking. I promise you that I'll always be listening. I love you so much." I bite down on my bottom lip to keep the tears at bay. I know babies can sense when the person holding them is upset, and I don't want that for him.

"There you go, little man," I praise when he finally burps. Settling him back in the crook of my arm, I give him the rest of his bottle. The second half he takes his time as his eyes droop and he falls asleep. Instead of calling for Seth or Mara, I hold him just a little longer. I know that my days of taking care of him are few and far between.

Softly, I start to sing "Godspeed" by the Dixie Chicks. Tears coat my face, and my chest aches. I have never loved someone as much as this baby in my arms. "You, my son, are my greatest gift and my greatest accomplishment in life. I'll love you always."

"Perfect," Mara says, lowering her camera and wiping at her eyes. "I recorded that, the song, that is. I hope you don't mind."

"N-No," I manage to reply.

"Come on, Ryder. Mommy, it's time to take a bath." She steps into the room, sets her camera on a small end table, and takes Ryder from my arms. "I'll bring him back." She leans in and kisses me on the cheek. I watch them leave, my heart cracking wide open at the thought of leaving him.

Fuck cancer.

Chapter 27

Mara

"I'm nervous," I tell the hot-as-hell guy who's covered in ink sitting next to me on a small stool. Don't get me wrong, he's not my Seth, but he's easy on the eyes.

"Just relax." His wife, Tatum, smiles kindly. "I was nervous too, but it's not as bad as some people make it seem. You've endured childbirth. You'll be fine."

"Relax, babe." Seth chuckles. He's sitting next to me with Ryder strapped to his chest. Finley is with his parents, so thankfully I don't have to worry about her being around the needles.

"You want one of my pain pills?" Amelia jokes.

"No." I stick my tongue out at her. She's looking down at her wrist where her tattoo resides. We all decided the small ink would go on our left wrists. "I guess it's not fair I had that small advantage, but really, you're going to be fine."

"I'm done," Kendall says, showing me her ink. Blaise's brother, Asher, did hers.

"I'm going to need your number," Reagan tells him. "As soon as this baby is born, I'm coming to get mine. No way are these ladies having all the fun."

"I'll take you to him," Tyler assures her.

"You're the last to hold out," Kent teases.

"No, Dawn still has to go," I defend. He nods toward the other chair, and Asher already has Dawn's design on her wrist and is bent over placing the needle to her skin. "Do it," I tell Blaise, closing my eyes.

Squeezing my eyes shut, I grit my teeth when the needle hits my skin. I wince, but it's not as bad as I was thinking.

Not long after, Blaise's voice startles my eyes open. "You're all set." Blaise grins down at me.

"Really?" I ask, surprised.

He laughs. "Yeah, it's a simple small outline."

"Huh, not so bad. Maybe I might get more."

"Your husband knows where to find me," he tells me, still laughing.

"It's hot, babe." Seth leans in and kisses me.

"So are you, especially with your little man there." I smile at him. He's taken so well to being the daddy of his baby boy. I'm honored to call this man my husband.

"You guys want to stick around?" Seth asks Blaise.

"We'd love to, but our twins both have games tomorrow. We need to get home and get them in bed. My mom can't seem to say no to them."

"I really appreciate you doing this," Seth tells him.

"Anytime. Don't be strangers," he responds.

Seth peers down at me. "We'll be coming for a visit soon. I have to get some ink for my kids." He smiles down at me and I grin back. We got the final documents in the mail yesterday. He's officially Finley's dad in the eyes of the law. The adoption is final. He grinned from ear to ear all day. He snuggled with both kids pretty much all day.

We say our goodbyes to Blaise and Asher, and their wives, Grace and Tatum. The rest of the night, we sit around laughing and talking. The girls and I all take a ton of pictures of the guys goofing off with Amelia.

She laughs and smiles and snuggles baby Ryder, but her eyes tell me what she won't. She's tired, she's in pain, and this is all too much excitement for one day.

"I'm beat," I say, faking a yawn and stretching my arms above my head. Kendall catches my eye, and I give a subtle nod toward Amelia, who has her eyes closed, with Ryder lying on her chest.

"Yeah, we should be getting home. It's rare we have a night without the kids." Kendall lightly bumps her shoulder into Ridge, and that's all it takes for him to stand and take her hand in his. Not that she needed the innuendo. That man would ask how high if she said jump. They all would. We're all really lucky to have each of them in our lives.

Couple by couple, our friends leave until it's just Seth, Kent, Amelia, me, and baby Ryder.

"Let me help you to bed," I tell Amelia. I hand Ryder off to Seth and help her stand.

"You need help?" Kent asks.

"Nah." Amelia waves him off even when she wobbles on her feet.

"Stubborn-ass woman," he grumbles. Standing, he scoops her up in his arms. She doesn't protest. Instead, she rests her head against his chest, loops her arms around his neck, and accepts the fact that walking is harder and harder for her.

"Thank you, Kenton." Amelia's voice is soft, pained that she needs help.

"Anything for you, beautiful." He winks and leaves us alone.

"I'm going to miss that." She half laughs, half coughs the words.

"Miss what?" I ask, confused.

"Kent. When he finds the one who brings him to his knees, I'm going to miss it. It's been fun watching each of the guys with their wives and kids. I just hate that I'm going to miss it."

What do I say to that? I can't tell her to think positive. I love her too much to lie to her. We both know she's fading fast. Instead, I nod like I understand, and I do, but telling her that does nothing for either of us. Instead, I help her change into her pajamas and tuck her into bed. I double-check her oxygen tank, making sure she's good through the night. Reaching into the bedside table, I pull out the locked box where we store her medication. It's not worth the risk with Finley in the house.

Standing, I grab the key from a high hook, that even if she climbed or tried to she could never reach, and unlock it. Gathering her nightly medications, I hand them to her one at a time and hold the glass of water with a straw for her.

"Mara." Her voice cracks. "I love you. My entire life I was surrounded by the guys; they were my closest friends. I was the girl who had more guy friends than girls, and I was scared as hell to go to college and leave them behind, but then I met you, and it was all okay. I need you to know what you mean to me, what our friendship means before I can't."

"I love you too." I want to tell her that we have time, that she's just hit a rough patch and things will be better, but we both know that's not true.

"Can you do something for me? I want to finish his scrapbook. The one of up to his birth and his birth. Can you and the girls maybe help me with that? I just don't know if I can do it on my own."

"Done."

"And could you maybe go shopping for me? I want to get him birthday cards for each birthday, and a graduation card, two of them because I'm not sure if he'll go to college, and wedding, and baby, and—" She stops when a sob breaks free. "God, I'm going to miss so much."

"I'm sorry," I say, not knowing what else to say. It sucks. Cancer sucks. "Fuck cancer," I say, and she giggles through her tears.

"Look at you dropping F-bombs."

"It was fitting."

"Yeah," she agrees, wiping at her eyes.

"I guess I just need to do the milestones, maybe not cards. Some nice stationery maybe? I'll do a few cards, the big birthdays, and letters for the big events. I just… I want him to know how much I love him."

"He'll never go a day without knowing. I give you my word."

"He's so lucky to have two mommies who love him."

"I'm good with being Mara. I don't want to fill your shoes. I never could." It's true. I have no problem being Mara to Ryder. He has a momma.

"No. You're his mother. I know you're going to love him and nurture him as if he was your blood. I want that for him, for all of you."

"He'll never not know who you are, Amelia. I promise with everything in me, he will always know what you did to give him life."

"I wasn't taking treatments regardless."

"But even if you wanted to, when you found out about him, you wouldn't have. I know you."

She shrugs. "I was always going to be here. He will always be the best thing I've ever done in my life. Giving him life. I'm sorry for how it all turned out with Seth, I just—" I hold up my finger to stop her.

"There is nothing to apologize for. He and I weren't together. You did nothing wrong, and neither did he. We've been through this. It's done."

"I know, but my time is short—" I cut her off again.

"Exactly. Let's not dwell on the how or why. Let's live these days. Make some memories, take some pictures, and snuggle the hell out of your son."

"I like that." She closes her eyes, and I know I'm losing her to sleep and the pain medication.

"Sleep, my friend. I love you always," I whisper, kissing her cheek. Careful not to disturb her, I stand and make sure the baby monitor is turned on in case she needs me in the night, something she fought me on, but I won in the end. I head back to the living room.

Once there, I settle beside Seth, who's still chatting with Kent, who is holding Ryder.

"I hate this," I whisper, unable to fight back the tears that fall.

"I know, babe. We all do."

"You guys need a break. Go." Kent waves us off. "Go do what married people do. I'll hang here with the little man. I'll listen for Amelia too. Go take a nap, or you know, do married things." He wags his eyebrows.

"Kent." I stop talking when Seth stands and offers me his hand. "Let's take a nap."

"Is that what the kids are calling it these days?" Kent teases softly, mindful of Amelia sleeping in the dining room. Not that she would wake up. The pain meds knock her out.

"Just wait until you have a new baby." Seth shakes his head.

"I can only hope to have what you have one day," Kent tells him.

Something passes between the two of them, but I'm too tired to try and decipher it. "Thank you, Kenton." I use his full name as I bend to kiss him and then Ryder on the cheek. "He just ate, and I changed him so it should just be snuggling, but if you need us, come and get us."

"We're all set. I've done this with my other nieces and nephews. I can handle this little guy. Go." He waves again.

This time we go. We drag our tired asses to bed. Seth curls up behind me, and in his embrace, I let the exhaustion and the worry win as sleep claims me.

Chapter 28

SETH

Palliative end-of-life care. That's what the hospice nurse called it. Ryder is six weeks old today, and the nurse tells us it will be within twenty-four hours. Twenty-four hours and my son's mother will leave this earth. A disease that has affected far too many taking her life. My fucking chest aches, a literal tightening, iron-fist gripping my heart kind of ache. She's one of my closest friends, we grew up together, and she's dying. I've known this was going to happen. Thought I was prepared for it. How do you prepare yourself for death? I'll tell you how. You don't.

You're never prepared.

It's a challenge I wasn't prepared for but have to face.

"Seth," Harold calls my name.

I turn to face him. He's aged another ten years more than his seventy-one in the last month. I can't imagine having to watch Finley or Ryder go through this. I can't even fathom it. "Hey, Harold," I greet him. I don't bother with pleasantries. They've been staying here the last two weeks. He knows to make himself at home.

"You're a good man, Seth. Ethel and I have been talking. Amelia was our only, and we're not getting any younger. Everything we have will go to Ryder."

I nod. I would expect nothing less from them. They're great people. "Okay. What do you need from me?"

"His social is all we'll need to make it official. We've already had our attorney set up a trust for him. I just wanted to let you know."

"Thank you."

"College, whatever he needs, there will be more than enough to take care of it all."

"I'll make sure it goes to him."

"He gets access at twenty-five, but you and Mara will have access whenever you need it. If it's for him, health or school whatever, it will be there."

"That's not necessary."

"Maybe not, but we want to. You've given her so much. All of you have. It's what we want. It will make us feel better, like we're helping in some small way. We can't care for an infant at our age."

"You're welcome here anytime. Hell, you can stay in your room as long as you want, even after...." My words trail off. I can't bring myself to say what we both know is happening just inside.

"H-Hey," Kent says, interrupting us. "You guys better come inside."

Harold and I follow him in the house and to the dining room. Everyone is there. The guys, their wives, my parents, as well as Amelia's. Sonia has Finley, but we kept Ryder with us. He's too little to understand what's going on, and well, I thought it might help her to know he was here with us. Not that she knows. She's been out of it for days, unless you count late last night when she told us that she loved us. When she held our son and told him he was her world, the love of her life, and her greatest gift.

She fell asleep shortly after and then turned from bad to worse. When the hospice nurse arrived early this morning, she told us to call our family and prepare for what's to come. She said she couldn't be sure, but her guess was sometime today.

As we enter the room, I find Ethel sitting next to her daughter's bed, tears coating her wrinkled cheeks. She too has aged so much this last month. Mara is sitting next to her with Ryder in her arms. My wife's face is also wet from her tears. Reaching into the economy pack of tissues we purchased, because there have been a lot of tears shed in this house in recent weeks, I pass a few around, making sure everyone has what they need. Then I go to my wife. She stands, and I take her seat so she and our son can take a seat on my lap. Together, we reach out for Amelia's hand.

"Thank you, A," I say softly. "Thank you for Ryder, for being the amazing human being you are. I'm honored to have known you my entire life. I can't wait to tell our son about you. About how his mom never let the guys do anything without her." I pause to swallow back my tears. "I'm going to miss you, but it's okay. You can go now. You've fought hard, and you saved our little boy. He loves you. He can't tell you that right now, but he does. He loves you."

"Please God," Mara says as she cries softly. "Stop making her suffer. She doesn't deserve this." She holds tight to Ryder and kisses his forehead. "Amelia Anderson, you were my first true friend, my family. I will never forget you. I love you, my bestie."

One by one, our friends come up to the bed to say their tearful goodbyes. There is not a dry eye in the house as we sit with her, waiting for her pain to be taken away. "What are you doing? You just gave her some," I question the nurse as she places yet another drop of liquid morphine under her tongue.

"This will help her relax. She's fighting to stay here. This will help her go peacefully."

"You're drugging her?" Harold asks.

"I'm taking away her pain so she can relax and let her body take the natural progression," she replies calmly, her voice soothing.

"How long?" Ethel asks.

"Within the hour," the nurse explains. "Her breathing is shallow, and her pulse is slow."

I rub my thumb softly over Amelia's hand while Mara rubs her arms soothingly. Ethel and Harold are in a similar situation on the other side of the bed. Our friends gather around us and strong hands grip my shoulders. I don't turn to see who it is. I know it's one of my brothers. One of *her* brothers, as we stand strong, silent, giving her our strength to let go.

One hour.

One minute.

One second.

One breath.

"Time of death, 6:15 p.m.," the nurse states.

There are sobs around the room. I don't know which one is mine, which is Mara's. Hell, her parents, our friends, they all mix together with our tears and our hearts that break as we accept this new reality.

Amelia is gone.

Her memory will be alive in our hearts, and in our son. The pain of losing her will eventually dull but never fade, and the hole she leaves in our lives will never be filled.

It rained today. Not just a sprinkle, but an all-out downpour of rain. It poured all the way to the cemetery, and while we sat through the service, and with the final goodbye, it rained. However, when the minister stood before us and told us that Amelia would forever be watching over us, the rain stops. Suddenly, not gradually. It stops and the sun peeks through the dark clouds, and I smile.

Amelia.

I didn't need the sunshine to know that she's here with us. All I have to do is look at our son or in my heart for the memories that will forever remain there. I stand still, Ryder in one arm, Mara on the other, long after they've lowered her casket into the ground. My feet won't work. They don't seem to want to let me walk away. I hear a sob and look around to see that everyone is still here with me. My brothers, their wives, my sisters, her parents, my parents, everyone is still here. It's not just me that misses her and hates the gaping hole she left in our lives. It's all of us.

What do we do now? How do we move forward? I think about Amelia and can almost hear her reply.

"Seth, you take it one day at a time until you learn to live with our unexpected bond. It's not something we planned, but it's the hand we were dealt. I live on through Ryder, through you and Mara, and the guys, their wives. You take it one day at a time."

"She wouldn't want this," Mark says, his voice gruff.

"She wouldn't," Tyler agrees.

"She'd want us to remember the good," Ridge adds.

"She told me…" Kent clears his throat and starts again. "She made me promise that we would celebrate her life. That we would tell stories of our time with her, that we would write them down so we never forget."

"Like that's possible," I say, kissing the top of Ryder's head.

"You're right," Mara speaks up. "She lived her final days how she wanted. She made me promise to make you all come back to our place. Her only request was to include her parents." Mara pulls away from me and walks over to Harold and Ethel. "Our home is open to you always. Ryder is your grandson, and we want you in his life. You're welcome to stay with us as long as you want or need."

"Thank you, dear," Ethel says. "We'd like to come and visit, but we need to go home. It's our home and where we raised her. That's where we belong."

"Well, today you're coming back to ours. You're going to eat some food and snuggle that baby boy. You're going to listen to us tell stories about how incredible Amelia was as we celebrate her life." She wipes at her eyes. "That's what Amelia wanted."

"She was so lucky to have all of you," Harold speaks up.

"Well, I'm going to go call Sonia, and tell her to head that way," Mom says, her arm linked through Dad's.

"Thank you."

"You're welcome, honey."

"Get your babies," Mara tells our friends. "We're celebrating life, and we all need to be there. We'll meet you back at our place."

And just like that, my wife once again has proven how strong she is. Her heart is broken with the loss of her best friend, but she's fighting through the sadness and the pain to give Amelia the final goodbye, the final celebration of her life that she wanted.

"We love you," I whisper, taking one last look at the grave, before turning. And with my family by my side, I head to the car. "We're going to celebrate your mommy, Ryder," I tell my son softly.

That's exactly what we do. Until the early hours of the morning, we sit around, eating and talking and telling stories. Everyone takes a turn with Ryder; he's getting all the love today, but that's okay. He's lost something huge, something he doesn't understand, but one day he will. One day when he's old enough, we're going to tell him about his first mother.

"He go down okay?" Mara asks, covering her yawn as soon as I walk back into the bedroom.

"Yeah, he didn't even stir when I put him in his crib." I grab the baby monitor and make sure it's turned on.

"What took you so long?"

"Oh, I was in Finny's room."

"Is she awake?"

"No, I was just watching her sleep. Next week can't come soon enough." In the eyes of the law, Finley is already my daughter and we have the papers to prove it, but we're still waiting on her new birth certificate with my name as hers. We're going to have a daddy-daughter day. I'm going to make it something we do as often as possible for as long as she'll let me. She's independent now, so I can only imagine how headstrong she will be as a teenager.

She smiles at me. "Yeah, I can't believe it took so long, but it's done now and soon she'll have it on paper that she's a Jennings too."

"Finally," I say, stripping out of my jeans and sliding under the covers. "Come here, you," I say, holding my arms open. My wife doesn't hesitate to come to me. I hold her close and close my eyes. This past year has been hell, but having Mara by my side has kept me sane. Today was hard, saying goodbye to an old friend, a best friend, an aunt, a daughter, and a mother. It took a lot out of all of us. We weren't ready to say goodbye.

"Do you want to open it now or later?" Mara asks.

The envelope. Amelia gave it to us and told us that we couldn't open it until after her funeral.

"You decide."

"Can we do it now?"

"Sure." Pulling away, I turn on the lamp and reach into the nightstand and pull out the blue envelope. "You want me to do it?" I ask.

"Yes." Mara snuggles up to my chest and I drape an arm around her, then slide my finger under the seal and open it. I pull out the card and the outside makes me chuckle. It's balloons and confetti with *Congratulations* written on the front.

"She's crazy." Mara laughs while wiping under her eyes.

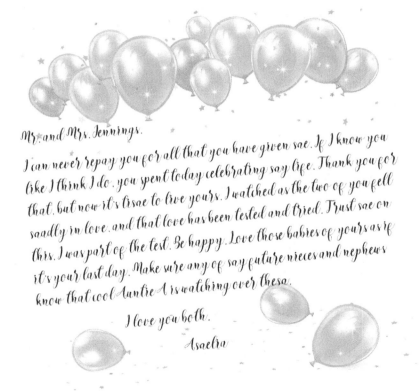

Mr. and Mrs. Jennings,

I can never repay you for all that you have given sae. If I know you like I think I do, you spent today celebrating say life. Thank you for that, but now it's time to live yours. I watched as the two of you fell sadly in love, and that love has been tested and tried. Trust sae on this, I was part of the test. Be happy. Love those babies of yours as if it's your last day. Make sure any of say future nieces and nephews know that cool Auntie A is watching over thesa.

I love you both.

Asaelia

"Damn her," Mara says as she reaches for a tissue.

"She always did have to get the last word in." I can't help but smile. "You okay?"

"Yeah." She waves me off. "I miss her."

"I know. I do too." I place the envelope back in the nightstand and turn off the light. We lie in silence as the heaviness of the day and her final words to us set in. "Do you want more? Babies, I mean?"

"We have two healthy and happy children, but if we should be lucky enough to have more, yeah, I'd be happy about it. You?"

"Yes." I pause, thinking about Mara and her belly growing round with our baby. "How soon?"

"What?" she says with a chuckle.

"How soon can we have another one?"

"Ryder is still an infant."

"Okay?"

"That's a lot of diapers."

"I'll be there every step of the way."

"Seth, are you being serious right now?"

"Yeah, I mean when you're ready. When our family is ready, I want more. If we decide it's now that we start trying, then we do. If we decide to wait, I'm okay with that too, but I don't want to wait too long. I want them to be close in age, so they can play together and be close."

"Let's give it a few months. Let's adjust to our new reality, then we can talk about it."

"We should practice," I say, kissing her neck. "You know, for when the time comes."

"Seth Jennings, what am I going to do with you?"

"Make lots of babies."

"Goodnight, crazy man."

"Goodnight, my wife." I pull her closer, and with a smile on my face, sleep claims me.

Epilogue

Mara

It's his first Christmas. It's only been five weeks since we laid Amelia to rest, but the pain is still there. It lingers in our daily lives, but we keep pushing through. Ryder is thriving. He's happy and healthy, and his little chubby cheeks, they light up our life. Finley loves him to pieces, and it's her favorite thing in the world to make him laugh or smile at her.

I have a framed picture of Ryder and Amelia in his room, every night, sometimes multiple times a day, we stop and tell her how much we love her. Finley has one too. She loved her aunt A something fierce.

Today has been good. Harold and Ethel stayed here last night so they could watch the kids open gifts from Santa. Sure, Ryder is too small to know the difference, but Finley isn't, and that little girl, she's captured their hearts just as Ryder has. They spoiled both our kids rotten, and their smiles are huge because of it. I'm glad to see them smiling, living. I can't imagine burying a child, but they are working through it.

"Mommy, wook!" Finley holds up the five-dollar bill that was in her Christmas card from Grandma and Grandpa Anderson.

"Wow, look at you. You better go put it in your piggy bank." She's up and racing toward her room before the words are even out of my mouth.

"You're an amazing mother, Mara. Thank you for loving him," Ethel says, nodding to a sleeping Ryder in her arms.

"He's my son," I tell her. "My heart doesn't know the difference between him and Finley. I promise you that."

"We know, dear," she assures me. "Thank you so much for having us, but we need to get going. It's going to be dark soon, and we don't like to be out after dark."

"Thank you so much for being here with us. We'll bring him by soon."

They nod and head to the guest room to pack up their things. I hear them stop by Finley's room to tell her goodbye, before joining me once again in the living room for a hug. "Tell Seth, thank you. You kids have fun with your friends."

"Be safe. Call me or text if you can when you get home so I know you got there okay."

"Oh, we'll call. I can't seem to see those little letters," Harold grumps.

I smile, saying, "Thank you." With that, they're out the door. I send Seth a quick text letting him know that they left. He stepped out to grab a few things for tonight. Everyone will be here at seven to hang out. We want the kids to play together and grow up in a tight-knit group just like their daddies. With Ryder being the youngest of the brood, and with Ethel and Harold stopping by, we're hosting this year. I have a special surprise for everyone. Amelia started everyone a family scrapbook. Inside on the first page is a picture of her with their families. It's her way of keeping us girls going with the scrapbook nights. I love it, and I know that Kendall, Dawn, and Reagan will too.

Glancing at the clock, I see it's just before five. I put on a princess movie and grab a sippy cup of milk before making Ryder a bottle. With any luck, Finley will take a quick nap before her friends get here. It's late in the evening, but it's been a long day and she skipped her nap earlier. "Finley!" I call for her. I hear the pitter-patter of her little feet racing down the hall. "How about some milk while Mommy feeds Ryder?"

"Okay, Momma." She happily accepts the sippy cup and curls up next to me on the couch.

That's how Seth finds us half an hour later. Both kids passed out from today's excitement. "Let me take her to her room," he whispers, lifting Finley in his arms.

"Wuv you, Daddy," our daughter says sleepily.

"I love you too, Finny."

I trail along behind them, placing Ryder in his crib before we meet in the hall. "Come here, wife." Seth pulls me into a scorching kiss that I feel all the way to my toes. "Let's go take a nap while they do."

"Is Kent rubbing off on you?" I tease.

"That's not the kind of nap I meant, but we can make that happen." He smirks.

"Not happening. I'm exhausted, so this time we're really napping too."

"I figured." He chuckles and follows me into our room. Within minutes, we're curled up under the covers, in each other's arms as we drift off to sleep.

Epilogue

Seth

Standing in the corner of my living room, I watch as my wife, and the other wives laugh and cry over the gifts from Amelia. I'll admit I got choked up myself, and if the throats that were clearing and the beers that were being tilted back are any indication, my brothers were just as affected.

Speaking of brothers, they're all headed toward me. "What's up?" I ask them.

"Just getting to the corner where there seem to be fewer tears," Tyler says, looking over his shoulder. "I hate when she gets upset like this. It's not good for her or the baby."

"It's okay," I assure him. If I know anything, it's that just because a woman is pregnant, it doesn't mean she's fragile.

"I know, I just can't help but worry about both of them."

"I can't blame you after what the two of you have been through, but they're a few sad tears over missing a friend. She's going to be fine," Mark assures him.

"So, I have some news," Ridge says. The girls squeal and he grins. "Looks like I'm not the only one letting the cat out of the bag. Kendall's

265

pregnant. We're having another baby."

"Congratulations." I shake his hand, as do Mark, Kent, and Tyler.

"Thanks. We're excited."

"Damn, I need to get moving," Mark says. "Daisy is not going to be an only child," he says with certainty. He's looking at his wife, and I'm thinking we're going to have another baby announcement pretty damn soon if he has anything to say about it.

"So," Kent says, laughing under his breath. "Where's the next job?"

"The Nottingham Estate."

Kent coughs, choking on his beer. "Say again?"

"The Nottingham Estate. I got a call from the family attorney. Seems old man Nottingham passed away and the family wants to fix it up to put it on the market."

Kent nods but doesn't say anything else.

"Ridge," Kendall calls out, and he doesn't spare us a glance as he goes to his wife.

"Dawn," Mark calls out, and Tyler and I laugh as he stalks toward her.

"He's on a mission." I laugh.

"What about you? You want more?" Tyler asks.

"Yep. As soon as my wife says it's a go. Ryder is only three months. She doesn't want them too close together."

"I get that. Beckett, Benjamin, no!" Tyler calls out as he rushes toward the twins who are trying to pull ornaments off the tree.

"You good?" I ask Kent.

"Yup."

"Liar."

"This is another one of those 'don't want to talk about it' moments."

"Fine, but one day you're going to want to, and I'm your guy," I tell him.

"Pussy," he says with a cough.

"I'll own that." I laugh. "After the year I've had, I know that it helps not only to talk but to know there are people willing to listen."

"Sorry, man." He winces.

"Not necessary. I just want you to know we're brothers and I've got your back. We all do."

"I know. Maybe one day. I just need to… work it out in my head."

"Uncle Kent, come play with me!" Knox yells. He rushes away to get a break from the heavy, and I get it. He's all twisted up inside, but he'll get there, and when he does, we'll be there for him because that's what we do.

Life has thrown me some curveballs, and there have been times when the unexpected changes have literally knocked me on my ass. I had to learn to live one breath, one second, one minute, one hour, one day at a time. I've learned that the best things in life are truly unexpected. I've embraced it and learned to live with the unexpected bond.

Thank you for taking the time to read

Unexpected Bond

Want more from the Beckett Construction Crew?
Look for Kent's story in the Winter of 2020.

Never miss a new release:
http://bit.ly/2UW5Xzm

More about Kaylee's books:
http://bit.ly/2CV3hLx

Contact
KAYLEE RYAN

Facebook:
http://bit.ly/2C5DgdF

Instagram:
http://bit.ly/2reBkrV

Reader Group:
http://bit.ly/2o0yWDx

Goodreads:
http://bit.ly/2HodJvx

BookBub:
http://bit.ly/2KulVvH

Website:
www.kayleeryan.com

Other Works

BY KAYLEE RYAN

With You Series:

Anywhere With You | More With You | Everything With You

Soul Serenade Series:

Emphatic | Assured | Definite | Insistent

Southern Heart Series:

Southern Pleasure | Southern Desire | Southern Attraction | Southern Devotion

Unexpected Arrivals Series:

Unexpected Reality | Unexpected Fight | Unexpected Fall | Unexpected Bond

Standalone Titles:

Tempting Tatum | Unwrapping Tatum | Levitate
Just Say When | I Just Want You
Reminding Avery | Hey, Whiskey | When Sparks Collide
Pull You Through | Beyond the Bases
Remedy | The Difference
Trust the Push

Co-written with Lacey Black:

It's Not Over

Acknowledgements

To my readers:

This book killed me. I've never cried while writing as much as I did with this one. I think there are a lot of factors that play into that. My dad had the same kind of cancer as Amelia had. He lived twenty-one months from the day of his diagnosis. #FuckCancer

I'm also so invested in these characters. They've been with me for a while now, and their pain is my pain. Not that it's not like that with every book I write, but the Beckett Construction Crew, they're weaved tight into my heart. Thank you for taking the time to read Seth's story. Although I broke your heart, I hope that I also put it back together. Thank you for staying on this journey with me.

To my family:

I love you. You hold me up and support me every day. I can't imagine my life without you as my support system. Thank you for believing in me, and being there to celebrate my success.

Wander Aguiar:

Thank you for an amazing image that brought Seth to life!

Zack Salaun:

Thank you for doing what you do, so authors can bring their characters to life for readers.

Tami Integrity Formatting:

Thank you for making The Unexpected Bond paperback beautiful. You're amazing and I cannot thank you enough for all that you do.

Sommer Stein:

Time and time again, you wow me with your talent. Thank you for another amazing cover.

My beta team:

Jamie, Stacy, Lauren, Erica, and Franci I would be lost without you. You read my words as much as I do, and I can't tell you what your input and all the time you give means to me. Countless messages and bouncing idea, you ladies keep me sane with the characters are being anything but. Thank you from the bottom of my heart for taking this wild ride with me.

Give Me Books:

With every release, your team works diligently to get my book in the hands of bloggers. I cannot tell you how thankful I am for your services.

Tempting Illustrations:

Thank you for everything. I would be lost without you.

Julie Deaton:

Thank you for giving this book a set of fresh final eyes.

Becky Johnson:

I could not do this without you. Thank you for pushing me, and making me work for it.

Marisa Corvisiero:

Thank you for all that you do. I know I'm not the easiest client. I'm blessed to have you on this journey with me.

Kimberly Ann:

Thank you for organizing and tracking the ARC team. I couldn't do it without you.

Bloggers:

Thank you, doesn't seem like enough. You don't get paid to do what you do. It's from the kindness of your heart and your love of reading that fuels you. Without you, without your pages, your voice, your reviews, spreading the word it would be so much harder if not impossible to get my words in reader's hands. I can't tell you how much your never-ending support means to me. Thank you for being you, thank you for all that you do.

To my Kick Ass Crew:

The name of the group speaks for itself. You ladies truly do KICK ASS! I'm honored to have you on this journey with me. Thank you for reading, sharing, commenting, suggesting, the teasers, the messages all of it. Thank you from the bottom of my heart for all that you do. Your support is everything!

With Love,

Kaylee Ryan
AUTHOR

Made in United States
Orlando, FL
09 April 2022

16655320R00153